Here
After

BOOKS BY SEAN COSTELLO

Eden's Eyes (1989)

The Cartoonist (1990)

Captain Quad (1991)

Finders Keepers (2002)

Sandman (2003)

HERE AFTER

by

Sean
Costello

Your Scrivener Press

Library and Archives Canada Cataloguing in Publication

Costello, Sean
       Here after / Sean Costello

ISBN 978-1-896350-29-5

       I. Title.

PS8555.O73H47 2008   C813'.54   C2008-904464-9

Book design: Laurence Steven
Cover photo and design: amy Bradley www.amalyn.net
Author photo: Alfred Boyd

Published by *Your Scrivener Press*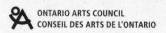
465 Loach's Road,
Sudbury, Ontario, Canada, P3E 2R2
info@yourscrivenerpress.com
www.yourscrivenerpress.com

We acknowledge the support of the Canada Council for the
Arts and the Ontario Arts Council for our publishing program.

 Canada Council   Conseil des Arts
for the Arts   du Canada

 ONTARIO ARTS COUNCIL
CONSEIL DES ARTS DE L'ONTARIO

Dedication

This book is dedicated to my colleagues: Dave Rideout and Don Wallis, in loving memory; Brent Kennedy, who ferried my son safely through the scariest day of his life, and went to bat for me on one of my own...thanks, Brent, more than you'll ever know; the handsome and gracious Elwood Dunn, professor of neuroanesthesia; les deux Lamberts—the eloquent and charming Wayne-o, trusted friend and advisor, and his uncommonly sexy sibling, Swaide; Sylvain Cote, magazine model– and proof that life truly is stranger than fiction (something to do with bio-glue); the lovely ladies of gas: Jo-Jo, Cheryl B and Kristy G; the impossibly gorgeous Jeff Sloan; Pedro Z, my old windsurfing buddy; Julien Marti, one of the most fertile men I know (Stash, you still got him beat, though, buddy); Jamie D...just so goddam cute you wanna hug 'im; Derek Manchuk, director of Sudbury's Marineland; Tony 'Toner' Hick,one of the brightest and most generous people I know; Sanj Mathur, just plain groovy guy; the two Robs, charmers both; Martin Shine, probably the toughest man alive; Walter Morrow, who got out alive; Norm Hey, who took on an awkward task on my behalf and pulled it off with patience and grace...thanks for that, Normy; David Boyle, another beauty you just wanna hug; and finally, Carlos 'Santana' Nanaya and Arsenio 'Booger' Avila, deserters...but still much loved.

Thanks, guys, for everything.

1.

Thursday, February 8

"Dad, I'm afraid."

"I know, sweetheart, but I'm right here. I won't let you go through this alone."

Doctor Peter Croft snuggled closer to his son on the stiff hospital bed, spooning the boy's wasted body against his own. It would be only a matter of minutes now.

"What if I fall asleep?"

"I won't move from this spot, David. I swear."

"Okay, Dad. 'Cause I'm really tired."

The boy drew a ragged breath and Peter could hear the fluid that saturated his lungs, a wet crackle under the steady hiss of oxygen.

Drowning him.

David adjusted the green oxygen mask on his face, rubbing at the reddened furrows the rigid plastic had dug next to his nose. Peter watched his son's movements, the huge effort it cost him to simply raise his arm, and the terrible loathing he felt for God rose to his throat in a barely suppressed roar.

He glanced at the door to the private room, securely locked now from the inside. The drugs he would need were in his hip pocket, already mixed in a single syringe. He'd taken them from the OR days ago, when he made his decision.

"Dad?"

"Yeah, little buddy?"

"Can you tell me a story?"

"Sure," Peter said. He came up on one elbow, leaning over his son so he could see the boy's face. "Had a little doll, stuck it on the wall, and that's all."

And there it was, the tiny smile he'd hoped for. It was a 'story' his grandfather had told him, a man Peter barely remembered. Peter had used it many times on David when he was younger, glad now for the hundreds of nights he'd lain next to the little guy, coaxing him off to sleep. *Lie down with me, Dad? Just for two minutes?*

David was almost ten now, two days away from a birthday he would never see. Peter had arranged a small party for him last weekend, right here in the room, inviting a few of his closest pals from school, telling David they were doing it early this year because his best friend, Thomas, couldn't make it any other time. The kids came bearing gifts and good intentions, but when they saw David, how much he'd deteriorated in the weeks since they'd last seen him, things quickly turned awkward. With surprisingly adult grace; David let the boys off the hook, saying he was too tired to spend more than a few minutes with them. Two of them were in tears before they reached the hallway.

"A real story, Dad. Something funny."

"Okay, let me think." But his mind was a black pool of despondency, and when he reached in for something to say he came up empty.

David said, "Remember when I cut my head?"

And miraculously Peter laughed out loud. He reached over his son's shoulder to show him the index finger of his right hand. "How can I forget?"

David took his father's hand in his own, gently rubbing the unnaturally smooth pad of Peter's finger, and Peter thought of how precious those little hands were, the instruments of his son's industry and curiosity, the parts of him Peter had enjoyed most when David was a baby.

"That was pretty funny, eh, Dad?"

"It sure was." Though neither of them thought so at the time.

Four years ago David had struck his head on the edge of the coffee table and opened a small gash. Typical of scalp lacerations it had bled like crazy, and in a barely restrained panic David's mother, Dana, had pleaded with Peter to rush him to the ER for stitches. Wanting to avoid the unpleasantness of the experience for his son, Peter had decided to deal with the problem on his own.

"You had that glue stuff in your first-aid box," David said. "Remember?"

"Derma-Bond. Yeah, I remember."

"You called it human glue."

"Was I lying?"

David released a small, asthmatic chuckle. "Nope."

Peter had calmly reassured Dana, telling her stitches were over-kill, he'd have their son fixed up in a jiffy. The look she'd given him should have been enough, but by now he was on a mission.

The bio-glue was expensive stuff, and though he'd never actually used it himself, he'd heard the ER docs sing its praises. Besides, how hard could it be? He'd bought a tube of it for this very reason. So with Dana standing over him, fidgeting and huffing, and David sitting stock-still on a kitchen stool, he'd gone to work.

Now David coughed, a wracking wet hack, and Peter held him and felt tears sting his eyes. They were huddled together on a cliff-edge, clutching each other for dear life, trying not to look down.

The cough subsided and David said, "It was a pretty cool idea, though."

"I suppose."

Peter had squeezed a small amount of the stuff on the wound edges, coaxed them together with the tip of his finger and smiled—a little smugly—at Dana.

David was chuckling again. "You glued your finger to my head."

Peter laughed now, too, a tear tracking warmly down one cheek. David wasn't kidding. He *had* glued himself to his son's head. For keeps. Like crazy glue, only worse. No matter how hard he tried, he could not free his finger. Dana's renewed efforts to get them to the ER were met with even more vigorous resistance from Peter, who could only imagine the ribbing he'd suffer at the hands of his colleagues if he showed up at the hospital glued to his son's head.

David said, "Get a razor blade, hon," mimicking his dad's deep voice, his desperate solution on that ridiculous day. "Cut us apart."

Peter said, "You're never going to let me live that down, are you."

Dana got a razor all right, and she did cut them apart—but the first time David even squeaked the blade began to err on the side of Peter's flesh, Dana's gaze warning him that if he made so much as a peep she'd separate the two of them at the first knuckle.

David caressed his Dad's fingertip, his weak chuckles fading. "Your fingerprint never grew back," he said.

"Don't imagine it ever will."

David fell silent now, and Peter could feel the light mood slipping away as irretrievably as his son's life.

Leukemia. A cold bullet of a word born of a nose bleed that wouldn't stop. A month of aggressive, crippling chemo. A brief remission and then relapse. A fucking nose bleed in a kid who only six months ago could do fifteen chin-ups and run like the wind.

So much suffering. But it would be over soon.

"Will I see Mom?" David said. "When I die?"

"I don't know, sweetheart. I hope so."

At the urging of a counselor they'd discussed death openly in the weeks leading up to this day, but this was the first time David had asked about his mom. Dana had died a month to the day following the bio-glue fiasco, slamming face first into a bowl of cereal at the kitchen table, an aneurysm in her brain choosing that comic moment to claim her life. Peter had almost roared with laughter before he realized she wasn't kidding. Thankfully David had slept at his cousin's the night before. Telling him had been the hardest thing he'd ever done. Until now.

Strangely, he recalled something he'd overheard an OR nurse say when she thought he was out of earshot. His son had been diagnosed only the week before.

How much misery can one man endure?

Peter thought: *No more.*

"I love you, Dad," David whispered. "And don't worry, I'm not afraid anymore."

Then he stopped breathing.

With a steady hand Peter took the syringe from his pocket, poked the needle into the plump vein in the crook of his arm and injected a lethal mix of morphine and muscle relaxant into himself. Then he tightened his grip on David's limp body and in seconds he stopped breathing, too.

Wherever his son was going, Peter was going with him.

* * *

Peter Croft awoke in a dark, strange room, groggy and disoriented. David was spooned against his chest, trembling uncontrollably, his cotton pjs matted with sweat. They were on a narrow bed—the top section of a child's bunk bed, Peter realized—and as he lifted his head to speak to his son, David's clammy hand tightened on his encircling arm.

"Shh," David whispered, and Peter realized his son was terrified. The terror burned in his flesh like dry fire and now Peter was terrified, too. The feeling was pure and elemental, but without focus, coursing into Peter as if they shared the same skin, the same racing heart.

"David...?"

"*Shh.*"

His son's voice was a low hiss and Peter realized that he had never experienced such utter, unmanning fear. He was paralyzed, only his eyes moving in concert with his son's to focus on the dull brass gleam of the doorknob across the room.

The door inched open on silent hinges and Peter felt the air leave his lungs. Now a figure appeared in the doorway, its shadow long and bulking in the dim light from the hall, and Peter smelled something primal infect the homey scent of this room...the musty reek of pelt, wet with the blood of a recent kill.

Dense and faceless the shape moved, gliding toward them in the chancy light. Peter felt his son's fingernails dig stinging crescents into the skin of his forearm. He wanted to move, to protect his son, but he was unable. His nerves had come unstrung.

He blinked sweat from his eyes and now the figure was *right there* and Peter felt his son wrenched away, replaced by twin impacts around his heart like the hooves of a raging stallion. He opened his mouth to scream David's name and felt something snake into his throat, muting him. Far off, he heard a single, frantic word—*Clear*—then there was nothing.

* * *

Dr. Lisa Black felt her own heart race even as Peter Croft's stubbornly approached death on the pediatric bed in front of her. He had progressed from V-tach to V-fib in spite of a series of shocks and two boluses of adrenalin, and that surprised her. When she had security unlock the door, less than five minutes ago, Peter's colour had still been reasonably good, his pulse irregular but strong. She should have been able to get him back with the first shock—he was healthy as a horse, a runner, slim and muscular—but his heart was behaving like that of a much older man. The exhaustion he'd suffered through the ordeal with his son, though severe, wasn't enough to explain it. Maybe it was whatever he'd given himself. As an anesthesiologist hell-bent on self destruction, his choices of lethal cocktail were many. From his totally flaccid state Lisa was betting he'd used a combination of a long-acting muscle relaxant and a narcotic or hypnotic. That would have led to an abrupt respiratory arrest followed by the arrhythmia she was currently attempting to reverse. Every instinct told her she'd reached him before irreversible harm could be done, and yet he was completely unresponsive. It was almost as if his desire to die with his son had instilled itself in his physical heart too, as if his body was simply refusing to go on.

"Give him three hundred of Amiodarone," Lisa said to the resident assisting her in the resuscitation, then charged the defib paddles and positioned them again on Peter's chest. "*Clear,*" she said and discharged the paddles. Peter's upper body arched off the bed, froze there briefly then fell flaccid again.

Lisa checked the monitor. Still in V-fib.

"Come on, Peter," she whispered. "Don't do this."

"Lidocaine?" the resident said.

"Do it."

As the resident injected the drug Lisa glanced at David's pale, wasted body, stretched out on a gurney where they'd lain it, the morgue crew attending to it now. Then she looked back at Peter, his shirt torn open to expose his chest, dark blood still tricking from the injection site in his arm, the discharged syringe lying next to him on the bed. She should have seen this coming, should have acted sooner. Peter had asked her to give him a few minutes alone with his son after the remote monitors went flat. As David's physician she'd had the power to grant that wish, not an uncommon one, but her instincts had twitched at the reso- lute expression that had hardened Peter's eyes when she agreed. She'd known Peter since med school, had dated him briefly early in their respective residencies, and though they'd decided they were a better fit as friends, she knew the man well. Knew how much his son meant to him. She'd been sitting at the bank of monitors at the nursing station when David's vitals faltered then flat-lined, and had lingered there for at least two minutes, torn between her promise to her friend and the growing certainty that something terrible was going on in that room. Then a nurse had approached her on another matter, breaking the spell, and Lisa jumped out of her chair shouting, "Get security up here *now*," then dashed down the hall to David's door, David's locked door, and she'd *known* it and had simply sat there on her backside.

Lisa refocused her attention on the resuscitation. Peter was still in V-fib.

"Okay," she said, recharging the paddles, "I'm going to shock him again. *Clear.*"

Peter's body bucked, the muscles in his chest bulging into tortured striations.

And the resident said, "Good job, Lisa. You got a rhythm."

"Alright," Lisa said, watching the morgue attendants wheel David's sheeted form out of the room, "let's get him to the unit."

* * *

Consciousness came all at once, a dash of cold water in the face, and Peter sat bolt upright in his ICU bed, a violent birth from a darkness that was vast and barren. In that first instant he knew only terror, the details of his life erased by it, and he lashed out against it, ripping the IV from his arm, dislodging the tube from his throat to give voice to his scream. His first awareness was that of hands pressing him down, and overlapping voices, and though his eyes were open he could discern only shape and shadow.

"David?" he said, his voice a dry rasp, his eyes wild now, leaking pain. *"David?"*

"Peter, it's Lisa."

A familiar voice, silencing the others.

"Please, try to stay calm."

The hands restraining him relaxed and he sagged back on his elbows, his gaze focusing on Lisa. She was a touchstone in the midst of his confusion and he let her words guide him the rest of the way into the world. His last clear recollection was of trying to think of a story to tell David. The rest was a swirl of muddy water.

"You're in ICU," Lisa was telling him, and now he could see that he was. He lay back against the pillow. "You're going to be fine."

"What happened? Where's David?"

He watched Lisa turn to the other people in the room— staff members, Peter realized, concerned faces resolving into familiarity—heard her say, "Leave us."

When they were alone Lisa sat on the edge of the bed and took his hand. In this merciful fog of amnesia and bewilderment, Peter managed a wan smile.

"Did I have an accident? There's no pain."

Lisa squeezed his hand. "Peter, David's dead. He passed just over an hour ago."

"That can't be." He was up on his elbows again, his eyes glazing over. "They promised to call me...I wanted to be with him."

"You were with him, Peter."

And even before she said it he remembered David's last little smile, his breathless reassurance that he was no longer afraid, then the sting of the needle and his unspoken promise to his son, to follow him into the unknown, to protect him if he could. After that there was nothing.

He looked into Lisa eyes. "You said you'd leave me alone with him."

"Peter, I—"

"You *promised*. You fucking *promised* and now he's out there all alone..."

Lisa got to her feet, jerking her hand from the tightening vise of Peter's fist.

"How dare you," he rasped, struggling in his weakened state to climb out of bed. "You had no *right*." Then he was over the edge, crashing to the floor beside the bed, an IV pole laden with med pumps tipping into the monitors. He continued to rail against Lisa even as the staff lifted him onto the bed, restrained him and drugged him back into oblivion.

When he was quiet Lisa fled the unit in tears. It would be months before Peter spoke to her again.

2.

Wednesday, May 30

"Good morning, Peter, it's Wendell."

Peter hit the pause button on the DVD remote; he knew he should have ignored the phone. He breathed and said, "Hi, Wen."

Wendell Smith was the head of the anesthesia department. He'd been calling twice a week for the past month, trying to get Peter to commit to a date for his return to work.

"Sorry to bother you about this again," Wendell said, "but we need a decision here, manpower being what it is."

Peter's first impulse was to tell him to forget it, he was done with the whole damned rat race. Though he was only forty-two, he'd been smart with his money. He could retire today if he chose to, not lavishly, but comfortably. And comfortable would be a welcome sensation right now. But the department had been good to him, giving him plenty of time to get his act together—it had been almost four months since the funeral—and like most people in the medical community, for Peter the pull of duty was a powerful one.

He glanced at the room around him: the bed unmade since the cleaning lady had last done it a week ago; the curtains drawn against the daylight; every available surface littered with fast food containers and empty pop cans. Since David's death he'd spent the majority of his time in here, the bedroom he'd shared with his wife.

And just down the hall, David's room.

"I'm not ready yet, Wen. I can't even tell you when I will be." Then he was saying it. "If ever. To be honest, if you need to fill the slot, I'd say go ahead and do it. You've got some promising recruits, I know that." He felt an unexpected lightness in his chest. "Maybe you should just go ahead."

Silence. Then: "Do you know what you're saying here, Peter?"

"I believe I do."

"Tell you what. Take a couple more weeks. We'd hate to lose you. If it's time you need, you should have it. We'll get by. I'll check back with you around the middle of June. Okay?"

"Okay. Thanks. If anything changes, I'll let you know."

"I appreciate that. Talk to you soon. And take care."

"Shall do. Bye for now."

He replaced the handset in its cradle and returned his gaze to the TV, a thirty-two inch flat screen built into the wall unit Dana had loved so much. He'd been half-watching an episode of I Love Lucy on DVD, one of many gifts people had given him in the months since David's death, all of it thoughtfully designed to lift his spirits. Looking now at the screen—Lucy still frozen in the midst of stomping around in a tub full of grapes— Peter understood that since his son's death what he'd been desperately trying to avoid was the pauses, the lulls in the stream of input he'd been exposing himself to through every waking moment, sleep coming only when his eyes could no longer endure the light, his mind the ceaseless chatter. He'd jacked into the tube and let it zombify him. He could lose himself in it, ride it downstream, forever if need be. The pauses were the hard part.

He thumbed the play button and the chatter resumed, numbing him.

* * *

Hunger. That gnaw. There was the animal part of him— bladder, bowels, hunger, thirst, fatigue—and the rest was emptiness, the absence of drive or enthusiasm, the simple baseline energy required to power a life. His friends had been after him to seek counseling, all of them doing their level best to snap him out of it, set him back on the path. But the path to where? What was left after family? His family had been his engine, the centre from which all things flowed and into which all of his energies were directed. What was he supposed to do now, pick up and start again? He just couldn't see it. A family was not a car, an item you simply replaced if it got trashed. It was over and he could see no path.

His younger brother Colin, a marine biologist with the University of British Columbia, had spent the first two weeks after the funeral here at the house, helping Peter box up all of David's stuff. After convincing him it was time to deal with David's possessions, Colin had been firm, telling him to get rid of it all. "The last thing you need," he'd said, "is stuff like this jumping out at you, breaking your heart all over again." Colin had been thorough, almost brutally so, moving furniture, running his hand around every seat cushion on the couches and chairs, looking under beds, even touring the grounds for lost balls or toys. Peter had to argue with him and finally insist on keeping the family photos in place. "I managed after Dana died," he told Colin. "I'll manage now." They stored some of it in boxes in the attic, things Peter just wasn't ready to let go of yet. The rest, clothes and toys mostly, Colin drove to the nearest Salvation Army drop station.

Like most people who cared about Peter, what concerned Colin most was his apparent suicide attempt. Peter could read the questions in his eyes: Why had he done it? And if left to his own devices, was he at risk for trying it again? One night near the end of Colin's stay the two of them had sat at the kitchen table and Colin had put those very questions to him. And Peter had explained that it hadn't been a suicide attempt, at least not in the accepted sense—ending his life had not been the point. He'd been trying to accompany his boy on his journey into eternity or oblivion or whatever it was that awaited him on the other side. Misguided, perhaps, but he told his brother he felt certain it would have worked. Colin, a realist who believed that once you were dead you were dead and that was the end of it, said he understood and they left it at that.

Peter swung his legs off the bed, the hunger working on him now, giving him a headache, a familiar throb in his temples. The trigger levels for his biological imperatives had ramped way up. To eat he had to be starving, to relieve himself required a bladder full to bursting. Otherwise he couldn't be bothered.

He was starving now.

Dressed only in his skivvies, he padded into the kitchen. He'd made a survivalist grocery run about a month back, stocking up on canned soups and stews, cereals, snack foods. Empty calories to fill a hole that couldn't be filled. He opened a can of beef barley soup and popped it into the microwave. When the oven beeped he retrieved the steaming bowl, scalding his fingers as he hustled it toward the nearest counter. The pain made him lurch, the action slopping more soup onto his fingers and the shin of his left leg. Peter screamed and the bowl slipped his grasp, shattering against the ceramic floor tiles, the soup splattering his ankles. He cursed and felt something malign rise up in him, rending its restraints in a single massive pull. By reflex he danced away from the spatters of hot soup and skidded in the puddled liquid, losing his footing and falling backward into the tight space between the microwave and the cook island. His left buttock came down on a jagged shard of bowl and now the fury was loose in him, rampant, and he cursed and thrashed in a slick of cooked barley and fresh blood, cursed and roared and wished for death. Now he rolled onto his side, away from the pain in his backside, and his fist found the metal drawer beneath the oven and pummeled it without pause, blow after senseless blow until blood flowed from his knuckles too.

And when it seemed his rage could not be tamed, that he would thrash and wail until his body imploded from the force of it, he noticed something under the fridge, cocooned in a dust kitty, just within reach of his fingers. Tears standing in his eyes, he retrieved it and sat up with it in his palm, plucking it free of its shroud. The smile the sight of it brought felt pleasant on his face, a beam of August sunshine in the pit of January cold.

It was a tiny crystal figurine of a cat he'd bought for David when he was five or six. David had spotted it in a downtown boutique and had all but begged Peter to get it for him. It had seemed to Peter an odd thing for a small, active boy to want, but he'd bought it for him just the same. And David had treasured it, holding it up to the light in the daytime, storing it at night in a toy safe only he knew the combination for. He'd been playing with it one evening some months later and had gotten distracted by an episode of *The Simpsons*, his favourite TV show. After that it was lost, just...gone, and it had stayed that way until this very moment. How it ended up where it did Peter couldn't imagine, but the loss of it had broken David's heart. Even Peter's offer to replace it with an identical one had failed to mend the blow. "It's okay, Dad," David had said. "I'll keep looking for it." And he had. Even a year later, Peter would sometimes find his son searching for it. He finally gave up when they bought him the twenty gallon fish tank that still bubbled away on a stand in the family room. David had wanted just the one fish, a gold, bubble-eyed, genetically engineered monstrosity that waddled around the tank gobbling flake food and shitting on the plastic plants. That stupid creature had outlived its keeper. One of the most devout promises Peter had made to his son before his death was to make sure his fish got fed every day and its water got changed once a month. Not trusting his dad's memory, David had written the instructions down in an open, carefree script that was just beginning to reflect his personality.

Peter held the figurine up to the glow of the kitchen window. He saw that one of its ears was missing. He rotated it slowly in the light, as David had done, and a reflected needle of sun-light stung his eye, shattering a floodgate of misery the depth of which Peter would never have imagined possible. Terrible, breath-less sobs wracked him, tears as hot as the soup streaming from his eyes, and Peter was swept away by it. In the months since the funeral he had shed barely a tear, letting his anger at God and Medicine and Lisa Black—the woman who called herself his friend yet sabotaged his only hope of being with his son—sustain him. He had bitten the bullet, stoically plodding on while turn-ing his face from the truth each time it reared its ugly head.

But all of that was behind him now. He was caught in this undertow of pain and grief and he could no longer summon the fight to escape it.

He let it come.

* * *

Lying on the kitchen floor, the rhythm of his breathing al-most normal now, Peter imagined that the way he felt in this moment must be much the way a woman feels following a diffi-cult labor that produces only a stillborn. There is no joy in it, but the relief at having it over with is immeasurable.

He picked himself up, found a bucket under the sink and mopped up the mess. Then he got in the shower, his hunger gone. The wound in his buttock was still leaking blood and would prob-ably require stitches. This made him think of bio-glue and in-duced a bout of crazed laughter that scared him a little. The skin on three of his knuckles had peeled off, leaving flaps of tissue he would coax back into place with band-aids. The hand hurt like hell.

He lingered under the stinging spray until it started to chill, watching the pink water swirl down the drain, then toweled himself off and attended to his wounds, using the bathroom mirror to guide the repair on his backside, drawing the jagged wound edges together with Steri-strips he'd pilfered from work. If the sticky strips held, he might get away without stitches. He dressed in T-shirt and jeans, tucked the crystal kitty into his pocket and went out the front door for the first time in three weeks.

* * *

The street was slick from an earlier rain, the blacktop steaming in the sun, and it occurred to Peter as he focused on the day that he'd missed the part of spring he enjoyed most, that sudden, abundant renewal after months of sub-zero temperatures. He'd moved to Sudbury from Ottawa thirteen years ago, the winters so cold here he sometimes worried there would be no spring, that nothing could survive such relentless, barren cold. The day three weeks ago that he'd last left the house—he couldn't even remember what had taken him out on that day—there had still been isolated mounds of snow in the yard and not a leaf or a new blade of grass in sight. Now, in this brilliant sunshine with everything freshly scrubbed, it seemed a different world, a world in which his son might still be alive, and for a moment he half expected David to come romping around the corner of the house, smiling and saying, "Hey, Dad, what a day..."

He leaned against the porch railing and took the crystal kitty out of his pocket, standing it upright in his palm. He supposed there would be moments like this for the rest of his life, instants in which holes appeared in the fabric of reality and anything seemed possible. In these moments his son could be alive, all that had come before just a grinding nightmare extinguished at last by a beautiful day or a treasured object; his first instinct upon finding the kitty had been to run tell David about it, knowing how delighted he would be, even now, all these precious years later.

He pocketed the figurine and looked down the street. He lived in a quiet, upscale neighbourhood in the Moonglow sub-division, elegant homes built shoulder to shoulder, the crab apple trees the city had planted on each lawn just beginning to blos-som. As he watched, a school bus chuffed to a stop across the street and a group of kids piled out, laughing and chatting, backpacks stuffed with books and empty lunch pails. One of them was David's best chum, Thomas, a rail thin redhead with ears like jug handles. He broke off from the pack to tag along with a tall girl named Sophie. Thomas and David had both been a little sweet on Sophie, an eleven year old who won math contests and played the saxophone, her nightly practice ses-sions setting the neighborhood dogs howling. The two of them were giggling about something and Thomas happened to glance Peter's way. Their eyes met and Peter saw the boy's happy ex-pression flee his face; it seemed to actually sheer away, the change so abrupt it stole Peter's breath. Thomas jerked his gaze away and now Sophie's eyes found him, and she looked away too. Stricken, the kids quickened their pace, heads bowed in silence, until they reached Sophie's house and hurried into the open garage. The experience heightened Peter's dread of re-turning to work, the awkwardness of the whole process of bereavement, the culture's total lack of meaningful words or interactions in approaching those left behind. In a way, the kids' reaction had been the more genuine one. No one wanted to face it. The bereaved was someone you hoped to avoid, but realized that ultimately, particularly where friends or co-workers were concerned, you simply could not. So you had to come up with something, some statement, some thoughtful gesture. Peter was not looking forward to it. He worked with more than a hundred people at different times and was acquainted with a couple hundred more. And however well intentioned their efforts might be, each encounter would be a fresh kick in the stomach.

He made his way gingerly down the steps, the puncture wound in his butt starting to throb, and eased into his gray Corolla.

* * *

Peter was a lapsed Catholic, but when the issue of where to bury his wife had come up he hadn't objected to her parents' wish that it be consecrated ground. Saint John's was a well maintained, isolated cemetery near the town of Warren, where Dana had grown up and her mother still lived. When Peter purchased the plot, the funeral director suggested he reserve an adjacent one for himself, which he had. It had never occurred to him he'd be using it for his son. In making David's arrangements, he'd reserved a third plot for himself.

He parked in the empty lot and limped along a cobbled path toward a gaudy mausoleum, since 1973 the final resting place of one Donald Brushwood Jr., who had once been mayor of Warren. During David's funeral Peter had absently noticed it, deciding it was a perfect landmark in this hilly suburb of the dead, David and Dana's graves almost in its shadow. The last thing he wanted was to end up wandering around this dreadful place in search of his family.

David's marker was beaded with rainwater, striking in its newness next to Dana's, which had already begun to weather and fade. Peter had decided on a glossy, black marble finish that resembled the lobby floor in a Toronto hotel David had loved staying at, not because of the spacious rooms or the heated pool, but because of that polished floor. *Look, Dad, you can see yourself in it.* Peter could see himself now, a husk of a man perched on the rim of a rectangle of sod that was slightly sunken, sadly out of place in its smallness. The inscription was rendered in gold, David's favourite colour. It read simply, *David Croft, Beloved Son of Dana and Peter.* And the dates, *February 10, 1998 – February 8, 2008.*

Peter took the tiny figurine out of his pocket, pixies of refracted sunlight capering around it in his palm. He held it up between his fingers.

"Look, bud," he said, a curious peace in his heart. "I found it."

David's voice, in his mind. Warm, pleased. *Thanks, Dad. Where was it?*

"Under the fridge. Can you believe it? We looked everywhere, didn't we?" He walked along the edge of the plot to the headstone and set the kitty on top. "I'll leave it right here, okay?"

He stood there for a long time, deciding. Then he turned away. Fresh clouds had gathered in the interim, and as he made his way back to the car fat spits of rain struck the cobblestones around him.

3.

Monday, June 4

He arrived early on his first day of work, intending to change quickly and get to his room, thereby limiting the number of people he ran into. By some strange blessing, the first person he did see was Brent Chamberlain, a chubby guy who smoked too much and worked on the cleaning staff. He and Brent had grown close over the years, sharing an offbeat sense of humor and an abiding love of movies. And though they rarely socialized outside of the hospital, they were always pleased to see one another. At the funeral Brent had approached Peter with tears in his eyes. "I'm only gonna say this once, chum," he said, "then I'm never gonna talk about it again, unless you tell me you want to, in which case I'm there for you night or day." He wrapped his big hand around Peter's arm. "This is unbelievably shitty. And if I could, believe me, I'd trade places with your boy this very minute. No man should have to bury his child. I love you, Pete. You're a good friend. Decent. I can't tell you how sorry I am." Then he hugged Peter and said, "That's it." He'd been the last to leave before Peter, who asked him for some time alone with his boy.

He met Brent in the hallway outside the Ophthalmology suite, which was located one level down from the main OR, in an older part of the hospital. Wendell had seen to it that Peter got an easy room his first day back. A list of fourteen cataracts was usually finished by one o'clock.

Brent, who'd been servicing a sterilizer, smiled when he saw Peter coming. "You dog," he said, gripping Peter's hand, shaking it hard. "Good to have you back."

"Good to be back," Peter said. "I think."

"I hear that," Brent said. He released Peter's hand, then, eyes twinkling, told him a goofy joke—something about a Newfie, a leopard skin Speedo and a potato—and Peter lost it. For a moment he feared it would be the same breed of crazed laughter that had possessed him in the shower the other day, but it turned out to be just a good old belly laugh, and he wanted to hug Brent for bringing it out of him.

Shaking his head, Brent picked up his mop and headed off down the hall. "See you around, Doc," he said without looking back.

"You bet," Peter said and walked into his room, feeling human for the first time since his son got sick.

* * *

The staff in Ophthalmology seemed to sense Peter's apprehension, and each in their own way got it over with quickly: a whispered, "Good to have you back," an affectionate hug, a brisk handshake and it was done. Surprisingly, the familiar rhythms of routine had a soothing effect. Unlike the numb hours spent in front of the tube, the work brought a sense of purpose, and at times Peter found himself distanced from the pain, a welcome but strangely guilt-inducing sensation. He'd grown so accustomed to the weight of his loss, setting it down even for a moment seemed a betrayal. Still, it was a relief to concentrate on the needs of others for a change. Cataract patients were often elderly, old school in their attitudes, and Peter welcomed their warm expressions of gratitude.

One old gal in her eighties squeezed his hand while he was starting her IV, and when Peter met her milky gaze he thought he saw something there—pity? empathy?—as if the years and her own losses had allowed her to see beyond the visible. She startled him further when he tried to take his hand away and she held on with spidery strength, saying, "It'll be okay," through a toothless grin. She released him as the nurse started to prep her eye, leaving Peter to wonder if the old woman had been referring to her surgery or if she was somehow privy to what he was going through. He wanted to ask her about it later, but her son was waiting for her in the recovery area and the turn-over in Ophthalmology was brisk. By the time he started the IV on the next patient, the woman was gone.

They broke for lunch at eleven-thirty and Peter took a back staircase to the basement-level cafeteria. A few people who knew him glanced his way, but no one approached him. He had the girl at the deli counter make him a salami sandwich and started back along the main hall to the stairwell, thinking he'd find a quiet corner upstairs in which to eat. There was a big message board along one wall, papered with job postings, bake sale flyers and the like, and as he passed it something caught his eye: a *Child Find* poster, an artist's rendering of a boy of maybe eight with huge doe eyes that seemed to stare right through him. Surrounding it were dozens of photos of smiling children, each displayed under the same stark banner: MISS-ING. Peter found himself focusing on one of them in particular, an adorable little boy with a full head of blond, popcorn curls. He was clutching a beat up teddy with button eyes and a heart-shaped nose, the brief text saying he'd vanished from his own back yard six years ago. And here was another, a girl of about David's age, missing since the summer of 2000. Eight years.

And so many others…

Standing there, looking from face to face, Peter thought of how horrible it must be, the wondering; how it would work on your nerves without mercy or pause. Were they still alive? Six years later? Eight? Would their loved ones ever see them again? With David's death so fresh in his heart, he found himself thinking that losing his son in this manner would have been much worse. So few of these kids ever turned up alive. The hope would be unendurable, a shoreless sea with only the slenderest of reeds to cling to.

To gaze on these lost faces was torture, yet he couldn't look away.

This one, the curly blond. Peter's eyes were repeatedly drawn to him. What an angel. Almost six when he was taken. He'd be

nearly twelve now. Peter could picture himself as the boy's father, still wandering the streets, scanning the faces of every
curly headed kid he saw—*What if they dyed his hair?*—realizing
the boy could be buried in the neighbor's basement next door
or sold into slavery in a Russian village and he'd never know
the difference. The mere thought of it made the world seem
impossibly large. Searching would be as pointless as it would be
fruitless. But search he would, without end.

Behind him people streamed by, going about their duties,
but Peter was unaware of them, in this moment as lost as these
children, these precious faces push-pinned to the wall. What
kind of monster stole a child? What aberration of human cir-
cuitry did it require to abduct, rape and kill an innocent *child?*
If he could get his hands on one of these bastards—

Cool fingers touched his elbow and Peter cried out, dropping
his sandwich, greasy discs of salami fanning out at his feet in a flurry
of chopped lettuce; looking at it on the worn green tiles, Peter wondered how he could have found it even remotely appetizing.

"Oh, my God, Doctor Croft, I'm sorry."

It was Rose, one of the orthopedic nurses, bending now to
scoop the ruined sandwich onto its paper plate. Peter squatted
to help her.

"Forget about it," he said, feeling as if he'd been slapped
awake from a nightmare.

"I'll get you another one," Rose was saying, "I'm such a klutz."

"It's not your fault," Peter told her, rising to his full height.
"I was day dreaming."

Rose was standing now too, red-faced, the remains of
Peter's lunch mounded onto the plate, a scrap of Iceberg let-

tuce stuck to her wedding diamond. She said, "It's just, they were paging you for the OR and I thought you mustn't have heard. They paged you twice."

It was true; he hadn't heard a thing. He glanced at his watch. He'd been standing here for fifteen minutes. "Better be off then," he said.

"Are you sure I can't get you another sandwich?"

He manufactured a smile. "Don't worry about it, Rose. I wasn't that hungry anyway."

He left her standing by the wall of posters.

* * *

Peter finished his day at one o'clock and left the building without going into the main OR. In the change room he considered it, just go ahead in there and get it over with, let them all have a look at him. But the posters had upset him. He didn't even know why he'd stopped to look at them. He'd walked past that display hundreds of times in the past and if he'd noticed it at all it had been only fleetingly; because when you had a child of your own, to ponder such things further was to plug your own child's face into one of those photos, and that was just too much to bear. So you glanced as you passed, felt a tug at your heart and then a flush of gratitude, your own child safe in his classroom or his bed.

He drove home in a light drizzle, thinking he'd pop a movie into the DVD player and maybe jump on the treadmill, get himself moving again. But five minutes later he drove past the video store as if the thought had never occurred to him, his mind drifting back to those photographs, one in particular prominent over all the others, the one of that curly-headed angel clutching his teddy. He couldn't stop thinking about him.

At home he sat at the computer and brought up the *Child Find* site, sifting alphabetically through dozens of thumbs until he found the boy's face, this time reading his name: Clayton Dolan. *Clay.* He had lived on a farm near Ottawa, six hours drive away, and it struck Peter now what was eating him. He wanted to *find* this boy, wanted it in the same way a kid wants to find a lost kitten. The urge—the *need*—to find this little boy had that same child-like intensity, the same obvious futility. Why he felt this way he had no idea. It made no sense. But he wanted to jump in his car right now and go. The power of this notion surprised him; he knew it was crazy and yet he could barely remain seated in his chair.

The desire ballooned in his chest, the certainty that he could pull it off so compelling his body thrummed with the force of it. A plan began to take shape in his mind, and he dragged the cursor to the Bookmark tab and clicked it, clicking again on a link to a site that listed dozens of Ottawa hotels, one he'd used in the past to book accommodations for the anesthesia conferences he sometimes attended in the area. The site opened and he commenced a search for a budget hotel with weekly rates, thinking he could set up his laptop there, pay for an Internet hookup and spend his evenings researching the case and his daylight hours looking for the child. He could start by interviewing the parents, maybe, tell them he was a special investigator or—

Then, under an almost crushing weight of disappointment, he realized how insane this was, really saw it, and he sagged back in his chair, tears rising to his eyes. And finally, he understood that no matter how much he wished it were different, he could no longer face his grief alone.

He left the computer and in his bedroom closet found the suit he'd worn to David's funeral, the material still smelling of flowers and that faint, funeral-home odour of putrescence, chemically sanitized and suspended. There was a scrap of paper in the jacket pocket a nurse had tucked in there, squeezing his arm as she did, telling him how much calling the number printed on it had helped her when her daughter's life was taken by a drunk driver. He took the number to the phone by the bed and dialed it. The woman who answered told him a new bereavement group had started two weeks ago, but they always had room for one more. She said the next meeting was Thursday night at eight in the basement of Saint Michael's Church on Paris Street, and she'd be happy to add his name to the list. Peter told her to go ahead, thanked her and hung up.

Then he went back to the computer.

4.

Thursday, June 7

In med school during a rotation in addiction medicine Peter had attended a series of Alcoholics Anonymous meetings. Members had gathered around long tables, introduced themselves one at a time, then said a few words about how their recovery was going. People drew on each other's experience, strength and hope, and honesty was a mainstay of the program. Listening to their stories, Peter had judged the process astonishing. Here were people whose addictions had dragged them to the very brink, robbing them of everything they held dear while riding roughshod over their often tragic efforts to free themselves of their compulsions. And yet, with the help of the group, they gave up drinking with apparent ease, many of them living out the balance of their lives without ever touching—or desiring—another drop of alcohol.

From what Peter could tell, the bereavement group func-
tioned along similar principles. The meetings were moderated
by a big, balding man who seemed familiar to Peter. He introduced himself as Roger Mullen—and again Peter felt that twitch
of familiarity, the details lingering just out of reach—then went
through what Peter assumed was a standard preamble: stating
the group's aims, outlining the benefits members could expect
from honest and patient participation, finishing up with a re-
minder to turn off all beepers and cell phones. Then, in the fash-
ion of the AA meetings Peter had attended, Mullen told everyone why he believed he was qualified to chair the meeting.

"Though the circumstances of my participation in this group
may be fundamentally different from yours," he said in a voice
that was deep and hollow, "I've attended dozens of these gather-
ings in the three years since my son's disappearance—" and in
that moment Peter made the connection "—and I believe I can
function as a guide to the healing benefits I mentioned earlier."

It came to Peter in a rush. Roger Mullen's six year old boy
had been abducted from his home. The details were sketchy,
but Peter recalled that David and Mullen's boy had attended
the same daycare for a few months when David was about five.
Dana had usually driven David back and forth, but Peter had
done it a few times before they switched to a different centre.
That was where he'd seen Roger Mullen. The man had looked
twenty years younger then, but Peter remembered those striking blue eyes. Thinking of it now, he seemed to recall Dana telling
him that David and the Mullen boy—Jason, that was his name—
had been close. Yeah, Dave had been upset when they switched
him to the new place. Poor kid, really got attached to people.

"I have no proof that my son is dead," Mullen was saying, "but common sense, and my heart, tell me that he is. Though I've never given up hope, to continue believing he'll turn up one day has become unbearable. So I grieve for him."

The room was silent, all eyes on Mullen, standing at the head of a single long table surrounded by the eight other participants that included Peter in this small, cement-floored church basement with the stations of the cross on the wall.

Now Mullen sat, the scrape of his metal chair breaking the spell. He looked at Peter and said, "For the benefit of our new member, Peter Croft, why don't we introduce ourselves and fill him in briefly on why we're all here." He shifted his gaze to the woman seated to his right, giving her a sombre smile.

Peter could feel the pain in this room in his chest, a low G force pressing in on him, making it difficult to breathe.

The woman looked across the table at him. "My name is Emily McGowan," she told him. "Welcome to the group, Peter." Peter thanked her and she said, "My son Sheldon was visiting a friend's house last August. I told him to be home in an hour. There was another boy there, an older boy, and he found a handgun in a closet. For fun he aimed it at Sheldon and pulled the trigger. The gun was loaded. Sheldon was eight." Her eyes welled with tears and the woman next to her clutched her hand. Then that woman looked at Peter and told her story.

Before they were halfway around the table Peter decided he'd made a terrible mistake. He could see nothing healing in this public exhumation of grief, a process that could yield only more grief, and he wanted to leave, was on the verge of doing so when Mullen said, "Maybe that's enough for now," looking directly at Peter as he said it. Then: "Peter, why don't you tell us about your boy."

Peter felt caught, the tension in his muscles refusing to abate.

"You're here now," Mullen said. "Why not give it a shot?"

Peter swallowed hard. His feelings for his son were deeply personal. He had no idea what he'd expected to achieve in coming here, but breaking down in front of a bunch of strangers was not a part of it.

"Please," Mullen said. "The first time's the hardest. Just take your time."

Peter glanced at the exit, then back at Mullen. "David had leukemia—"

"I'm sorry," Mullen said. "That's not what I meant. I meant, tell us about your son."

Something warm welled up in Peter. He looked down at his hands and said, "David was born by emergency Cesarean section. I was a mess. Knowing as much as I did about Obstetrics—I'm an anesthesiologist—I was beside myself. I should have been barred from the whole process. He was coming out the wrong way, facing up instead of down, and they tried to get him flipped around with forceps. But his heart rate dropped and they decided to operate." Peter could feel himself flushing. "We had to change rooms and things weren't moving fast enough for me. Suddenly I found myself alone in the delivery suite with my wife, the poor thing in agony and terrified, and I decided I'd lift her onto the stretcher to save a little time. But I forgot about the catheter in her bladder and when I shifted her over it popped out. The balloon on the end tore her urethra. Then everything went into overdrive. She had an epidural they topped up for the surgery and I sat by Dana at the head of the table with my face buried in her neck and I wept and prayed and made promises to whatever gods might be listening. I didn't look up again until I heard that precious little cry. And when they handed him to me wrapped in a blanket and he opened his eyes and looked at me, I knew why I was alive." Peter glanced at all the smiling faces and said, "Now I'm not so sure."

But he felt better.

And when Mullen said, "Tell us more," Peter did, his words scarcely able to keep up with the rush of memories.

He spent another ten minutes talking about his son, then a couple of other people shared some of the ways in which they were attempting to move on. In contrast to the introductions, the balance of the session was mostly upbeat and Peter found himself settling in, a comfortable feeling of belonging blooming inside him.

* * *

Mullen approached him at the break, offering his hand to be shaken. Peter took it, surprised by its gentle warmth. Mullen was a tall man with the powerful build of a laborer, his huge hand swallowing Peter's whole. Peter recalled Dana saying he was a miner, working underground at Inco. He offered Peter a coffee and Peter declined, telling Mullen he'd never developed a taste for it.

"A doctor who doesn't drink coffee," Mullen said.

"Or golf."

Mullen smiled, deep dimples showing now, giving him a boyish look. "So what do you think?" he said.

"To be honest," Peter said, "I was ready to bolt."

"I caught that."

"But it's alright. I can see how it might help."

"Glad to hear it," Mullen said. "Everyone has something unique to bring to the process. I know it's helped me a lot."

"It's got to be tough," Peter said. "Your situation."

Mullen nodded and looked away, his smile dimming. "I still hope I'll find him," he said. "It's impossible not to. Just last Sunday I spent the whole day driving around town just...looking for him. I can't count the number of times I've done that."

"I'm sure I'd do the same thing."

"Every once in a while I'll think I've spotted him," Mullen said, the smile gone now. "What a feeling that is. I've embarrassed myself more than once with that one." He returned his gaze to Peter. "The thing is, the times I think I've found him? He's still six years old. The way I remember him. He'd be almost ten now."

"It must be hard."

"No harder than what you're going through."

"I believe it is. I was just thinking about that the other day. I feel for you, Roger. I really do."

"Thanks, Peter. And thanks for hanging in. Your listening just now has already helped me."

"Any time."

Mullen set his empty coffee cup on the table by the chrome urn. "Shall we get back to it?"

"Sounds good to me."

* * *

On the drive home that night Peter tried to recall the details of the Mullen abduction. At the time it had been big news, the first incident of it's kind in Sudbury that hadn't eventually turned out to be just a deadbeat dad or a simple runaway. According to the FBI, who'd been called in to assist, this had been a bold, calculated abduction most likely perpetrated by an intelligent white male between the ages of twenty and thirty-five who had no connection to the Mullen family.

It occurred to Peter as he pulled into the driveway that he hadn't forgotten as much as he'd thought about Jason Mullen's disappearance; he'd simply put it out of his mind. Just like the MISSING posters he'd walked past so many times at the hospital. It was sad, it was horrible, but thank God it was somebody else's kid.

But he *had* thought about it, he realized now, for months afterward. Not in any concrete way, particularly once the news-worthiness of the crime began to fade. It had been more of a heightened wariness: a frequent, sometimes impatient rein-forcement with David of the rule that he must never wander off in a public place—and a gut-ripping panic on those occasions that he did; locking the doors at night, then lying awake fretting that he hadn't; letting David sleep with Dana and him nearly every time he asked. The details of the abduction had merely been supplanted, by fear, by loss of innocence. One of the things that had first attracted him to Sudbury was the low incidence of major crimes. Like any growing city there were homicides from time to time, but among people who invited that sort of thing: the criminal element, the druggies down-town. And the sporadic break-ins that occurred rarely amounted to more than a few stolen stereo components. In had seemed a community in which, even if monsters existed, they never came to your home.

One of them came to Roger Mullen's home, though. And when it came it was only seven short blocks from Peter's house. It made him wonder if the crime had been random or carefully premeditated. If what he remembered of the police profile was correct, it was likely the abduction had been planned, Mullen's boy chosen for some reason.

Once inside, Peter found himself back at the computer. He started where he'd left off, the *Child Find* site and that beaming face with the round blue eyes, curly blond hair and dimples bookending a delighted smile. He stared at the boy for a long time, little Clayton Dolan, feeling that same baseless connection, that same gnawing desire to find him where his parents, local law enforcement and the FBI had failed. Then he opened a new window and typed *FBI, missing children* into the search window. Another page popped up, this one entitled, *Kidnapping and Missing Persons Investigations.*

More photos, dozens of them. Kids from all over North America, their names listed next to their photos. He had no idea so many went missing every year. It struck him as he scrolled from face to face that each wore a sunny smile, each unaware of what would soon be coming for them.

Peter found himself imagining how Roger Mullen and his wife must have felt when they woke to find their son missing and he pushed away from the computer, his capacity for grief exhausted. He stood abruptly, that queasy feeling of pause flaring again, a sensation akin to teetering on a high ledge, and he turned his mind quickly to filling the hours before sleep.

He settled in front of the TV in the bedroom, a can of pop on the night stand beside him and a bowl of cheese-flavored popcorn on his lap. Munching his snack, he remembered the countless evenings he'd shared a big bowl of the stuff with David, the two of them cozied up to a movie or *The Simpsons*, and watched the news through shimmering prisms of tears.

* * *

Despite a restless sleep Peter awoke refreshed, a forgotten bud of optimism blooming in his chest. He'd always loved his job, the people he worked with, and he looked forward to immersing himself in that environment again. He'd been allowing his grief and his sunless home to entomb him; and this morning, though little had changed, he just...felt better, like a man with a protracted viral illness that breaks all of a sudden.

He showered briskly and got dressed, chased a toasted bagel with a glass of orange juice, then hustled out to the garage and backed the car into the driveway. The day was sunny, almost blindingly so, and he came close to running over an old doll walking a scruffy Pomeranian past the house. The woman clutched her bony breast and shot him a withering look, then dragged the yapping mutt along behind her. Peter rolled down his window to shout an apology, but the woman just waved him off. He left the window open, enjoying the cool morning air, and performed a careful shoulder check in each direction before trying again.

As he cleared the neighbour's hedge, sunshine beat through the rear passenger-side window, flooding the spot where David always sat, dutifully attaching his seat belt, chastising his dad when he forgot to do up his own. The warm beam of light was broken by four candied finger smears on the glass and Peter learned that his brother Colin had been correct, you really didn't need things like this jumping out at you, breaking your heart all over again.

He left the car where it was, the engine still running, and went back into the house, tears filming his eyes. He found a bottle of window cleaner under the kitchen sink and a roll of paper towels in the linen closet. He doused the finger smears with the tart-smelling liquid and polished the glass with a wad of paper towels, scrubbing it until it squeaked. Then he did it again. When the window sparkled he tossed the cleaner and the paper towels into the trunk and backed carefully into the street.

He wept quietly as he drove, and when the hospital came into view he considered driving past, void now of any desire to pursue the charade of his life. In that moment hopelessness deconstructed him, leaving an empty shell.

But duty pulled him, even now, and he turned into the doctors' lot and parked in the farthest spot, overlooking Ramsey Lake. There was a Dairy Queen napkin in the glove box— another stab in the heart—and he used it to dry his eyes. Then he waited, staring without seeing at the mirrored surface of the lake. When he could feel his body again, he climbed out of the car and went inside. Wendell had given him an easy room again, a list of vasectomies with a surgeon he liked.

He'd get it over with and go home.

* * *

In med school Peter had chummed with a guy named Trevor Ryan, a brilliant student who went on to become an emergentologist. One beery night in second year Trevor had introduced him to the film *Easy Rider*, a Jack Nicholson classic Trevor said he'd seen the night it opened, July 1969 at the Britannia drive-in theatre.

Peter spotted the film in the Drama section at the video store and decided to rent it. Work had turned into a nightmare, his list running late, recovery room full to overflowing, and at the end of the day he'd gotten stuck doing an emergency bowel resection on an elderly cancer patient who almost died on the table. Peter was worn out. A good movie, and reliving old times, seemed like a good idea. So did a few beers.

He picked up a club sandwich at Eddie's and settled in with the movie and a cold beer, Nicholson actually wringing a few chuckles out of him. After that he watched old re-runs, the images blurring without meaning one into the next.

Around midnight he got up to go to the bathroom. On his way back he stopped outside David's bedroom, noticing that some of the paint had come off the door when his brother peeled off the stickers David had collected there.

He put his hand on the cool chrome knob for the first time since he and Colin had stripped the room. It was empty in there now, nothing but a box spring and mattress, David's vacant dresser and a gaping, dusty closet.

Peter turned the knob, easing the door open...and for an instant all was as it had been, the curtains drawn against the night, David peacefully sleeping under his comforter, only his precious head showing in the glow of his computer screen, David's version of a night light. Peter had done this every night of his son's abbreviated life, looking in on him after he fell asleep, thanking God from the doorway for the privilege of being his dad.

The room was empty, of course, that instant, in spite of its vividness, existing only in Peter's memory. As he lay on David's stripped bed he remembered something he'd heard at the be-reavement meeting—*It's okay to hurt*—and he wept into the quilted fabric until exhaustion claimed him.

* * *

Dana had always been the one with the vivid dreams, ter-rifying ones involving snakes, which she feared and detested, violent storms or enraged psychopaths chasing her or David. Peter's dreams, the ones he recalled, were generally more mun-dane. A recurring theme was one of himself trying to reach some unknown destination, but stuck in a maze of hallways or endlessly branching tunnels. Only rarely did he have a dream that upset him or woke him up.

He knew he was dreaming now, though it seemed more like a trance, but he couldn't snap himself out of it. In one respect he didn't want to wake up. He was with David—and this part seemed so real—David lying beside him, spooned against his chest in a room that was strange yet eerily familiar. It was dark in here, the only light a pale glow from beyond the partially open door, but as his eyes adjusted Peter realized they were on the upper level of a child's bunk bed.

His son was terrified—the knowledge came to Peter through a kind of psychic osmosis—and now he was terrified, too. He tightened his grip on his son, the familiarity of this room triggering a memory…this was where death had come for them, but instead of taking them both it had taken only David, torn him from Peter's arms.

He said, "David…?" and David hissed, "*Shh,*" as the door sighed open on silent hinges. Now a figure appeared…backlit, faceless, a hunched silhouette pausing in the doorway, listening with a hunter's patience. Peter could smell it, wet and feral, a savage odour that doubled his terror. It was coming for David, and Peter tightened his grip on his son, powerless to do anything but wait.

Then the figure turned its head, just for an instant, and the dim light found its face—chiseled, baleful, sockets of pure night where there should have been eyes. David whispered, "Do you see?" and Peter awoke dripping sweat in the dark of his son's pillaged bedroom. He felt a tingling on his wrist and when he looked David was standing there in his funeral suit, touching him, terror etched on his young face. And when he saw his father looking he was gone and Peter's skin crawled in cold handfuls.

5.

Thursday, June 14

"The other night I fell asleep on David's bed and had a dream about that day."

Peter had already told the bereavement group about his attempt to go with his son when he died; and though break-time had come and gone, everyone was urging him on. One woman in particular, dark-haired with brilliant green eyes, had been staring at him the entire time, hanging on every word.

"When I woke up in ICU I couldn't remember a thing. I thought David was still alive. But even after they told me he was gone, I couldn't remember what happened in the minutes after he died. I knew there was something, I just couldn't put it together in my mind.

"The dream fixed that."

He told them about the strange room, the dark figure he believed had taken David. "It seemed so real. The dream, I mean. And the weird thing was, while I was having the dream, I finally remembered what happened after I injected myself that day. It was as if the dream was a window onto the world I found myself in with David when he died, and hence the only place I could remember what had happened there before. I don't know if I'm making any sense."

"Perfect sense," the green-eyed woman said. "Please, go on."

Peter focused on her and continued. "The thing is, I don't know whether that room or what happened in it was real or just an hallucination. I did give myself a big dose of morphine, and hallucinations are a common side effect of narcotics."

"What does your heart tell you?" the green-eyed woman said.

"I'm sorry," Peter said, "I've forgotten your name."

"Erika."

"If you don't mind, Erika, I think I'll finish before I tackle that question."

"Good idea. I'm sorry."

Peter cleared his throat, uncomfortable but determined to go on. "The dream I had the other night was different. The first time, that figure—death or whatever it was—it came right up to us. And though I didn't actually witness this part of it, I believe it took David. I was being resuscitated at this point so I can't be sure. Maybe my so called rescuers took me away from David." Tears burned his eyes. "Maybe, if they'd left well enough alone, I could have helped him…"

"Peter—"

"Let me finish, Roger. I need to get this out." Someone

handed him a tissue and he wiped his eyes with it. "This time, in the dream, the figure had a face. David asked me if I saw it, but I woke up before I could answer." He looked directly at Erika. "When I opened my eyes...David was there. Beside the bed, touching me. It was just for a second, but I swear I could feel his hand against mine..."

Erika reached across the table for Peter's hand, her grip dry and strong. "My Tanya came to me in the same way," she said. Her daughter had died at seventeen from complications related to mononucleosis. "In a dream...or on the tail of a dream, like you described. She'd been gone nearly six months and I was dreaming about a glorious afternoon we spent together at Cape Cod on her sixteenth birthday, just us girls. My, how we laughed. When I woke up she was sitting on the foot of the bed with her hand on my shin...it felt like butterflies. She was smiling, peaceful. She spoke to me, Peter," Erika said, her voice breaking a little. "She told me she was happy and that she didn't want me to be sad anymore. Then she was gone." She squeezed Peter's hand. "Your boy's in a good place. That's what he was trying to tell you."

Peter slid his hand away and stood. "I hope you're right, Erika. I'd give anything to believe it. But my son wasn't peaceful. He was terrified.

"I'm sorry, I have to go."

* * *

Roger Mullen waited until Peter had slipped out the door, then excused himself and went after him, catching up to him in the parking lot.

"Peter, hold up."

Peter kept walking. "Not now, Roger."

"Come on, wait up. Let's talk."

Peter stopped in a yellow circle of streetlight, his shoulders sagging. He turned to face Roger. "Look, I'm upset, I just want to go home."

"Is this a good time to be alone?"

"I've been upset for a long time. I'll manage."

Roger swiped a mosquito off his neck; his fingers came away streaked with blood, black in the streetlight. "Alright, but listen. About Erika. She's a sweet gal, but a little out there. You know…Tarot cards, tea leaves, the whole nine yards. She runs a small business out of her house, telling fortunes. She's harmless, but she can't wait to put a supernatural spin on things. She's been a regular at these meetings since her daughter died. Just keeps signing up."

Peter glanced at his car, edgy, saying nothing.

Mullen rested a hand on his shoulder. "Sure you won't come back inside?"

"I'll come back," Peter said. "I promise. But not tonight."

"Fair enough." Roger took his hand away to look at his watch. "I usually head over to Eddie's for a nightcap after the meetings. Care to join me? Say, half an hour? I'll beg off early."

A polite demurral came to Peter's lips and he cut it off. This big man, smiling at him in the dark with a squadron of mosquitoes circling his head, had been enduring the same breed of pain as Peter, only for a hell of a lot longer, and now he was standing here trying to help. To refuse the man's offer would be the worst kind of selfishness.

But it was more than that. As soon as David was old enough to grasp the concept of honesty, Peter had done his best to instill that quality in his son. "Truth," he would tell David, "is a powerful tool. Of all things, honesty is the clearest measure of a man." It was a principle David would adopt to a degree Peter could not have anticipated. Standing here now, he could think of dozens of examples of how truthful his son had become. Even recently, a few months before he got sick, David had shown his true colours. The phone had rung that evening while Peter was cooking and David had answered it. The call was for Peter, and when David covered the mouthpiece to tell him who it was Peter asked him to say he was out and take a message. David stood there a moment, his hand slipping away from the mouthpiece, the conflict evident in his eyes—Do I disappoint my father by refusing his request or do I tell a lie?—then handed the phone to his dad. Peter took the call, then went to David's room later to apologize. And there had been other occasions when David was with him and a lie seemed the easiest way to resolve a situation—the time a cop pulled him over, saw from his ID that he was a doctor and asked him if he was speeding because he was on his way to the hospital. A white lie could have saved him a couple of hundred dollars; the cop actually seemed to be offering him the out. But he had felt David's eyes on him, the little guy sitting stock still in the seat beside him, and he'd told the cop No.

Facing Roger Mullen now, Peter felt as if David were standing right behind him, watching to see if he'd do the right thing.

He glanced at his own watch and said, "Yeah, okay. Sounds good. I'll swing by the video store first and meet you at Eddie's around nine."

Roger nodded, saying, "Good," and jogged back to the church.

Peter stood there a moment longer, returning his gaze to the sky, thinking that the single greatest foible of the human condition was hope. Even now, with his wife and son in the grave, he couldn't help but hope they were together somehow, at peace, waiting for him. You could hate God, but the hate was impotent without belief.

Without hope.

He climbed into the car and drove out of the parking lot.

* * *

"Did youse want menus?"

Grinning, Roger said, "No thanks. Molson Ex for me."

"Root beer," Peter said. "Lots of ice."

As the girl took off Roger said, "You know, I don't believe a person can get a waitressing job in this city unless they use the word 'youse' at least once during the interview."

Peter chuckled. "Same thing in Ottawa. Same thing everywhere."

"You're from Ottawa?"

"Yeah. Grew up there, studied at U of O. I came up here to do a two month locum thirteen years ago and met my wife." He grinned. "The rest is history."

"How's your wife holding up?"

Peter told Roger about Dana's aneurysm and how close he and David had grown since her death.

Roger looked gray. "That's more than any man's share of shitty luck."

The waitress showed up with their drinks before Peter could reply, and that suited him fine. He didn't want to talk about this anymore tonight.

When the girl left Roger said, "Your boy and mine spent some time together at the same daycare. Did you know that?"

"Yeah. After I met you last week I remembered."

"Jason used to talk about David all the time. They really hit it off. He cried every morning for nearly a month after you guys left."

Peter said nothing. One of his principal regrets about a life in medicine was the amount of family time it had robbed him of. He knew that compared to many of his colleagues he'd done his best, reserving the majority of his time away from work for his wife and son. Still, he could have done so much better...

Roger poured half his beer into a frosted stein and took a gulp, a thin crescent of foam sticking to his lip. He wiped it away and said, "You into movies?"

"Love 'em. If I had to do it all over again I'd try to get into the business."

Roger grinned. "Star potential?"

"Hardly. No, the creative end. Writing, maybe. And the software they've got now? Fascinating. I was just getting David interested in a computer animation course for kids the university offers. He was a whip with computers."

"How do you feel about going to them? Movies, I mean."

"You and me?"

"Don't get worked up. It's not a date."

Peter snorted laughter. "Relax, you're not my type. When were you thinking?"

"That new Spielberg flick starts tomorrow. I'm on grave-yard shift tonight, so I'll sleep till one or so. Why don't you call me anytime after that?" He jotted his number on a napkin and gave it to Peter. "We could do the early show, beat the rush, then maybe catch a bite at Mr. Prime Rib."

"My favourite place in the world. I'm in."

"How do you want to work it?"

Peter glanced at Roger's vanishing beer and said, "You're the boozehound. I'll pick you up."

Roger smiled. "Deal."

The waitress came back all smiles with her tray and said, "Can I get youse anything else?" and both men broke into help-less laughter.

* * *

Peter felt good. He was watching *Tommy Boy*, a Chris Farley movie he and David had watched together about a million times. David had loved the film so much, he'd named his goldfish after the main character, and for a while Dana had made 'Tommy Boy' her pet name for David. Peter laughed out loud in a dozen places watching the film, and by the time it was over felt relaxed enough to call it a night. Brushing his teeth, he realized that a big part of the way he was feeling came from the prospect of a friendship with Roger Mullen. Roger was a good guy who understood Peter's situation. The other friends he had were mostly couples left over from the days he and Dana socialized with members of the medical community. A friendship with Roger would allow them to lean on each other, outside of the sometimes morbid circle of the group. He was actually looking forward to their outing tomorrow night.

Passing David's door on his way to bed, Peter considered going inside again; but in spite of what Erika had suggested at the meeting—and in spite of his own vain hope that what he'd seen in this room had actually been his son—he'd already reconciled himself to the belief that what he'd experienced was a dream…vivid, terrifying, heart-breaking, but a dream nonetheless. He could see no point in attempting to relive it.

He climbed into bed, pulled the covers up to his chin and slipped into a deep, dreamless slumber.

6.

Friday, June 15

Friday dawned damp and cool, interrupting an unseasonable, week-long heat wave. Peter drove to work under a dense cloud cover that looked more like snow than rain.

He was on Paris Street now, making a mental note to check the show times on the Internet at work, then call Mr. Prime Rib and book a table for two. He had to brake suddenly for the endless construction that went on every summer on this busy thoroughfare and his briefcase slid off the back seat, spewing books and papers everywhere. Reduced to a snail's pace, he steered through a cordon of orange pylons, shifting his gaze between the back seat and the road ahead while using his free hand to scoop up the scattered contents of his briefcase.

The third time he glanced back the morning sun found a rift in the cloud cover and flared through the passenger-side windows, dazzling him. Peter flinched away from the glare, checking ahead of him again, then squinting into the back seat. When he saw the four candied finger smears on the glass back there he felt an actual impact below his sternum and he gasped like a man with the wind knocked out of him.

He heard a shout and swung around in time to see the hood of his Corolla crunch under the tailgate of a huge dump truck. He hit the brakes hard and the airbag deployed, releasing a dusty gas that stung his throat.

A flag girl appeared at the window and started rapping on the glass. The truck driver climbed down from his cab and a half dozen workers converged on the vehicle.

Peter forced the airbag away from his face and turned to look at his son's smeared fingerprints on the window, still unable to catch his breath.

* * *

"Roger, it's Peter. Did I wake you?"

"Just getting up. What time is it?"

"Five after one."

"Damn. Still looks dark out."

"It's raining."

"You at work?"

"No, the Toyota dealership. I had an accident on the way in this morning; they're giving me a loaner."

"You okay?"

"I'm fine. Listen, I need to talk."

"Sure. Tell you what. When you're through there, why don't you drop by the house? Just give me a half hour or so to shower and get dressed."

"Thanks, Roger. What's your address?"

Roger told him and Peter jotted it on the back of a business card.

* * *

They sat at an antique oval table in the kitchen of Roger Mullen's tidy York Street home, Roger eating the bacon and eggs he'd been cooking when Peter arrived, Peter sipping listlessly from a glass of water. Outside a gentle rain fell from a white sky, a damp breeze sifting in through the small screen at the base of the kitchen window.

"So what's going on?" Roger said.

Peter told him about the finger marks he'd scrubbed off the car window last week, and how they'd reappeared this morning. "I just about polished a hole in the glass getting them off. There's no way I missed any. That glass was clean."

"So what are you suggesting?"

"I don't know. That's why I'm here."

"Do you think somebody's messing with you?"

"If so, I don't know how or why. The fingerprints were inside the vehicle, and unless I'm using it I keep it locked all the time."

"You haven't driven anybody?"

"Not since before David got sick."

Roger wiped the corners of his mouth with a napkin, his breakfast finished. "I don't believe in ghosts, Peter, so there's got to be a sane explanation. Maybe it was just one of those stubborn stains, you know? I'm always dealing with shit like that at work."

"It was candy, Lick-M-Aid or something like that. Clear but crusty; you could feel it. I saw the cleaner dissolve it. It was gone, Roger. Gone."

"I don't know what to tell you, chum, except I wouldn't make too much of it. My advice would be to just let it go. You've got enough on your plate already without giving yourself the willies."

"What about my dream?" Peter said. "What if it wasn't one?"

Roger stood, clearing his place at the table. "You know what? You might be talking to the wrong person." He opened the dishwasher and stacked his dishes inside.

Peter said, "Erika?"

"I have her number."

Peter stood now, too, handing Roger his empty glass. "Let's do it, then."

* * *

Erika Meechum lived in a basement apartment in the Gatchell area. There was a sign above her aluminum door, visible from the street: FORTUNES TOLD.

Peter pulled into the gravel drive and looked at Roger, who grinned and said, "Sure you want to do this?"

"You think I'm crazy."

Roger shook his head, the grin vanishing. "You want to talk about crazy? I walked into a bar one night a few months after Jason disappeared. I hadn't slept in weeks and at the best of times I'm an angry drunk. A biker-type kept eyeballing me, and the more I drank the more convinced I became he was the one who'd taken my son. I ended up beating that man almost to death, along with two of his friends. Spent a week in jail because of it."

"Jesus."

"Yeah. Turns out the guy had trained under me for a few days at Inco, years back. He was looking at me because he was trying to figure out where he knew me from. Luckily, when he and his friends found out about my situation, they decided to drop the charges. So if you think talking to a fortune teller'll help, or a snake charmer, I say go for it. I ended up seeing a shrink. Court appointed."

"Did it help?"

"No. But it led to something that did."

"The group."

Roger was grinning again. "You got it."

Peter glanced at Erika's door.

Roger said, "Want me to come in with you?"

Peter opened the car door, returning Roger's grin. "The voice of reason? No thanks. If you don't mind, I think I'll go it alone."

"Okay," Roger said, angling his seat back as Peter got out, "but leave the keys. I'm going to tune into the Q, maybe catch a few more winks." Peter handed him the keys and Roger said, "We're still on for tonight, right?"

"Are you planning on drinking?"

"Afraid I'll kick your ass?"

"Yes."

Roger laughed. "Then I'll try to keep it to a minimum."

Peter swung the door shut, watching as Roger tipped his ball cap over his eyes and eased back into the reclined seat of the tiny blue loaner. Then he turned to Erika's door and the chipped sign above it, hesitant now, wondering what he'd been reduced to. What could this woman possibly tell him? What Roger had said made sense. Maybe he hadn't cleaned the glass as thoroughly as he thought. He'd been a wreck for months, driven to distraction, crying his eyes out while he cleaned that window. The loss of his son, coupled with this chronic, grinding fatigue, could explain all of it: the nightmares about David, errors of perception. Maybe he was overreacting, giving himself the willies, like Roger said.

He put his hand on the cool metal door handle, thought, *Screw it* and got back in the car.

Roger raised the ball cap off his eyes. "That was quick."

Peter said, "Let's try the snake charmer," and keyed the ignition.

The two men shared a rare laugh as Peter backed into the street. Partway down the block he called Erika on his cell phone and left a message on her machine, apologizing for breaking the appointment.

* * *

Roger said he had a few chores to run in town, stuff he'd planned on doing before their get together this evening. Peter told him he had the rest of the day off anyway and offered to chauffeur him around. That was why, at shortly after two o'clock on that drizzly afternoon, Peter found himself in the New Sudbury Shopping Centre, picking up a pair of work boots from a shoe-repair kiosk with this man who stood a head taller than

him and could beat the tar out of three guys at once. The mat-
inee they'd decided on started at 4:15 and now, with the last of
Roger's chores done, Peter realized he was hungry. Roger suggested a plate of stir fry from a Japanese place in the food court.
Peter ordered the beef teriyaki and Roger followed suit.

They ate in silence at a table in the busy dining area, Roger
only picking at his food, his blue eyes constantly roving, the
eyes of a soldier on the alert for snipers. At one point he came
partway out of his seat, big hands closing into fists, and Peter
followed his gaze to a tall man in work clothes leading a cranky
blond kid of five or six through a stream of shoppers. The boy
was fighting the man, dragging his heels, verging on a tantrum.

Peter returned his gaze to Roger only to find his new friend
already looking at him, ghost pale, beads of sweat on his upper lip.

"See?" he said, then tipped the remains of his lunch into a
garbage bin.

* * *

The movie was great, the food even better. Peter drank
only rarely, but tonight he had a glass of wine with dinner and
now the alcohol was making him giddy.

"Goddam," Roger said around a jaw full of Black Angus
beef, "who's the drunk now? Looks like I'll have to do the driving."

"Nah," Peter said. "I'm already facing a reckless driving
charge, why not round it out with a DUI?"

"Crazy bastard."

They chatted comfortably through dinner, Roger saying he'd
grown up in Sudbury, married his high school sweetheart and

followed his father and three brothers into the mines. His wife Ellen had left him two years to the day following Jason's abduction, moving to Montreal to live with her sister. He said they rarely spoke anymore. Peter told him about growing up in Ottawa, his plans to work in the north for just a couple of months, and how his love for Dana had altered his course. The conversation lightened after that and Peter talked about an idea he had for a screenplay, something he referred to as 'the ultimate reality show'. He said the only reason he hadn't started it years ago was that he'd expected the whole reality craze to dry up before he got a chance to finish. They talked about how unlikely that was now, television riddled with the crap, and Roger told him he should go for it, the distraction might do him good. Peter said he didn't know the first thing about screenwriting and Roger told him he was lazy. Peter picked up the tab—he insisted—and Roger said he'd get the next one. Peter liked the sound of that.

They got to Roger's place just after nine and Roger invited him in. "I got all the Clouseau videos for Christmas about four years ago and I still haven't cracked 'em open." He asked Peter if he wanted a beer and Peter declined, asking instead if he could use the bathroom. Roger directed him upstairs, "Blue door at the end of the hall," saying he'd cue up the film while he waited.

The long stairwell opened into a dimly lit hall, the blue door at the end partway open, revealing a checkered ceramic floor and a glimpse of beige shower curtain. There were three doorways along the length of the hall, two on Peter's left, one on his right. The nearest on the left gave onto a small office with a computer table, an old couch and a couple of wooden chairs. The one on the right, centred between the other two,

opened onto what was clearly the master bedroom. The last door
on the left, closest to the bathroom, was shut. There were chips
of paint missing from the door and Peter thought, *Jason's room.*

He put his hand on the brass knob and looked back along
the hallway, listening for Roger. In that moment the TV came
on down there, startling him, and Peter went ahead into the
bathroom, locking the door behind him.

Though Roger had been separated for at least a year, Peter
saw signs of a woman's touch wherever he looked: the subtle flower
print on the shower curtain; the framed prints on the walls, continuing the botanical theme; the lavender cover on the toilet seat.

When he was done he rinsed his hands and dried them on a
bath towel. In the hall he walked past Jason's door...then turned
and came back, grasping the knob again, listening. He could
hear Roger downstairs, doing something in the kitchen now. And
though his heart was racing, he did not let go of the knob.

Standing outside this door, Peter found himself in the grip
of a compulsion he could scarcely comprehend. A trespass like
this was completely out of character for him. He was a decent
man who respected the privacy of others...yet the urge to open
this door, to see what was on the other side, was more powerful
than any in recent memory.

Sweating now, he turned the knob and pushed on the door;
it opened silently, releasing a pocket of stale air. The room inside was dark, curtains drawn against amber streetlight, revealing only shapes until his eyes adjusted. He found a light
switch inside the door, but didn't turn it on.

He stepped into the room, clearly Jason's: a child's painted
dresser by the window; a long folding table against one wall

supporting an elaborate electric train set; Spiderman wallpaper with matching comforters on the bunk bed...

Peter went to the bed and put his foot on the ladder.

* * *

Roger was preparing drinks when he heard a sound that made him drop the glass he was holding. The kitchen was directly under Jason's bedroom and sometimes, getting himself a beer or a late night snack, Roger would hear the squeak of the ladder on his son's bunk bed, a signal that Jason was restless and changing beds. Though the little guy had always preferred the bottom bunk, when he had a bad dream or just couldn't nod off, he'd climb up top all on his own, telling his dad it was cooler up there.

Roger heard that squeak now.

Time folded back on itself as he took the steps in bounding threes, the merciless guilt he carried for sleeping through his son's abduction welling up in him undiluted. He ran the length of the hall flat out and slammed his son's door open, flipping the ceiling fixture on, flooding the room with light.

Peter Croft was curled on his side on the top bunk, squinting at Roger against the light, tears streaming from his eyes. "I've been in this room," he said in a voice that sent chills up Roger's spine. "I've seen the man who took your boy."

* * *

Roger's left hand seized Peter's right arm at the elbow, the other closed around his throat. Peter heard the man grunt and then he was airborne, coming off the edge of the top bunk as if he weighed no more than a pillow. Clutching the vice at his neck, he landed on his back on the mat beside the bed and Roger's knee came down on his chest, pinning him beyond all hope of escape. He was suffocating, black dots swirling in his vision, his single attempt to speak producing only a strangled croak. He looked into Roger's slitted eyes, their usual sky blue shot through with red.

"Did I say you could come in here? *Did I?*"

Peter shook his head *no*, the swirling dots coalescing into solid black; he could feel himself going...

Then the hand came away, and the knee. Air rushed into his lungs and he coughed it back out. He clutched his throat, his skull throbbing from air hunger.

Roger took a step back from him, breathing hard through his nostrils, shoulders hunched. He pointed at the door. "Get out."

"Roger, I—"

"You can walk out now, under your own steam, or I can put you through the window."

Peter got to his feet, trembling, almost falling. Dazed, he made his way to the bedroom door, paused to look back at Roger—still breathing hard, gaze averted now—then shuffled down the hallway, using the wall for support.

Downstairs, on his way to the front door, he passed the family room and saw the TV in there. The movie was on pause, the Pink Panther cartoon grinning out at him.

Shattered and confused, he hobbled down the porch steps in the dark, to the ocean blue loaner parked at the curb.

* * *

The moon was a night or two away from full, a flawed gem in a tattered bed of cloud. Peter sat on a rocky outcrop on the shore of Lake Ramsey, feet dangling in the water, a silver contrail of moonlight dispersing around his ankles. The water was cold, numbing him, the breeze off the water keeping the bugs away. It hurt to swallow and his head was still throbbing.

He'd been sitting here a couple of hours now, the Day-glo hands on the wrist watch David had given him for Christmas telling him it was a minute after midnight. In the wake of what had happened at Roger's place his mind had whited out, his scrambled thoughts defying any reasonable translation.

Peter shivered now, his gaze drifting from the trail of moonlight to its shifting edge and the black depths beyond. It seemed an apt model for his confusion. His whole life he'd kept to the lit path, his innate fear of what might lurk beyond manifesting in a dozen different guises, from snobbish pragmatism to simple bull-headed dismissal. If he couldn't see it, touch it or smell it, it didn't exist.

But what about now? Had he gone mad? Suffered sufficient brain damage when his heart stopped beating to topple him over the edge? Or was it the loss that had undone him? The unending grief?

Or had his experience—technically, a near-death experience—made him part of a mystery? *The* mystery. That fearsome realm beyond death, closed to most people but for some reason opening to him? Should he trust his senses, no matter how bizarre the circumstances? Or dismiss what was happening out of hand, explain it away and risk losing it forever?

Bottom line, every instinct told him his son was trying to reach out to him. And if there was even a remote possibility of that happening, he had to do everything in his power to facilitate it. Seen in this light, there really was no question. As this logic grew clearer to him, Peter realized that his own closed-mindedness had been getting in his way. He'd given himself a lethal injection in the hope of following his son into the unknown; what clearer expression of belief, however confused, did he require?

He dug his cell phone out of his hip pocket and punched in Erika's number. She answered on the first ring.

"Hi, Peter," she said immediately. "I thought you might call."

His cell phone ID was blocked, but he was too worn out to ask how she knew it was him. "Did I wake you?"

"No, I was talking to my daughter."

He said, "The dead one?" and immediately regretted it.

Erika laughed. "The living one," she said. "She just left. But I do, you know."

"Do what?"

"Talk to her. The dead one."

"That's sort of why I'm calling."

"Are you coming over?"

"May I?"

"Of course. I'll put on some tea."

* * *

Peter wasn't sure what he'd expected—a crystal ball maybe, shelves of exotic herbs and potions—but Erika's place was a pleasant surprise, a cool, tastefully furnished apartment with a big sectional sofa and a spacious kitchen that opened onto the living and dining areas.

Peter settled in on the sofa and Erika sat next to him, pouring tea. There was something on the stereo, *Swamp music*, Peter thought, the kind of stuff acupuncturists and massage therapists played *ad nauseam*—birds chirping, brooks babbling—but this was the only thing even remotely fringe about Erika's living space.

A plump woman, she wore a shapeless, full length dress, her preferred look, this one dark blue denim. She had a wholesome face with a ready smile, showing perfect white teeth. Her hands and bare feet were small, the nails manicured, painted bright red.

She handed him a cup of tea and he thanked her, setting it on the coffee table in front of him. He wasn't a tea drinker either, but didn't want to appear impolite. Erika took a sip of hers then set it on the table next to his, shifting on the sofa as she did, facing him now.

"So tell me."

And he did, leaving out only the parts she'd already heard in group. Erika nodded throughout, the information seeming familiar to her, as if what he was relating was a shared reminiscence rather than a personal event. He finished by telling her of Roger's violent reaction and how badly he, Peter, felt for his trespass, one fueled by an impulse so powerful it had seemed almost involuntary.

Erika tilted her head and smiled. "Where do you suppose that impulse came from?"

"I know what you're thinking," Peter said, "but I can't get my mind around it. On the way over here I was convinced, but describing it to you just now...I don't know. It sounds so crazy. The mind's a tricky thing, particularly when stressed or fatigued; or in my case, both."

"You said Jason's room was the one you found yourself in when your son died? The one you dreamed about later?"

"It was dark…it was a kid's room with a bunk bed. How many of those are there in the city? In the world? Maybe it's just a random memory I dredged up from a magazine or a movie."

"I'm not going to try to convince you one way or the other," Erika said. "You have to listen to your heart and decide that part of it on your own."

"Fair enough…but what do you think?"

She took a sip of her tea, leaning back on the couch with it this time, holding the cup to her chin, blowing steam off the surface. She looked away from him for a moment, thoughtful, then said, "You and David were close?"

"Very."

"Did he talk to you?"

"All the time. What do you mean?"

"When something was eating him, would he bring it you?"

Peter averted his gaze. "It was better after he got sick; we talked about everything then. Before that the only person he really opened up to was his grandmother. Dana's mom. She owns a deer farm near Warren. Dave spent all his summers there from the time he was about two. He loved the place."

"You shouldn't feel bad about that. Boys often find a woman to confide in. On certain topics dads can seem a tad unapproachable."

"I always blamed it on my job. The long hours."

"You said your son and Jason were about the same age?"

"Yeah."

"When Jason disappeared, did you get a sense of how it affected David?"

"It was summer. He was at the farm. He hadn't seen Jason in months. I'm not sure David even knew about it."

"He knew about it, alright," Erika said. "And apart from the loss of his mom, I'm betting it was the single greatest trauma of his life."

"Why do you say that?"

"Isn't it obvious?"

"You think the man I saw—barely saw—you think he's really the one who took Jason?"

"When you were in Jason's room tonight, what did you think?"

"But how would David know about him?"

"I don't know, Peter. I only know that he does."

"So why doesn't he just tell me?"

"Imagine waking up in a place totally foreign to you," Erika said, an avid light coming into her eyes, "a place in which the sun never shines and all you can discern are shapes and shadows. Imagine then discovering that this place is actually the world you've known all your life, but for some reason you've been knocked out of sync with it, the ways in which you were previously able to interact suddenly closed to you. No one can see you and no one can hear you. It's as if you no longer exist. Imagine the frustration. The fear." She paused to blow on her tea, her gaze unblinking, then said, "But in the midst of these emotions you learn that sometimes, though you have no idea how or why, you can reach out and make something happen. Usually not what you intended, but something. I'm sure David would love to just whisper it in your ear or jot you a note, but his best effort might produce only a chill breath of air or—"

"Finger smears on a window."

"Exactly."

Peter looked into Erika's soft green eyes, as convinced as he was ever likely to be. "So what should I do?"

"If it were me I'd start with your mother-in-law. Find out if David said anything to her about it, if for nothing more than to convince yourself of the impact the event must have had on your son. Then, just...do what you've been doing. Keep your eyes and your mind open and eventually it'll work itself out."

"No séance or anything?"

"You watch too many movies."

Peter chuckled, exhaustion creeping up on him. "You're right, I do. Thanks, Erika."

She touched his hand. "Anytime."

At the door on the way out he said, "How well do you know Roger?"

"Give him time," Erika said. "He's an angry man doing his best to carry on. When he's ready he'll come around."

"Do you think I should keep going to the meetings?"

"If they help."

Peter nodded, stiffened a little when Erika gave him a sisterly hug, then went out to the car.

On his way home he drove past Roger's place. The house was cocooned in darkness, the only light a pale glow in an upstairs window. Peter knew right away the window was Jason's. He couldn't be sure, but he thought he saw a hunched silhouette on the drawn curtain, Roger standing where Peter had left him hours ago.

He went home and sat at the computer until the sun came up, staring at lost faces.

7.

Saturday, June 16

Just after seven that morning, Peter called his mother-in-law. She was a farm woman, wide awake when she answered.

"Hi, Katy, it's me."

"Peter. It's so nice to hear from you. How are you holding up?"

"It's hard, Katy."

"I know."

Peter took a deep breath. For a moment he'd forgotten she'd lost a child, too. And a grandson.

Katy said, "What's on your mind?"

"There's something I need to ask you."

"Fire away."

"Three summers ago while David was there, do you remember hearing about a Sudbury boy being abducted from his home?"

"Of course I do. David knew him. The news broke his little heart."

"He knew about it, then?"

"He saw it on TV. I'll never forget it. It was storming that day and I was making biscuits. David was lying on the couch in the living room. When the segment came on he sat right up, and when they said the boy's name he screamed for me. Gave me a terrible fright. I was days calming him down."

"Why didn't you say anything about it?"

"David asked me not to."

"Why would he do that?"

"Children are people, Peter. They have their secrets. Maybe he didn't want to upset you. He was fine after a week or so. He was a very mature boy."

"I know."

"Why are you bringing this up now?"

"No reason. Just curious. Something David said before he…"

"I understand."

"Thanks, Katy."

"When will we see you?"

"Soon."

"Okay, Peter. Whenever you're ready. Bye for now."

* * *

The headstone felt hot under the beating sun. The wind had shifted David's crystal figurine to the edge of the stone and Peter burned his fingers picking it up. He moved it to the raised base, centering it beneath the inscription, safely out of the wind.

There was a wrought iron vase spiked into the earth in front of Dana's monument and Peter tucked a dozen red roses into it, Dana's favourite. Sometimes the ache of her absence ran so deep he wondered if he could ever feel love for a woman again. Dana had been his ideal companion, his refuge, his heart and soul. He missed her humor, her sparkling green eyes flecked with gold, the perfect fit of her body with his own. In this place, the cruelty of her death, and that of his son, weighed terribly on him, making it difficult to breathe.

Eyes glazed with tears, Peter filled the vase with water from a plastic bottle then sat cross-legged on the grass at the foot of the adjoining plots, looking from one to the other in a species of numb disbelief. He'd opted for porcelain portraits on each of the headstones, the one of Dana culled from their honeymoon collection, Dana standing with the ocean at her back, a blush of rising sun soft against her skin. So beautiful. Almost impossible to believe she'd been gone four years. The photo he'd chosen of David was his absolute favourite, the little guy hamming it up in the yard at home, a ball cap flipped around backwards on his head, Terminator sunglasses hiding his eyes, David flexing a bicep in a black and yellow muscle shirt, smirking for the camera.

Peter spent the balance of the day sitting there, sunburning his neck and the backs of his arms. And though he held himself open, there were no signs, no visions, no feelings other than confusion and grief. To think of his son aware and frightened in some dark limbo between life and death was almost as unbearable as his loss. It made Peter feel helpless, the way the leukemia had made him feel helpless. He thought of prayer, but his prayers had already been ignored. Why waste time on a heedless God?

By the time he left, the air had cooled and the afternoon shadows had grown long. He hadn't slept in thirty six hours and it felt like he might never sleep again.

When he pulled into the driveway at home and saw Roger Mullen sitting on the porch steps, smiling guardedly at him, Peter felt something slacken inside him.

* * *

Roger stood as Peter approached, stretching to his full height on the third step, towering over Peter. Extending his hand, he came down the stairs to the stone walkway. Peter took his hand and shook it.

"I can't tell you how sorry I am," Roger said.

Peter was startled to see a glimmer of tears in the big man's eyes. "Me, too. I never should have gone into that room."

"I lost it. Overreacted."

Peter released Roger's hand and smiled, glad to see him. "You're lucky I didn't kick your ass."

Roger laughed and it was okay between them again.

Peter pointed at the steps. "Sit for a while?"

Roger said, "Sure," and they sat together in the heat of the westering sun, enjoying a comfortable silence. It was just past suppertime and the neighbourhood was quiet. Then a dog barked in reaction to a screech from across the street—Sophie on the saxophone, butchering what might have been "Proud Mary". Now a woman in running togs came around the corner from the park, pushing a baby jogger, a kid of perhaps two gazing at them as he rolled by. The woman smiled without breaking stride.

"My wife used to run with David," Peter said.

Roger nodded. "We had one of those bike trailers. Jason loved the thing. Even wanted to go out in the rain in it."

Peter smiled. "You know what I was thinking about on the drive home?"

"Cold beer?"

"I've got root beer."

"That'll do in a pinch."

Peter said, "Gimme a sec," and went inside, coming back a minute later with a frosty can for each of them.

Roger tabbed his and took a healthy swallow, then looked at Peter and said, "So tell me."

"What?"

"What you were thinking on the drive home."

Peter said, "Right," and told him about the bio-glue debacle, Roger grinning and saying, "You're kidding, right?" Peter saying, "Not a word of a lie."

When Peter was done Roger said, "I got a good one, too. Maybe not a match for that whopper, but still a doozy."

Surprised at how good telling that story had made him feel, Peter said, "Let's hear it," and opened his pop, the syrupy liquid cooling his throat.

"Jason was heavy into dinosaurs," Roger said, resting his elbows on the step behind him. "His first stuffed toy was a paisley T-rex. He wouldn't sit through a bedtime story unless there were dinosaurs in it. We had all the *Land Before Time* videos and Jase had them memorized. Me too, actually." Roger chuckled. "Anyway, we're at Science North this one day and it's almost closing time. I have no idea how old Jase was at the time, but he was still in diapers, holding a juice bottle with a nipple on it. All I know for sure is he could talk. I was carrying him around on my shoulders and when the five minute announcement came over the PA we were standing at the live beaver display. The attendant was getting ready to feed the thing a bunch of fresh fruit, and I guess Jason looked pretty unhappy it was time to go because the guy asked him if he wanted to feed the beaver before he left. Jase was a little shy in those days, but I could tell he was thinking about it. Then, a few seconds later in that serious little voice of his, he says, 'To what?'"

Peter sprayed a mouthful of pop onto the steps, almost choking on it, his laughter making an old couple out for a stroll stare at him from across the street.

The men were quiet for a while after that, each dwelling in his own thoughts. Then Roger said, "Ellen, my wife, she was out of town the night Jason was taken. She managed a boutique in the Southridge Mall, did all their buying for them. She called that night from Toronto and we got into an argument over an appointment Jason had for a haircut that I forgot about. She kept going on about it, how it inconvenienced the hairdresser, who was a friend of hers, how bad Jase needed it cut, and I ended up being short with her. Bad day at work, didn't think it was worth making a federal case out of. Finally, when she wouldn't let it go, I hung up on her, didn't let her talk to Jason." He looked at Peter with the most wretched guilt in his eyes. "She never got a chance to speak to him again.

"Next morning was a Saturday," Roger said, "and I slept late. Jase was pretty good about amusing himself when I was working shift and his mother wasn't around. He had his

Gameboy, a little TV in his room and his train set. I got up around ten and went to his room to see what he wanted for breakfast. When he wasn't there I figured he was downstairs. It wouldn't be the first time he'd fixed himself a bowl of cereal or an English muffin. So I went down to check on him."

Roger hung his head and went on.

"That moment, when you realize your child is missing, really *missing*...I can't even begin to describe it. It was as if my insides had turned to ice and started to shatter, one chunk after another breaking off until there was nothing left and I was running through the house shouting his name, knowing he'd answer if he heard me but getting angry anyway, thinking that if he was playing games with me I'd ground him until he was thirty. Praying that he was.

"Whoever took him came in through a basement window. I saw the busted pane on my second run around the house, thinking Jason might have forgotten the rules and gone outside while I was sleeping, still hoping it was something that could be remedied with a good talking-to. When I saw the broken glass, that was when it really hit me. My son was gone and someone had taken him.

"By noon that day the entire neighbourhood was in an uproar. Cops everywhere, evidence teams, K-nine units, hundreds of volunteers combing every square inch in a ten block radius. The media were on top of it right away, showing Jason's picture on national TV, interviewing anybody who'd talk to them. At the time I wasn't aware of the statistics, but I found out later that the victims in more than half of stranger abductions are dead within the first three hours. A couple of those dogs were what they call cadaver dogs; I found that out later, too. Trained to sniff out human remains.

"One of the investigating officers was a guy I play hockey with, Bernie Eklund. Good guy, really helped me through those first few days. He was the one who sat with me when I made the call to Ellen. What a nightmare that was. I mean, what are you supposed to say? 'Hi, hon, how's the business trip going? By the way, someone kidnapped our son out of his bed last night and I slept through the whole thing.'

"Ellen really lost it. She wanted to drive home right away, but Bernie got on the phone and told her not to. Told her he'd set up a ride for her with a cop friend of his down there. Guy brought her up in a cruiser. It was a good thing, too, because I'm sure she would've had an accident trying to get back here on her own. I've known my wife a long time, Peter, but I've never seen her that shattered. That...cold. She blamed me; still does. And I know that if she lives to be a hundred she'll never forgive me, not even if Jason comes walking down that street right now. It's torn our lives apart."

Roger took a ragged breath. "Every second that passed I could feel him getting further away. It was the most horrible sensation, wanting to take an active part in the search but not wanting to budge in case the phone rang. The cops set up a special line in case there was a ransom call, but no one really thought it was about money. I'm a miner, you've seen my house.

"By ten o'clock that night you could already see them starting to give up. Don't get me wrong, they were great, all of them. But you could tell that somewhere in that twelve hour period they'd gone from hoping for a living child to expecting a dead one. Most of the rest of it's a blur to me now. I have no idea how many nights I went without sleep, afraid that if I risked it some break in the case might come along and I'd miss it.

"It wasn't long before searching turned to hopeful waiting and even that didn't last very long. Pretty soon I started feeling like I was on my own. After the first few weeks Ellen decided she couldn't stay in the house any longer and moved in with her mother. A friend of mine set up a website for me, *findjasonmullen.com*. At first the site generated hundreds of hits a day—well-wishers mostly, people promising to keep their eyes open for Jason, some of them wanting to know where they could send donations—but that tapered off pretty quick, too, just the nutcases using the site after that. People calling themselves psychics, claiming to know where Jason was, offering to trade the information for cash. Religious types sending prayers, even a few sick bastards claiming they *had* Jason and were writing to let us know, in detail, exactly what kind of perverse shit they were doing to him every day. The cyber cops managed to track down a couple of these whack jobs—one out West and another down in Texas—but neither of them had Jason. Just heartless assholes with nothing better to do. One of them was arrested and charged with something under the Child Pornography Act."

Roger looked at Peter now, his eyes red but dry. "Eventually," he said, "after Ellen left for good and the investigators made it clear they were moving on to other things, the whole bubble of hope and pointless action I'd built around myself—the posters, the website, the days spent out looking for him on my own—it all just...collapsed. I started drinking heavily, screwing up at work, flying into fits of rage. If I hadn't found the group I can't say where I'd be right now, but I'm betting it'd involve either a rubber room or a casket. It's gotten to the point where any fresh hope is like a knife in the heart, because you just know it's going to end in disappointment. And you begin to wonder why you were given such a gift in the first place—this beautiful life, this sweet boy you love with every fibre of your being, whose safety you'd happily trade your life for—only to be singled out to have it all taken away.

"So this thing last night, Peter, the way I reacted. I wanted you to understand—"

"Of course I do," Peter said. "And you were right, I was way out of line."

Roger touched Peter's shoulder. "That's not what I meant. What I was going to say is, I wanted you to understand that in the end, I'll do anything to find my son. Alive or dead. There's nothing else in my life but that. And I would do *anything* to rain justice down on the one responsible. So what I wanted to ask you was…what you said last night…do you really think you saw the person who took my boy?"

"I honestly don't know," Peter said, sick to his soul in the face of what this man had endured. "But when I stepped into your son's room the sense that I'd been there before was overwhelming. I went up that ladder like a robot, and when I lay down I could almost smell David, that sick, medicinal smell that was always on him towards the end. And, Jesus Christ, when you came through that door, I thought it was the guy. It really freaked me out."

Roger swatted a fly off his arm, "You talked to Erika about it."

"How did you know?"

"I called her this morning. She told me how bad you felt."

"What else did she tell you?"

"She said you're not crazy. She said neither of us is. She thinks what you saw was real. She said there's dozens of examples of psychics helping police solve crimes and that in a way, you have that ability now."

"Come on."

"It's what she said."

"Better buy some lottery tickets, then."

"I know, it sounds wacky. But what if she's right? If you actually saw this guy and there's even half a chance you can ID him, shouldn't we go for it?"

Peter agreed that they should. "But what can we do?"

"Call my cop buddy, Bernie," Roger said. "He could show you some mugs shots, maybe. Have an artist do a composite."

"It was just a glimpse, Roger. A big scary guy. It was dark, I was terrified. I don't know."

"Would you be willing to give it a shot?"

"Sure, I guess. What are you going to tell your friend?"

"I haven't worked that part of it out yet," Roger said. He stood. "Can I use your phone?"

"You're going to call him now? It's Saturday."

"Cops work weekends. Got anything better to do?"

Peter said he didn't and brought Roger inside, leading him to the phone in the family room. Roger managed to get Staff Sergeant Eklund on the line and, after a brief explanation, arrange an appointment for a half hour from then.

On the way out to the car Peter said, "You were a little evasive with the guy about why you wanted to see him."

"You said it yourself," Roger said. "What am I going to tell him? Let's get our foot in the door first, then play it by ear from there." He caught Peter's arm, leading him toward the street. "Let's take my rig," he said. "I don't think I could stand another ride in that sardine can of yours."

The two men climbed into Roger's black Suburban and headed downtown.

* * *

Sudbury Regional Police headquarters stood on the corner of Brady and Minto, a beige five story structure annexed to the provincial government building. At Roger's request, the officer in the reception booth paged Sergeant Eklund to the lobby. A few minutes later Eklund came through a door to the left of the booth, wearing casual clothes. He and Roger shook hands and Roger made the introductions.

"Bernie, I'd like you to meet a friend of mine, Doctor Peter Croft."

Eklund shook Peter's hand. "Pleased to meet you, Doctor Croft."

"Same here, Bernie, but please, call me Peter."

"Peter, then. You guys want coffee or anything?"

When both men declined, Eklund led them through the door next to the booth, then down a short hallway to a bank of elevators. He thumbed the UP button, the doors slid open and all three stepped aboard, Eklund selecting level four. "We'll use my office," he said. "It's quiet and there's a computer in there." On the way up he and Roger bantered about the old-timers hockey league they played for, Eklund asking Roger if he planned on coming out again in the fall, Roger saying that he did.

On the fourth floor a series of short corridors took them to Bernie's office, an angular space with an oversized desk, a crammed book case and a computer table, most of the available wall space plastered with wanted posters.

Sitting behind the desk, Eklund told them they'd picked a good day to drop by, business being quiet at the moment, then invited them to sit down. There were a couple of metal chairs facing the desk and the two men settled in.

"So, Roger," Eklund said, "you were a bit vague over the phone. How can I be of help to you?"

In the beat of silence that followed Peter glanced at Roger, wondering if Roger felt as awkward about this whole thing as he did. Sitting here now, in front of this sober-faced police sergeant, Peter felt himself cringing inside, sweat breaking out in his armpits.

Roger said, "Peter here lost his son David to cancer a few months ago."

"Sorry to hear it," Eklund said, and Peter nodded his appreciation.

"As it turns out," Roger said, "David and Jason knew each other from daycare, and I guess they got pretty close. Around the time David died, Peter had a…what would you call it, Peter? A vision?"

"That's as accurate a description as any," Peter said, grateful to Roger for avoiding the more extreme details of that day.

"Anyway, in this vision he found himself and his son on the top bunk of Jason's bed."

"How did he know the bed was Jason's?" Eklund said.

"He didn't at first," Roger said, going on to explain that Peter had seen Jason's room for the first time the night before and had made the connection then. He said that in the vision Peter got a glimpse of the kidnapper's face. He said he knew it sounded crazy, but that they'd been told by someone who knew about such things that when all else failed, the police sometimes used psychics to help solve certain crimes, and though Peter wasn't a psychic per se, they were hoping that if he were allowed to see some mug shots, maybe, or get a sketch done by a police artist, he might get lucky and make a hit. The whole thing came out in one breathless rush and Roger was red-faced by the end of it, clearly glad to have it over with.

At first there was no discernable reaction from Eklund, then he nodded and turned his attention to Peter, who found the man's gaze uncomfortably intense.

"You look familiar," Eklund said. "What part of town do you live in?"

"I'm over in Moonglow," Peter said, the question, in view of what Roger had just told the man, tipping him off balance. "Gemini Crescent."

Eklund was nodding again. "Nice area up there. Peaceful. The wife and I have a place out in Lively. It's a bit of a commute, but the kids love it."

Peter returned Eklund's nod, saying nothing.

"So tell me, what kind of doctor are you?"

"I'm an anesthesiologist."

"You put people to sleep."

"Yes, that's part of it."

"Stressful work I gather."

Peter said, "At times, yes," wondering where he was taking this.

"How did you and Roger meet?"

"Roger chairs a bereavement group I joined recently. We met there a couple of weeks ago."

"Yeah, your boy. How long was he sick?"

"Three months."

Eklund frowned, suspending the proceedings for a moment in what Peter decided was a show of regret. Then he said, "Okay, gentlemen, I'll do what I can for you." He swiveled his chair toward the computer monitor and clicked on an icon, bringing up a screen broken by a series of narrow horizontal boxes used for inputting data. "Believe it or not," he said, "I was the lead investigator in a case that involved a psychic, indirectly at least, and her advice turned out to be not only helpful, but dead-on accurate." He said, "Peter, why don't you come around here."

Peter moved around the desk to stand behind Eklund, looking over his shoulder at the screen.

"This is what we call the *Niche* system," Eklund said. "It taps into a nation-wide criminal data base. If there's a bad boy in this country who's been charged with anything more serious than jaywalking, you'll find him in here. Using the program is dead easy. Just type in as many of these descriptors as you can...Peter, your guy was what, short, tall? Heavy set?"

"Tall and very big," Peter said. "Solid, like one of those old time strongmen."

Eklund keyed the information into the appropriate boxes, then asked for more: race, hair colour, eye colour, a half dozen others. Peter was beginning to feel foolish, answering so many of his questions with, "I'm not sure," or "It was dark," realizing how little detail he'd actually registered.

When they were done Eklund struck the ENTER key and the computer began crunching data. "With a description this vague," he said, "we're likely to wind up with hundreds of hits." He stood, giving Peter his chair. When the first picture came up—a huge, dark haired Caucasian with deep set eyes and prominent cheekbones— Eklund said, "We call this a photo line-up. Scroll through them to your heart's content. If you come across anything that strikes a chord, I'll be in the outer office."

"Thanks, Bernie," Roger said, shaking the man's hand.

"I hope it helps," Eklund said. "Why don't you drag your chair over and join your friend. This could take a while." He paused at the office door. "The sketch artist we use is in today. If you're still interested, we can take a run down to her office when you're through here."

Peter heard Roger say thanks and pull a chair up behind him, but he paid no heed. He was already busy scrolling through mug shots, one sullen looking face after another.

* * *

An hour later Peter was still clicking through photos, the whole process degenerating into a blur of mean eyes, bitter mouths and crude, jailhouse tattoos. Earlier, during the drive downtown, he'd been thinking about Clayton Dolan and his strange reaction to the boy's photograph, wanting so badly to find him, and it occurred to him then that perhaps what he should be alert for here might have less to do with recognition than with any similarly unexpected response; but he'd already flipped through better than three hundred files—nearly the entire batch his vague description had generated—and not a single face had triggered a reaction.

And through it all Roger sat quietly behind him, watching over his shoulder. Peter could feel his frustration, could hear it in the quickening rhythm of his breathing.

Discouraged himself, he leaned back in the chair and stretched, trying to work a kink out of his back. It was Roger who said what they both were thinking.

"This is pointless."

Peter swiveled around to face him. "There's still a few more to go," he said, knowing Roger was right but reluctant to quit. "And if this doesn't pan out, maybe we can approach it from a different angle, ask Bernie if he can thin these guys out according to the type of crime they committed or—"

Bernie knocked once and came in. "How's it going, fellas?"

Roger stood, twisting his neck, irritated. "Piss poor."

"I told you it could take a while. Listen, the reason I came in, the sketch artist has to leave in about an hour. If you still want to take a shot at that, it'll have to be now. She works a circuit through the north and won't be back in town for a couple weeks."

Roger said, "Peter, what do you think?"

"I'd like to give it a try."

"All right," Roger said, "but if you don't mind, I'm going to wait here."

"That's fine," Eklund said. "Sara prefers to work alone with the witness anyway."

Peter turned back to the monitor to flip through the last few mug shots and Eklund said, "Sorry, Peter, we gotta go."

As he came around the desk Peter glanced back at Roger, hoping to give him an encouraging nod; but Roger was looking out the window now, his gaze directed at the park on the other side of Minto, at the kids playing on the swings.

* * *

After making brisk introductions, Eklund left Peter with the sketch artist, Sara MacKay, in Sara's second floor office, saying he'd check back in a half hour or so. Sara was an attractive woman of perhaps thirty with an odd quirk Peter noticed right away: when she blinked, one eyelid came down a fraction of a second ahead of the other. At first he found it disconcerting, like looking at someone with a lazy eye, but he quickly got used to it. On this cheerful, freckled woman it actually seemed to belong.

Sara was a chatty gal, and as she led him to a long table cluttered with sketches and photographs she apologized for rushing him, then outlined her tour of duty, saying it took her from as far west as Thunder Bay to as far south as Barrie.

"I'm on the road a lot," she told him. "Occasionally I consult with the Toronto police, but less so as time goes by. The bigger centres are moving to computer-generated composites now. Damn things are going to put people like me out of business. Forensic artists are a dying breed."

She sat at the table with her back to the window and Peter sat across from her in the only other chair, watching as she squared a piece of paper on the angled tablet in front of her, then picked up a stick of charcoal with delicate fingers.

"So," she said, "tell me about this man you saw."

And Peter did, responding to her prompts to the best of his ability, encouraged by the steady hiss and scratch of charcoal against paper.

When she was done, Sara held the page up in front of him and Peter felt spicules of ice sprout through the flesh of his thighs and up the middle of his back. What she'd drawn was exactly what he'd seen: a negative, a ragged sculpture in two dimensions, dark against dark.

"I'm sorry, Peter," she said, misreading his reaction.

"No," Peter said. "That's it. That's exactly what I saw."

* * *

Roger didn't say a word on the way out to the truck, wouldn't even look at him, and Peter felt as if he'd failed his new friend. Though the sketch had unnerved him in its eerie likeness to what he'd seen, he hadn't been able to recall enough detail— wasn't even sure he'd seen any—for the artist to render anything more than an indistinct hulk, mere shape and shadow. As a means of identifying a real person, it was next to useless. Why else would Eklund allow them to take it with them? The whole thing had been a waste of time.

Roger unlocked the Suburban with his remote and climbed in, starting the engine as Peter walked around the hood, startling him. Peter got in and sat stock still, the sketch in its brown envelope resting on his knees. Barely breathing, he stared out the windshield, the tension in the vehicle thinning the air.

He heard Roger put the Suburban in gear, then heard him sigh. He glanced over and saw him shift back into PARK, then touch the envelope on Peter's knees.

"May I?"

Peter said, "Of course," and handed him the envelope.

Roger pulled out the single sheet of white Bond and rested it on the steering wheel. "Looks like the bogeyman," he said.

"I'm sorry I couldn't remember any more."

Roger smiled, the expression joyless, defeated. His shoulders slumped, seeming to deflate him. "Let's not kid ourselves," he said, tilting the sketch toward Peter. "This is evidence, alright, of how desperate I've become."

"Roger—"

"You dreamed this guy," Roger said, staring at the sketch now, his shattered demeanor changing as he swelled with rage. "Can't you see the trap I'm in, man?" He wadded the sketch in his fist. "My son is dead and I know it. God Himself could appear and *tell* me Jason is dead and I'd *know* He was right...but I still wouldn't believe it. Couldn't." He gazed at Peter with the most fathomless torment in his eyes. "Now can you see how dead is better? I can never let go."

He opened and smoothed the ball of paper and glared at the wrinkled image. Peter was becoming intensely uncomfortable.

"This motherfucker. What gives him the right? What gives him the right..."

Roger lost it then, and it occurred to Peter as he looked helplessly on that he had never seen a man this big, this tough, cry so hard. Feeling both powerless and responsible, he put his hand on Roger's shoulder, waiting for the storm to pass.

Outside on the sunny street a few passers-by glanced in, then quickly looked away.

* * *

Staff Sergeant Eklund sat at his computer and typed Peter Croft's name into the DMV data base. A page came up with Peter's photo on it and all the information pertinent to his driver's license, including his home address. It showed the make and model of his vehicle, its plate number, and listed his wife, Dana Croft, as next of kin.

Eklund printed out a copy on a colour LaserJet and returned to the DMV home page, typing in Dana Croft's name now. The page that came up showed her as deceased. Eklund printed this one out, too. Then he called the hospital and punched in the extension for Dr. Russell Paul, Chief of Staff. After two rings Russell picked up and said a gruff hello.

Eklund said, "Russ, you grumpy bastard, what are you doing there on a Saturday?"

"Sickness never sleeps. Shit, Bernie, are we golfing today?"

"No, this is more of an official call. And confidential."

"Sounds ominous. What's going on?"

"How well do you know Doctor Peter Croft?"

* * *

Once Roger had collected himself, he put the Suburban in gear, refusing Peter's offer to drive. He handed Peter the crumpled drawing, then merged responsibly into traffic. He didn't apologize for his loss of control and Peter was grateful for that. It gave him permission to do the same should the need arise...and he was almost certain it would.

They made the ten minute trip to Roger's place in silence, sitting for a moment in the driveway after Roger turned the engine off. Peter had been sure Roger would take him home. Instead, he glanced at his watch and said, "That Clouseau movie's still in the VCR. Wanna order a pizza and check it out?"

Peter grinned. "I'd like nothing better."

They ordered a deep dish pie from Pizza Hut, half double cheese, pepperoni for Peter, the other half with the works. Without asking, Roger poured beers for them both and Peter thought, *What the hell.* It was a delicious combination and both men ate ravenously. The movie was *The Pink Panther Strikes Again*, one of Peter's all-time favourites, Sellers prancing around as the bumbling Clouseau, avoiding through sheer dumb luck the attempts of twenty-six different assassins—hired by his arch enemy, former Chief Inspector Dreyfuss—to end his witless life. Sitting in a reclining chair by a crammed wall unit, Peter had pizza juice running down his chin and a pretty good buzz on when he noticed a framed photograph of a boy who could only be Jason Mullen, smiling for the camera, a boy with thick blond curls, sky blue eyes and huge dimples, just like his dad's.

Peter wiped the juice off his chin and came out of the chair like a bullet, snatching the photo off the wall unit. Behind him

Roger said, "What the hell?" and paused the movie with the remote.

Peter turned to face him, his reflection ghost pale in the decorative mirror on the wall behind Roger's chair. Staring at Roger with unblinking eyes, he pointed mutely at the boy's picture.

Roger stood. "What is it, man?"

"Do you have Internet access?"

"Of course. What—?"

"In the office upstairs?"

"Yeah."

"May I?"

"Sure, if you tell me what's up first."

Peter said, "It's better if I show you," and headed for the staircase, still holding Jason's picture.

Roger followed him into the office, watching as he Googled the *Child Find* site, then scrolled through rows of snapshots to the one of Clayton Dolan. When Roger saw the boy he leaned in closer, shock closing his windpipe for a beat, Peter lining up Jason's picture next to Clayton's now to drive his point home.

Peter said, "They could almost be twins."

Roger took a slow breath, the startle Clayton's picture had given him beginning to fade, replaced by irritation. He said, "This your idea of a party trick?"

Peter turned in the chair to face him. He'd have to handle this carefully. Their experience at the police station had shattered Roger's already tentative belief that David was trying to reach out to Peter, direct him somehow. Truth be told, it had shaken his own faith, too. But this reaffirmed it beyond any shadow of a doubt. He said, "When I talked to Erika she told me to keep my mind open, avoid dismissing any odd coincidences or feelings."

"I thought we agreed Erika was a bird."

"Why did you call her, then?"

"So what's your point? They look alike."

"They don't just look alike, Roger. They're practically identical."

Roger took a step back from the chair, glancing over his shoulder at the doorway.

Peter said, "Okay, listen. Before I even met you, my first day back at work, I noticed a display on the wall outside the cafeteria. Posters, this *Child Find* stuff. This little boy, Clayton Dolan, he was one of them and he caught my eye. No, it was more than that. Once I'd seen him I couldn't put him out of my mind. When I got home that night I went on the website and found him again, and I was gripped by this bizarre desire to *find* him, just get up out of my chair and start looking. It was the craziest thing. In the end I passed it off to David, you know. Missing him." He turned back to the screen and lined up the pictures again, Jason and Clayton, the stark light of the monitor casting his face in haggard shadow. "But look at them, Roger."

Roger remained that extra step away from the screen. "Coincidence," he said. "I don't see your point."

"They're connected. Don't you see? David *wanted* me to see him. He tried to show me the kidnapper and couldn't, not in enough detail, anyway. So he showed me this little boy, Clayton Dolan...and he led me to you." He turned again to look at Roger, standing with his arms folded now, staring at the floor. "David loved your son, Roger. They weren't together very long, but that's how David was. He got attached. He would have made a great husband and father. My point is, I think these kids were taken by the same man."

"The faceless guy in your dream."

"Yes."

"Do you know how fucking whacked that sounds?" Roger reached past him to push the power button on the monitor. Then he took the picture of his son. "I'm sorry, Peter," he said. "I'm not angry. Just disappointed. If you don't mind, I think we should call it a night." On his way out the door, into the hallway that led to his son's empty room, he said, "I hope you don't mind letting yourself out."

Peter heard the door to the master bedroom latch shut. He sat for a moment in the hum of the computer tower, then turned the screen back on.

Clayton Dolan was there, smiling out at him.

Peter thought, *David, sweetheart, what are you trying to tell me?*

He got no answer.

He left the room without clearing the screen and let himself out of the house. It didn't occur to him until he was on the porch that he didn't have his car. He thought about going back inside to call a cab, then decided the walk would do him good.

* * *

Roger lay on his bed staring with parched eyes at Jason's picture, his body braced against a fresh assault of fury. He was caught in a place from which there was no escape, a fly lying helpless on its back, its wings mired in glue, denied even death's blessed release. He owned a shotgun, knew the feel of that cold steel pressed to his throat; but a dead man couldn't search, and above all that was his mission, to search a world that had forgotten him and his boy. The enormity of it, this demoralizing task, made him feel microscopic, without consequence.

Looking into his son's shining eyes, he imagined him locked away somewhere, suffering unspeakable terror and abuse, wondering why his dad hadn't come for him yet, losing hope where Roger could not. And as horrible as this thought was, it was better than imagining him dead…yet at times, God forgive him, he'd been guilty of far worse. At times, in the cellars of his anguish, he had *wished* his son dead, prayed that the next time the phone rang it would be the police telling him they'd found Jason's body and it was over at last. He could grieve now or he could get his gun and pull the trigger, his son's remains at least giving him the choice.

And now, this demented shit with Peter Croft, stuff he would have scoffed at when Jason was around…he couldn't let it go. Having a child brought you face to face with thoughts and fears you might never have considered otherwise; but losing one, having him stolen not by death but by some faceless savage visible only through the fever dreams of a grieving stranger, that was crossing over into territory from which there might be no safe return. Yet, where else did he have to go? Three *years* had gone by and conventional means had yielded nothing. What choice did he have? The truth was, he'd go down any road, no matter how narrow or perilous, in pursuit of even the most tenuous hope. The trick was knowing when to turn back.

Roger returned to his office, to the face Peter had left smiling on the screen, a face which, at first glance, could have been Jason's. He sat in the chair and held his son's picture next to Clayton Dolan's, thinking, *Uncanny*. Now he stood the picture on the desk and rolled his chair closer to the monitor, clicking on the HOME PAGE button. The *Child Find* site was laid out in alphabetical order and he started with the A's, going through them one by one, struck as Peter had been by the beaming smiles nearly all of them wore. He knew the majority of them were either parental abductions or runaways, most of those turning up eventually, but many more had simply vanished off the face of the earth.

When he got to the M's he found Jason, the picture identical to the one on the desk, and wondered why Peter hadn't come across it while searching the site. Probably never looked further than the D's, his weird obsession with this kid preventing it.

And wasn't that all this was? A grieving man's obsession? A well-intentioned but ultimately hopeless deflection of the pain he was feeling? Busy-work for the heart, twisted into something 'mystical' by the depth of his grief? He must have seen Jason at least once in the past—at the daycare, probably—and just forgotten about it, the picture of this other kid jogging his memory, all these wild connections he was making products of nothing more than fatigue, confusion and a broken heart.

And I let him suck me into it.

He liked Peter; liked him a lot. Under saner circumstances he could see the two of them becoming close friends. But all this...it was too much. It could only lead to more heartache. He'd been doing fine until Peter came along, going to his meetings, getting by. There was really only one solution: it was time to cut the man loose. He'd call him in the morning and ask him to find a new group, no hard feelings.

Roger closed the *Child Find* site and turned the computer off. He picked up Jason's picture and took it downstairs, replacing it on the wall unit. Then he poured a half bottle of vodka into a third-carton of orange juice and returned to the movie, sipping the sweet mix until his thoughts ceased and the credits scrolled out of a peaceful sea of blue, and the blue disintegrated in a rasp of gray static.

* * *

When Peter got home he shook a sleeping pill out of the bottle his family doctor had slipped into his pocket at the funeral. "Use these if you need them," he'd said, then added, "One at a time," fearful Peter might use them for darker purposes.

He needed one tonight. Needed to shut down, fade to black. To ponder things any further tonight was to court a breakdown. He could feel something bending in his mind, on the verge of snapping like a greenstick.

The pill was tiny, bitter on his tongue as he washed it down. He thought of sitting at the computer until the drug kicked in but forbade himself, turning instead to the tube and his comfortable bed. He caught Leno doing an interview with Alec Baldwin, Baldwin doing an hilarious impersonation of Robert de Niro, and he fell asleep giggling, still half drunk from the beer, the tiny blue pill finishing him off.

He awoke in gray dawn light with a sensation like butterflies on his hand from a dream in which Jason Mullen was drowning.

Drowning in shallow water.

8.

Sunday, June 17

Peter stood hunched in the shower and tried to erase from his memory the image of Roger's son drowning, staring up at him from two feet under, round face fish belly white and those vacant eyes, sky blue gone to black. It had been so *vivid*, so starkly real, the dark water green with algae, an arc of sunlight finding the boy's lips, deathly purple against the pale of his skin.

And that lingering touch on his hand...

The steam. The steam was filling his lungs, making his head spin, and now he shut off the faucet and stepped out of the tub, popping a couple of curtain rings as he lurched for the door and swung it open, stumbling naked into the hallway to gasp for air. Standing in a puddle on the cold tiles, he leaned against the wall and pressed an open hand to his chest, trying not to hyperventilate, the swarming specks in his vision signaling a black out.

He put his head down and slowed his breathing. And when his vision cleared and his racing heart settled he went into the bedroom and got dressed. Then he dialed Erika's number on the kitchen phone. He didn't know what else to do.

Erika picked up on the third ring and said hello.

"Erika, it's Peter Croft."

"Peter, hi. You sound out of breath."

"I had another dream…it's difficult to explain over the phone. Can we meet?"

"Of course. Why don't you drop by here? Say, half an hour?"

"Okay, thanks. I'll see you then."

As he cradled the receiver the phone rang, startling him. It was Roger.

"Roger, I'm glad you called, I wanted to—".

"Stop."

The word was cold, final, and Peter did as he was told.

Into the tense silence Roger said, "I can't do this anymore."

"Roger—"

"Please, Peter, hear me out. I'm asking you as a friend to let it go. This whole thing…I can't be involved in it anymore. It's as simple as that. And if you don't mind, it'd be better for me if you found another group. There's a new one starting Tuesday at the hospital, so it'll be handy for you. If you insist on going to the Thursday group—and you're well within your rights to do so—tell me now and I'll find something else."

Peter felt a surprising weight of disappointment. "No...I can switch groups. Anything you want. I'm sorry you feel this way, though, Roger. I still think—"

"I don't want to hear it, okay?"

"Alright."

There was a pause, then Roger said, "Goodbye, Peter."

Peter said goodbye and hung up, feeling ill, this new loss compounding his others, threatening to topple him. He leaned against the counter and hung his head, wondering why all of this was happening. His son was dead, wasn't that enough?

But God, that feeling of him, present in the room, that ethereal touch...it was impossible to ignore. And if it was madness he was slipping into, then he'd embrace it. If his son was in its midst, even in spirit, he'd embrace it.

There was a drawing on the fridge Peter had decided to keep on display, something David had done in the second grade. It showed the Croft family all in a row—Dana, Peter and David—stick hands linked, round, Crayola faces smiling, the three of them standing forever joined on the beach in Barbados, a palm tree angling in on one side, the sun beating a yellow path across the breaking surf. It was David's rendering of their favourite vacation spot, a private, beachfront home they'd rented for two weeks every year until Dana died. All three of them had loved the place, and he and Dana had dreamed of one day retiring there.

Peter straightened the drawing under its banana-shaped magnet and studied the careful strokes, David a natural artist even at this early age, blessed with an almost eerie sense of scale and perspective. Peter looked at their joined hands and for a heartbeat felt the sensation from his dream, that delicate brush of wings on his palm, and his hand closed around it, trying to capture it…and it was gone.

He plucked his keys off the counter and went out to the car.

* * *

When Peter told Erika about the extraordinary resemblance between Jason Mullen and Clayton Dolan—and his belief that they were somehow linked—Erika went to her computer and brought up the *Child Find* site, searching it for Clayton's image. Then she did the same for Jason Mullen, something Peter admitted he hadn't actually tried. It turned out to be the same photograph he'd seen on the wall unit in Roger's living room. Erika made copies of the pictures on a colour printer, then returned to the couch.

"My God," she said, switching her gaze from one smiling face to the other, "this is incredible."

"I thought so, too, but Roger got really upset," Peter said, telling her about Roger's reaction last night and his follow-up phone call this morning. "Now I wish I'd minded my own business."

"No," Erika said, meeting eyes with him now. "There's no way you could have ignored this." She glanced again at the pictures. "And you had another dream?"

"Yeah," Peter said, pointing at Jason's image. "It was about Roger's son. He was drowning, maybe already drowned. Just…staring up at me from underwater. That's all I remember. But when I woke up I got that feeling again, of David's presence. I didn't see him this time, but…"

"Butterflies?"

Peter nodded. "Do you think it means Jason's dead?"

"I don't get that feeling."

"What do you mean, feeling? Based on what?"

"Just a gut feeling. Don't you ever get those?"

Peter nodded, realizing he'd come here looking for easy answers and would have taken at face value almost anything this woman told him. The realization made him feel guarded, renewing the internal conflict that had formed a backbeat to his every waking thought since David first 'appeared' to him: Was what he was experiencing merely a product of grief and exhaustion? Or was his son—his *dead* son—actually trying to tell him something from beyond the grave? For a moment he couldn't believe he was here, hoping to pluck from the ether answers to impossible questions through this strangely serene woman…and in the same moment understood there was no place else for him. No matter how hokey the realist in him tried to make these things sound, he couldn't deny what his heart told him was true.

"Alright," Erika said. "Maybe 'gut feeling' isn't entirely accurate. When I first met Roger he'd already been through the wringer. He didn't come to group voluntarily at first."

Peter said, "Yeah, he told me that story. The guys he beat up."

"Jason had been missing for several months by this time and Roger's marriage was already in trouble. He was drinking heavily, disappearing for days at a time, out looking for his son. The official search had long since ended, but Roger was still out there, stapling posters to telephone poles, distributing flyers in the mail, monitoring a website and just wandering the streets, driving himself crazy.

"When he came to group and found out who I was, he dropped by the house one afternoon and asked for my help, which for a man like Roger illustrates how truly desperate he'd become. I told him I wasn't sure I *could* help, but there was one thing we could try."

Peter looked into Erika's eyes and saw wisdom there, but also a kind of torment. He said, "What was that?"

"When I was a kid I could sometimes see things other people couldn't. Scary things, for a kid, anyway."

"Like what, ghosts?"

"I prefer to think of them as spirits. The doctors thought of them as hallucinations and I spent some time in institutions, learning the joys of anti-psychotics and electro-shock therapy. And that taught me to keep what I saw—and felt—to myself."

"Jesus."

"Yeah. I was eleven. When I was thirteen my best friend's dog went missing, a beautiful Samoyed named Booker. Booker had slipped his collar one night and run off. He'd been gone a couple of days and Terry, my friend, was beside herself, carrying the dog's collar with her everywhere. We were sitting on the steps at my house one morning and Terry started crying. She dropped the collar and when I picked it up for her I saw Booker dead in a ditch—just a flash—the same way you might be able to close your eyes and picture it, but my eyes were wide open. The experience terrified me. I dropped that collar like a hot potato and threw up in my mother's azaleas. I didn't breath a word about it to Terry—to anyone—just said I had the flu and went to bed. They found Booker a few days later in a roadside ditch about a mile from Terry's house. He'd been hit by a car.

"Since then I've learned to control the 'ability', for want of a better term; practitioners call it psychometry. So when Roger asked for my help I told him to come back with something of his son's, something the boy had cherished. He brought over the engine from a toy train and we sat right here on this couch."

Peter said, "I saw the train set in Jason's room."

"When I touched the toy I saw Jason in a dark place. He was afraid, but he was alive and safe. When I told Roger he was overjoyed, hugging me, dancing around the room. But then he wanted to know where the boy was. When I couldn't tell him, things got pretty scary in here. He was furious, started calling me a fake and a parasite for taking people's money and feeding them lies. When I reminded him that I hadn't asked him for a cent and that we had both lost children, he grabbed the train and stormed out."

"Roger can be pretty scary when he's mad."

Erika gave a nervous chuckle. "Anyway, he didn't show up at group for a few weeks after that and we all thought he was gone. Then he came in one night and apologized to me in front of everyone. He said he needed hope, but not false hope and we left it at that. He's stayed pretty cool toward me ever since, though. That's why I was surprised to learn he'd suggested me to you.

"So to answer your question, my feeling that Jason isn't dead comes from that, from the fact that my original feeling hasn't changed. The only way I could be sure would be to go through the process again, but for obvious reasons I've never suggested it to Roger."

"Can't say I blame you," Peter said. He felt tired now. Tired and disappointed.

"Which still leaves the question of what your son is trying to tell you," Erika said. "And that I can't say. But he *is* trying to tell you something." She looked at the pictures of the two boys, their features so much alike. "These kids *are* linked somehow, Peter. Probably victims of the same kidnapper, I agree with you there. Beyond that, your guess is as good as mine. The only thing I can tell you with any certainty is that your son needs you to bring some sort of resolution to this thing. Exactly how you're supposed to do that I can't even begin to imagine. All you can do is wait; keep doing what you've been doing. I'm sorry I can't offer you more."

"No," Peter said, standing, "I appreciate you taking me seriously. This isn't exactly the kind of thing I could bring to a family member or a friend. I can hardly believe it's even happening. Sometimes I think I'm losing my marbles."

"That's the last thing you're doing," Erika said, standing now too. "Right from childhood people get so caught up in the business of life—keeping up, fitting in, a million pointless distractions—they quickly lose sight of their spiritual side. Often it takes some major dislocation, even something catastrophic, to wake us up to it again. That's what's happening to you now. And no matter what you do, it's going to run its course. If you can keep your mind open to it you're already more than halfway there."

She opened her arms to hug him and this time Peter hugged back, the innocent contact an unexpected comfort.

"Thanks, Erika," he said. "Can I stay in touch?"

Erika smiled. "I'll be very disappointed if you don't." Walking him to the door she said, "What are you going to do about group?"

"Give it a rest, I think. Maybe check out the new one Roger mentioned. I really don't know yet."

"Don't blame Roger, okay? He's in a tough spot."

"I don't. Of course I don't. I just wish I'd been more careful. I was starting to depend on our friendship."

"It's still there. It just needs time to heal."

At the door Peter thanked her again and stepped out into another muggy day, the click of the latch behind him one of the most lonesome sounds he'd ever heard. It felt absurdly like abandonment.

He had no idea what to do with himself.

* * *

The weather during the last half of June and the first three weeks of July was some of the most extreme ever recorded in the Sudbury district, day after day of sweltering heat, stifling humidity and not a single drop of rain. The region was placed under a strict fire ban and severe watering restrictions were imposed, along with daily smog alerts, the effluent from the Inco superstack cloaking the city in a sulphury haze. Lawns died, gardens shriveled and tempers ran hot. Air conditioners collapsed under the strain, a half dozen seniors were found mummified in their apartments, and the emergency room was clogged with bronchitics and asthmatics. The operating suites were ovens, staff members tacky with sweat standing still.

For Peter, each new day at work became an increasing burden, the stress and challenge of the job intensified by escalating dread and growing inattention, his ability to concentrate almost obliterated by the constant ache in his skull. He asked Wendell Smith, the department head, to exclude him from the call schedule until further notice and to avoid attaching residents to his lists. Even then, there were times, sitting at the head of the operating table with a patient under anesthesia, when Peter could barely keep his eyes open.

And while work was bad, home was much worse. His primary source of distraction had shifted from rented videos and favourite sitcoms to a stack of home movies he found in a box in the attic, something his brother Colin had missed in his sweep of the house. Dana had been a maniac for recording family moments—everything from Easter egg hunts and birthday parties to David playing with his friends in the pool or just sleeping peacefully in his bed. Peter watched them constantly now, slipping them into the player at random, sitting in the dark with an empty stomach and a full bladder, alternately laughing and crying. He and Dana had taken turns doing the filming, and when he saw his wife and son together on the screen, alive and happy, he wished he could somehow crawl in there with them, escape the empty shell of his life and just *be* with them again.

Here was one from the beach house in Barbados, March 14, 2002, David coming up the path with a wriggling sand crab, his lean body rippling with muscle, a miniature man at the age of five in his baggy Homer Simpson trunks, fearlessly gripping the crab. Everyone was always commenting on how much they'd love to have a six pack like David's, and David would just grin and look away. Now here came Dana, hurrying up the path behind David in a big floppy sunhat, a breezy shawl hugging her hips, her excited voice crisp and electronic sounding as

David swung on her with the crab, making her squeal. Peter could almost feel the tropical air whisking past the microphone.

Hours of the stuff. Like the world's finest wine laced with strychnine.

And when sleep finally came it was a fresh breed of torment, fretful and dream filled, Jason's submerged face haunting him night after night. The only thing that made these harrowing night sweats even remotely tolerable was the recurring sense Peter got of his son when he awoke from them: sometimes that feathery touch, sometimes a fleeting glimpse of him, and sometimes—and these instances were at once the most wonderful and the most heartbreaking—the same warm rush of love he'd felt every time David hugged him or said, "I love you, Dad," the sensation arising seemingly at random, Peter sitting at home or at work, driving the car or lying wide-eyed in his bed praying for the refuge of dreamless sleep. There and then gone, the feeling was at times so tangible Peter could close his eyes and imagine David standing right next to him in the room.

One Friday morning late in July, Peter awoke gasping in dawn light from the same maddening dream...except this time a white hand had broken the surface of that dark water from above and settled on top of Jason's head, holding him under until his weak struggles ceased.

Peter sat bolt upright and knew exactly what he must do.

9.

Friday, July 27

Peter sat in his Corolla a half block down the street from Roger's house, tucked behind a camper in the night shadow of a sprawling oak. It was ten thirty-five and Roger's Suburban was parked in the driveway, the main floor of his house still brightly lit. If he was working the graveyard shift tonight, he'd be leaving in the next few minutes. If not, Peter would try again tomorrow.

At ten to eleven, just as Peter decided it was time to leave, Roger came running down the front steps, buttoning a blue work shirt. Peter hunkered down in his seat and thought, *Good.* Roger wouldn't be back for at least twelve hours.

He waited another ten minutes after the Suburban roared away, then found a parking spot closer to the house. He emerged into the sticky night air and checked the street in both directions, finding it peacefully abandoned. Though Roger had left without turning off the lights, the houses on either side of his were dark, save porch lights and a few dim sources inside, a pilot light over a stove, maybe, or the shifting blue glow of a television set. The neighbourhood had settled in for the night.

Heart racing, Peter strolled up the walkway as if he belonged there, then veered right at the base of the porch steps along a cracked cement path that led to a side door, a rickety fence separating Roger's property from his neighbour's. Here, between the houses, it was pitch dark and a few degrees cooler, and Peter realized he was trembling.

He continued past the side door, crouching now, and stepped onto desiccated lawn, dead grass crunching under his feet. The sound startled him and he paused, listening, watching the neighbour's place for a light or a shifting curtain; but there was nothing, just the distant bark of a dog, a single lone volley and then silence.

Stepping as lightly as he could, he made his way to the small back yard, a low deck back here with a barbeque and some patio furniture, four chairs and a circular table shaded from the moonlight by a striped parasol. The deck creaked when he stepped onto it and Peter froze, thinking, *What am I doing here? Thinking, Is this what it's like to be insane? Is that what I've become?*

But he crept up to the kitchen window—the one he'd noticed on his first visit here, that damp breeze sifting in through a ten inch screen, the kind that just stood there, wedged between the window and the sill—and slid the window open, catching the screen before it could fall and make a racket. He rested the screen against the wall and took a last look around.

Nothing had changed.

He stood for a moment with his back pressed to the brick, waiting for the voice of reason to intervene, telling him to re- place the screen and go back home, see a shrink and be done with it. Then he slipped into Roger's kitchen through the open window, his heart a tripping jackhammer in his chest, his cloth- ing sticky with sweat.

His first thought inside was, *Motion sensors*, and he froze again; but he'd been in Roger's front hall a couple of times now and hadn't seen an alarm panel. Still, he looked around for the telltale red glow and saw none. He took a deep breath and kept going, through the kitchen to the main hall and the front entrance, then the staircase to the second floor, trying not to think about what Roger would do to him if he came through that door right now.

He started up the stairs, every footfall creating a dry creak that echoed through the empty house. Then he was in the hall- way at the top, the same hallway the kidnapper had trod with the same deliberate stealth. Had he felt the raw fear Peter was feeling now? The same withering sense of trespass? Somehow Peter didn't think so.

He crept past the master bedroom and picked up his pace, his fear of getting caught doubling with each frantic breath. Jason's door was closed and Peter got that same whiff of stale air when he pushed it open. The room was dark, the only light that eerie orange wash from the streetlights outside, filtered through gauzy curtains. He gave his eyes a few seconds to adjust then tip-toed to the train set, as if Jason were asleep in here rather than lost to the world. He did not look at the bunk bed.

The train cars were small, each an easy fit for a child's palm, and Peter reached for the shiny black engine. Then he paused, wondering if Roger came in here at night, the way he, Peter, sometimes did in David's empty room. Wondered if he'd notice the missing engine.

There were about a dozen boxcars between the engine and an authentic looking caboose, and Peter took one of these, joining the remaining ones together to hide the gap. Then he tucked the boxcar into his pocket.

He left the house quickly, replacing the screen in the window then briskly retracing his steps to the front of the house, trying not to run. Halfway down the front walk he saw a police cruiser roll to a stop at the curb, the passenger window humming open. Hesitating only slightly, he continued his strolling pace to the sidewalk, returning the nod of the female officer who looked up at him from the shotgun seat. From this angle he couldn't see the driver. Absurdly, he found himself picturing which way he'd run if it was him they were after.

"'Evening, sir," the officer said.

"'Evening," Peter said.

There was a burst of chatter over the radio in there, then the woman said, "You didn't happen to see a gang of about five boys run by here in the past few minutes, did you?"

"Afraid not," Peter said, pointing back at the house. Sweat was running into his eyes. "I was just visiting a friend. Watching a movie."

"Where are you parked?"

He pointed at the Corolla across the street. "Right over there."

"All right. Get to your car quickly, sir. These boys just assaulted an elderly gentleman walking his dog. Beat him up pretty bad. We'll wait right here until you're safely inside."

"Will do," Peter said, starting away on legs made of rubber. "And thanks."

The woman nodded again, her expression sober, and Peter wondered if that was part of their training, that stern look they all wore, like those palace guards in Britain who stood like mannequins no matter what distractions were aimed at them.

Verging on hysterical laughter, he gave the cops a wave and climbed into his car, starting the engine as they pulled away, Jason Mullen's tiny metal boxcar digging into his hip.

* * *

Peter said, "Sorry to call so late."

"No problem," Erika said, sounding wide awake. Peter heard the bright chatter of ice cubes against glass. "Just having a drink and watching the tube. Where are you?"

"In your driveway."

Erika laughed. "Are you stalking me, Doctor Croft?"

"You're right, I'm sorry, it's late."

"Nonsense. I was kidding. Come ahead in."

Peter hung up and went to the door. Erika was already there, waiting for him in the narrow foyer. She led him inside and offered him a drink, which he gratefully accepted. "All I've got is gin and tonic," she said and Peter said that would do fine. She brought it to him on the couch and Peter took a long swallow, the liquor bringing water to his eyes.

"Whoa," Erika said, settling in beside him. "Rough night?"

Peter said, "You have no idea," and dug the toy boxcar out his pocket.

Erika gazed at it with widening eyes. "He didn't give that to you, did he."

Peter said, "No," and held it out to her. "Can we do this?"

Erika put her drink on the table but didn't take the boxcar. She said, "He hasn't been back to group, you know," and Peter lowered his arm. "Not since the last time you guys were there together. Have you seen him lately?"

"No."

She pointed at the boxcar. "Then how did you get that?"

"You don't want to know."

"You broke into his *house?*"

Peter held the toy out again. "Please, Erika. Can we do this?"

Erika was silent for a beat, her eyes unreadable. Then she looked firmly at him and said, "If we do, Roger can never know."

"Of course."

"I mean it, Peter. No matter what the outcome. My instincts are telling me to refuse you. This is very personal stuff, and if it was me I'd be furious to learn that people I trusted had gone behind my back."

She was right, of course, and though Peter's own instincts were screaming at him to pocket the stolen toy and just forget the whole thing, he said, "You have my word."

"The only reason I'm even considering this is that you've got a vested interest. Like it or not, you're involved."

"I understand."

She stared at him a moment longer, as if reading him, then began rubbing her palms against her thighs, shifting her gaze to the boxcar now, a prosaic object that had once brought happiness to a child. Her breathing deepened and slowed, and Peter heard her whisper something, like a monk at prayer. Then she picked up the boxcar, her hand folding into a fist around it, and her whole body stiffened, a pained gasp coming from her throat. Just as abruptly she relaxed and a tear escaped one staring eye. As she turned to face Peter, she dropped the boxcar into her lap.

"Jason is alive," she said, her voice breaking. "I saw him... sleeping in the dark. But he's in danger, Peter. They're going to let him die..."

"Who's going to let him die?"

Erika was sheet white now, breathing hard. She pointed at the boxcar in her lap, saying, "Take it. Please."

Peter picked up the toy and put it back in his pocket. "*Who's* going to let him die? Where is he?"

"I don't know," Erika said, rising now, stumbling over his feet as she brushed past him, heading for the back of the apartment. "I need you to leave now, Peter," she said. "Please. Just twist the lock on your way out." She paused by the planter separating the living area from the rooms beyond; to Peter she appeared on the verge of collapse. "That's all I can tell you right now," she said. "Really. But if you'd like, maybe we can talk about it more another time."

Peter stood. "Are you all right?"

"Just go," Erika said.

Then she was gone and Peter heard her footfalls, heavy and fast, and now a door slamming shut followed by the unmistakable sound of retching. He considered going back there to check on her, but decided against it. She was a grown woman.

He let himself out, locking the door behind him. The night sky was flawless, a vast indigo vault flecked with diamonds,

122 · SEAN COSTELLO

and Peter walked beneath it to his car, feeling even more be-
wildered than he had when he came over here. He wasn't sure
what he'd expected from all of this, but what he'd just witnessed,
authentic or otherwise, was of little value to him. The only thing
he knew for certain was that David—his spirit, his essence, some
immutable part of his son—was trying to tell him something. And
about that part of it Erika had been correct: he needed to keep
his mind open, do his best to decipher the signs. What he could
not do anymore was sit passively by and wait. Whatever this was,
it was about Jason Mullen and his missing look alike, Clayton
Dolan. That seemed as good a place as any to begin.

Peter knew he wasn't a detective or even particularly in-
tuitive. He'd spent the better part of his life believing only in
what his senses told him was real. And what that brand of self
reliance had taught him was that knowledge was power, and
that the path to knowledge was simple: research. He also knew
that a hundred different people could examine the same body of
evidence and see it in only one light—and that sometimes, all
that was required to uncover the truth was a fresh pair of eyes.

He drove home and opened the *Child Find* site, bringing up
the image of the boy who had lured him into this nightmare in
the first place. Little Clayton Dolan.

* * *

The information on the site was surprisingly scant, something Peter hadn't noticed before, his attention at the time focused almost exclusively on the boy's image. What he did notice now was the age-enhanced photo of Clayton Dolan, dis-

played next to the one he'd first seen on the hospital bulletin board. Clayton had been almost six when he was abducted. The age-enhanced photo depicted him at twelve, digitally bridging the years since his disappearance.

At first glance the twelve year old Clayton bore little resemblance to Clayton at six. The facial features were longer and more lean, the hair style modified to reflect current trends, the kid's missing baby teeth replaced by a more mature set. And yet, on closer inspection, one could easily discern the likeness, most notably in the eyes, but also in the shape of the nostrils and ears, and in the way the boy's smile altered the rest of his face. Peter could see how it might be a useful tool.

He printed the page in colour, then did the same for Jason Mullen—whose photo had not yet been age-enhanced—starting a hardcopy file for each of them. He turned up similar information on another site, *The National Center for Missing & Exploited Children*, but learned little more beyond the salient details of time and place.

He wanted to find out more about the Dolan case in particular, the kind of in-depth information Roger had given him about Jason's abduction that day on the porch. It occurred to him then to look for any pertinent news articles. The abduction of a child was always big news, at least for the first several weeks.

He referred again to his printed information on Clayton Dolan. The boy had been taken in broad daylight from the back yard of his parents' farmhouse in the Ottawa Valley, near the village of Fitzroy. The contact numbers at the bottom of the page included one for the *Center for Missing & Exploited Children* and a second for the Arnprior Detachment of the Ontario

Provincial Police. Peter had been to Arnprior a few times during his residency, visiting a respiratory tech who'd moved there
after completing her training in Ottawa. He remembered it as
a quaint rural town west of Ottawa, about an hour's drive from
the U of O campus. Fitzroy he'd never heard of.

He typed 'Arnprior' into the search engine and came up
with a site called *Welcome to Arnprior*. Under Municipal Serv-
ices he found a map that showed the town nestled along the
south bank of the Ottawa River. Using the zoom function, he
located the village of Fitzroy about fifteen miles east of Arnprior.
He printed a copy of the map and added it to the Dolan file.

He thought of another site he wanted to check, one David
had introduced him to called *Google Earth*, and as he opened it he
recalled his son getting off the bus one day last fall, excitedly digging through his school bag, bringing out a dog-eared satellite
photo of a residential street. "Look, Dad," he'd said, standing on
the lawn with his school bag sliding off his shoulder, pointing at
the greenish printout. "Know what this is?" Peter studied it briefly
before admitting he had no clue. "It's our *house*, Dad. See?" And
there it was, the brown-shingled roof he'd paid a fortune for the
previous spring, and the pool in the back yard, a turquoise gem in
a bed of green. He thought he could even see his car in the laneway.
It made him think of some of the things he and Dana had done in
what they'd believed was the privacy of their own back yard. He
and David had spent hours on the site that evening, zooming in on
everyone's house they could think of, making copies David wanted
to give them later. They'd had a ball with the thing.

He typed Fitzroy into the search window and a lifelike globe
of the earth spun slowly toward him, the focus sweeping out of

the northern United States to zoom in on a rectangle of land
centred by the village of Fitzroy, the illusion of movement giving Peter a brief sensation of vertigo. The place looked small
and remote, an oval-shaped collection of quiet streets and rural souls, perched like its nearest neighbour, Arnprior, on the
bank of the Ottawa River. Zooming out, Peter could see little
for miles around but farmland, a tidy quiltwork of open fields
and scattered homesteads.

Somewhere in this idyllic setting a monster had surfaced
and taken a child.

Peter reopened the Arnprior site, searching without success
for the name of a local paper. Trying a different tack, he entered
'Canadian Newspapers' and found a comprehensive list arranged
by province, but the only ones he could come up with for the
Arnprior area were weeklies. Getting discouraged, he scrolled
down to the listings for Ottawa, the nearest major city, and
opened a link to *The Ottawa Citizen*, a paper he'd delivered as a
boy. The site offered a 7-day archive, which Peter opened in the
hope of accessing a wider time frame. Next to the 7-day search
window was a second option offering articles from 16 major papers ranging as far back as 1997. The catch was, full text printouts cost $4.75 CDN per document, plus applicable taxes. The
documents, once chosen, were then delivered by email.

Peter grumbled his way through the registration process and
carried on.

Soon he was into the meat of the story, a deluge of information detailing the early days of the case, then, over the course
of the ensuing weeks, the gradual—and inevitable—tapering off.

* * *

By sunup Peter had compiled a fairly comprehensive profile of the Dolan case, many of the details of which filled him with sorrow. The boy's mother, Margaret Dolan, was clearly the hardest hit by the child's disappearance. For this unfortunate woman, it was as if one tragedy spawned another, an insidious ripple effect that engulfed everything in its path.

Prior to her son's abduction Mrs. Dolan had been the family's principal breadwinner, her spouse, Lionel Dolan, on long-term disability due to chronic back problems. The Dolans had one other child, Aaron, twelve at the time of his brother's kidnapping. According to one article from a tabloid called *The Seeker*, Aaron had been playing outside with his brother that day, the kidnapper striking the older boy from behind with a rock and leaving him for dead, the whole incident taking place not ten feet from the house. Though Peter had always shunned the tabloids, *The Seeker* article was among the most detailed he could find, providing a thoughtfully worded account of that terrible day and the lengthy ordeal that followed. The website also gave access to a photo gallery that included ground-level and aerial views of the farm itself, and a video clip of the tearful appeal the boy's mother had made on national television just hours after the abduction. Watching the video, Peter couldn't help but imagine Roger and his wife making a similar plea, using their son's name repeatedly during the interview, as Margaret did, attempting to humanize the child to a faceless deviant who almost certainly didn't care, who was perhaps even amused by the entire spectacle, or in his own mind, deified by it.

From other sources he learned that Margaret Dolan later spent thirteen months in a psychiatric hospital following a vicious attempt she made on the life of her husband, whom she blamed for allowing the abduction to occur. Apparently Lionel Dolan had been in the house at the time of the incident, nursing his back pain with a bottle of scotch. According to another article, Margaret's break with reality progressed from a period of unappeasable rage to a state of catatonia, which persisted for the first three months of her incarceration. And though her husband's lawyers pushed for an attempted murder conviction, Margaret was remanded to the care of a team of psychiatrists until such time as she was deemed fit to return to her home and her remaining son. A few weeks after the brief trial, Lionel Dolan went on a drinking jag with a couple of his buddies and slammed Margaret's car into a bridge abutment, killing all three of them instantly.

Peter ran the video clip again, his heart going out to this tall, big-boned woman left to face this tragedy alone. She stood in sunlight on the steps of a quaint, well-kempt farmhouse, whitewashed clapboard with lush flowerbeds and a cane rocker on the porch, doing her best to dam back the tears until she'd had her say. "I'm begging you," Margaret Dolan said, the camera gliding in smoothly to lock on her dark eyes, her trembling, down-turned mouth, "whoever you are. Please, let my son go. Let Clayton go. I'm his mother and he needs me, Clayton needs his ma. Clayton's a brave boy and he's smart. Just let him go. He knows his phone number and his address. Let Clayton go now and he'll find his way home. Do that and I promise, I'll do anything you ask. I'll—"

Unable to stand any more, Peter clicked on the pause button and stared at the woman's face, thinking, *What now?*

And then he knew.

He dug the boys' pictures out of the files he'd created and lined them up on the desk in front of him. What he needed was a willing confederate, someone with nothing to lose and everything to gain from the resolution of this maddening puzzle. And since Roger had withdrawn his involvement, his next most logical ally was staring out at him from the computer screen, her plain face frozen in torment.

Peter closed the video window and returned to the photo gallery on *The Seeker* site, finding an aerial shot of the Dolan property that had caught his eye earlier on. Though the shot was blurry, he could discern the general layout of the area—a dirt road cutting in from route 22, ending in a T with a short arm on the right that led to what Peter assumed was another farm, the arm on the left, this one much longer, running on a gentle curve to the Dolan place. He flipped back through his notes until he found the name of the cutoff from route 22: Muldoon's Crossroad.

Now he brought up the *Google Earth* site and typed Fitzroy, Ontario into the search window. When the image resolved into focus he found route 22 and followed it east, zooming in closer as he soared overhead, pulling the smaller side roads into focus.

And there it was, Muldoon's Crossroad, neatly bisecting route 22. Peter followed it north to the T, zooming in to bring the Dolan farm into focus at the centre of the screen. A sidebar showed the viewing altitude at twelve hundred feet, but when he tried to move any closer the image started to blur. He printed a copy and added it to his files.

It occurred again to Peter Croft as he tossed a change of clothes into an overnight bag and climbed into his car—about to embark on a six hour drive with no sleep and an empty stomach, intending to approach a complete stranger with a bizarre and baseless theory—that perhaps he was losing his mind. Perhaps the best thing for him was a nice long stay in a private room at Algoma Psychiatric.

But by the time he got the car up to cruising speed, rolling east on Highway 17, what he was doing seemed not only sane, but inevitable. As crazy as it might appear to an outside observer, Peter was convinced his son was guiding him, and that he was on the right path. He wasn't a stupid man. He had a degree in medicine, had at one time even considered a career in psychiatry. And on a strictly clinical level, he understood that everything he'd experienced up to this point could fairly be ascribed to the complex fallout of unresolved grief and the accompanying phenomena of sleep deprivation and flagging nutrition. He'd pondered these truths countless times and, as a clinician standing on the other side of the fence, would have used these very arguments weeks ago to explain this all away. But living it, *feeling* the truth of it in his every fibre, he had no choice but to act. Exactly what he hoped to achieve by sharing his beliefs with Margaret Dolan had not yet fully crystallized in his mind. Maybe when she saw the boys' pictures, their unmistakable likeness, she'd recall something that had escaped her before, some apparently inconsequential detail which, in this new light, unearthed a link, however fragile. And maybe she'd just send him packing, as Roger had. He didn't know. Right now he was simply following his heart.

He got a rock station blaring and settled back in his seat, running through different scenarios in his mind, how he'd approach Margaret Dolan, never doubting for an instant that he could find her, never fearing that she might run him off her farm, have him arrested for trespassing or worse.

* * *

After stopping for gas and a late breakfast in Mattawa, two hours east of Sudbury, Peter made the balance of the trip non-stop, pulling into Arnprior at two forty-five that afternoon. Using a map of the area he'd purchased in Mattawa, he followed route 22 past the turnoff to the village of Fitzroy, checking every side road until he realized he'd gone too far. None of the roads up here had signs, and when he failed on his second pass to find Muldoon's Crossroad he pulled into a homestead that edged on the highway, a two story farmhouse in a cluster of shade trees, an assortment of sagging outbuildings arrayed haphazardly around it.

There was an old guy in a straw hat and faded coveralls sitting on the porch in a weathered Adirondack chair, and as Peter climbed out of the car the man nodded and said, "Help ya?" through a toothless grin.

Peter said, "Yeah, if you wouldn't mind. I'm looking for Muldoon's Crossroad."

"Figured," the old man said, tugging that brimmed straw hat a little further down over his eyes. "Seen you go by the first time. Reporter?"

"No."

"Writer, then?"

Something told Peter to say, "Yes."

"Figured that, too. The Dolan boy, right?"

Peter turned the engine off and shut the car door. "That's right. How did you know?"

The man grinned again. "Hers's the only place up there. And you ain't the first come up here tryna get her story. Word to the wise, though, chum. You can go on up there and try, but I can tell you right now, you'll be lucky if Maggie gives you the time of day. She thinks people like you're bloodsuckers, aiming to get rich off the misery of others."

Peter thought, *Shit, why did I lie?* and the old man patted the arm of the chair next to his. "But if you got a minute," he said, the grin cagey now, "I can tell you most of it. It was my place she run to the night she took the pigsticker to ol' Lionel."

Peter made his way up the steps, trying to clear the fog of exhaustion from his head. As he passed the screen door he heard a clatter of pans in there and caught a whiff of fresh bread.

The old man came partway out of his chair, stuck his hand out and said, "Wife's baking. Name's Albert Muldoon, pleased to meetcha. Crossroad's named after my daddy. He's an Albert, too."

Peter felt his hand swallowed in Albert's iron grip, the man's hand all knuckles and grizzled callous. "Peter Croft," he said, trying not to wince. He liked the old guy right away, those clear blue eyes shaded by the brimmed hat he kept adjusting like a cowboy, that gummy grin and laid back way of talking.

Peter slumped into the empty chair and sighed.

"Long drive?" Albert said.

"Six hours."

"Can't hack a run like that anymore," Albert said. "Hips are gone." He picked up a beer can from the porch beside his chair and showed it to Peter. "Get you one of these?"

"Thanks, no. I've still got some driving to do."

"Some of Myrtle's fresh lemonade, then. Myrt's the wife. If I'm swift, I bet I can snag us a couple tea biscuits, too, fresh outa the oven."

Peter didn't want anything, but the old man was already out of his chair, his hunched gait arthritic but spry, hinting at the young man he'd once been. At a glance, Peter put him at around eighty years old.

"Besides," Albert said, opening the screen door, "if we're gonna have us a chinwag out here, I'll be needing my teeth." He gave Peter that gummy grin again and Peter had to grin back. "You sit tight," Albert said. "I'll be right back."

The screen door clapped shut and Peter put his head back, the breeze cooling his light sweat, its chatter in the trees a gentle soporific. With his eyes closed he listened to the crickets' chirr and now the rising buzz of a cicada, the sound impossibly loud in this blessed rural quiet. In an instant he was fast asleep.

Though it couldn't have been long, when the screen door clapped again and Peter opened his eyes, he felt better, dreamy and relaxed.

"Country air," Albert said, the grin filled with perfect white teeth now. "Getcha every time." He handed Peter a tall glass of lemonade. Peter thanked him and Albert said, "Myrt'll be along in a minute with the biscuits."

Before Peter could comment a round, blue-haired woman in a plain cotton dress came through the door with a plate of steaming tea biscuits. Albert took the plate, saying, "Pete, this is Myrt," huffing when Myrtle started chatting with Peter, shaking his head as she waddled back inside. "You don't want to start that woman up," he said and took a biscuit, resting the plate on the wide arm of Peter's chair. Peter took one, too, butter already slathered through its spongy middle. He took a bite and said, "Delicious." Albert gave him a wink.

"Peter Croft," Albert said now, taking a slurp of his beer. "Not ringing any bells. You write anything I might've read?"

"If I decide to do this one," Peter said, feeling bad about the lie, "it'll be my first."

"I only read Westerns, anyway," Albert said, fiddling with his hat again. "Louis L'Amour, Zane Grey, that ilk." He angled himself in his chair, turning to face Peter head on. "So what do you wanna know?"

Peter said, "All of it."

Albert eyed him with a hint of suspicion. "You don't have a tape recorder or nothing?"

Peter raised a finger to his temple. "Never forget a word."

"If you say so," the old man said. Then he fixed Peter with keen, knowing eyes. "The way I see it, things started turning to shit for Maggie Dolan the day Lionel threw his back out and decided to go on the public tit. It wasn't long before that waste of skin was drinking every dime and Maggie had to look for work in Arnprior. This'd be twelve, thirteen years back now, Maggie still a presentable looking woman in them days, before she packed on all the weight."

Peter remembered the tall, angular woman he'd seen in the video and couldn't imagine her overweight.

"She lucked into an office job with a lawyer down there'd just hung out his shingle," Albert said. "Maggie didn't know the first thing about typing or computers, but she's a fast learner and a hard worker...and the way I heard it, lawyer boy's interest in the woman wasn't entirely professional, if you catch my drift."

Peter took a bite of his biscuit and did his best to suppress a smile, realizing he was in the presence of the county gossip. He nodded, urging the old boy on.

"In them days, word was little Clayton came compliments of the legal eagle, too. If you'd ever set eyes on Lionel, you'd know what I'm talking about. Must've been an Injun in the woodpile somewhere in that fella's clan. Aaron, Maggie's other boy, he come out the same way. Black hair, dark eyes and skin. That boy's not all there, though. Never has been. Maggie had him in school in the village the first year or so, then took to home schooling him, evenings mostly, as much as the boy could learn. By the time Clayton come along ol' Lionel was so addled with the booze he didn't seem to notice the blond hair and blue eyes. Or maybe he just didn't care. The lawyer fired Maggie the day he found out she was pregnant, and for my money that's all the proof a body needs. But that's neither here nor there. It all came out after the boy disappeared, the affair, but by that time the lawyer'd married and had two kids of his own. Cops cleared him of any involvement on day one."

Albert took a bite of his biscuit and washed it down with a slug of beer. Intruding on the quiet, an old Pony tractor came over the hill on route 22, hauling a load of manure. As it hummed past the house Albert waved to the young man sitting shirtless at the wheel, and the young man waved back. "Garnet Teevens' boy,"

Albert said and popped the last of his snack into his mouth. He looked at Peter and said, "Sure you don't want to jot a few notes?" spitting little missiles of tea biscuit onto the porch as he spoke.

"I'm good," Peter said, touching his temple again.

Albert grinned and gave his head a shake. Then his expression grew dark. "Hell of a thing, that kidnapping. The last thing folks around here ever expected. Son of a bitch come out of nowhere, brained young Aaron with a rock, opened a gash like that in his scalp—" he showed Peter a space between his fingers about two inches long "—then run off God knows where with wee Clayton. Cops tried to get a description out of Aaron, but the boy never even seen the man, it happened that quick. When Aaron come to, he run in'n told Lionel what happened— Maggie was at work by this time, waitressing for that Chinese outfit in town—but Lionel was already half in the bag and didn't believe him. Told him to go wash his face he was bleeding. Maggie told me the whole story the night she took the knife to Lionel, her sitting right where you are now, waiting for the cops to come arrest her. What a scene that was. Ambulance, cop cars tearing up the dirt. Myrt had Aaron in the kitchen back there, trying to calm the boy down. Maggie'd chased him through the fields with the knife, meaning to gut him too, I expect. Good thing the boy had the sense to head over here. Was all I could do to wrassle that woman down'n get the knife off her, she was that far gone. Snapped like a piece of kindling, that drunken fool setting her off. Clayton'd been gone a few months by this time and everyone'd pretty much given up hope of ever finding him. Everyone but Maggie. Lionel was stoked to the gills that night'n started in on her, telling her it was time she quit her whining, the kid was gone and that was the end of it. Told her if she wanted another he'd plant one in her right there on the kitchen table. That's when she snapped, and who could blame the woman?"

Peter just shook his head.

"There was a trial, but by that time Maggie'd pretty much closed up shop." Mimicking Peter, Albert pointed to his temple and grinned without humor. "That little boy meant the world to her. Had all her hopes wrapped up in him. Carted him around with her everywhere, even brought him to work a couple times 'til the Chinaman put a stop to it. Maggie's got a sister, Marie, runs the corner store in Fitzroy, and after Lionel's boozing got out of hand she took to leaving the boy there while she was working. Myrt helped her out a few times, too. That day, though, we was down to Arnprior for a funeral and Marie was in the hospital having a hysterotomy—"

From beyond the screen Peter heard Myrtle shout, "Hysterectomy," and covered his mouth with his hand.

Albert scowled at the door and said, "Nosey parker," then returned his gaze to Peter. "So that day Maggie was strapped. This was in June—goddam—six years ago now. And here's where the woman went wrong. She made Aaron responsible. Now don't get me wrong, the boy ain't that bad. Not all the way retarded. Just...slow. Can't stay focused."

From the kitchen Myrtle said, "Like someone else we know," and Peter laughed out loud.

Albert made an angry face, but his eyes were shining. He said, "Remember what I told you about that woman?" To Myrtle he said, "We're tryna have a conversation out here," and scooped up another biscuit. He took a bite and said, "This's the only reason I put up with her. Go ahead, have another."

Peter did, saying, "I did some research before coming down here. I know Mrs. Dolan was institutionalized for more than a year."

"That's right. Royal Ottawa, lockdown wing. Aaron spent that year in the village with his aunt. Boy seemed happier'n a clam down there, too, pumping gas, delivering groceries on his bike."

"I also read that Lionel died in an accident."

"Ejit *was* an accident. Took two mean bastards with him and good riddance to the lot. The only smart thing Maggie ever done where Lionel was concerned—besides putting a knife in him—"

"Albert."

This time the old man ignored his wife's admonition and went on, lowering his voice a shade. "The only smart thing she done was take out a term policy on the man. Gave her a nice little nest egg when she got out. That plus the fund the church set up. Myrt helped out with that. Amazing, really, once word got out about the boy, donations rolling in from concerned Christians all over the world. Tallied up a few hundred thousand before they was done. Far as I know, she's still living off that money."

Though Peter was enjoying the old man's yarn, he wanted to take a shot at meeting Margaret Dolan before it got too late in the day. Most of what Albert was telling him he'd already learned on his own. What he wanted to know now was how to find her.

He stood, reaching over to shake Albert's hand, the old man looking surprised and a little disappointed.

"There's a lot more," Albert said.

"I'm sure there is," Peter said, "and with your permission we'll talk again. But right now I'd like to go see if she'll talk to me."

Albert nodded, standing now too. "Fair enough. But if it don't work out and you're of a mind, come on back and we'll feed you supper. Myrt's got a roast in the oven, there's more'n enough."

Peter thanked him again and headed for the steps, saying, "Thanks, Mrs. Muldoon," as he passed the screen door. There was no reply.

At the foot of the steps Albert pointed up the highway and said, "Road's right there at the top of the hill. People always miss it 'cause they're too busy watching to see what's coming over the hill. Slow 'er right down and you can't miss it. Hang left, then left again at the foot of the crossroad. The old Misner place used to be up there on the right, but she burned flat back in '98. The Dolans've lived alone back there ever since. Hardly ever see Maggie anymore. The odd time at church or doing her groceries in town, but even then the woman keeps pretty much to herself. Never been the same since losing her boy."

Peter believed he understood. He thanked the old farmer again and got in his car, waving as he pulled onto route 22. At the top of the hill he turned left onto a narrow dirt road that angled sharply upward at first, then sloped gently down until it ended at the T he'd seen on the map. He glanced to his right, at the jutting, overgrown remains of the house Albert said had burned down, then turned left toward the Dolan farm, a quarter mile to the north.

* * *

A neglected looking L-shaped barn, the first thing Peter saw, stood in isolation far back to the right of the road, its sun-bleached boards roofed by rusted corrugations of tin. A broken line of trees blocked his view of the house, and it wasn't until he'd angled past it into the yard that he saw the rest of the compound. To his immediate right stood a tall, barracks-like row of three buildings joined end to end, the first of them clearly a garage, its faded white doors latched shut, the other two long since boarded up. Then came the house itself, a smallish two story wood-frame bearing little resemblance to the homey dwelling Peter had seen in the video. At a glance the place looked uninhabited, forgotten, the once lush flowerbeds overrun with weeds, the unmowed lawn scabbed with disease, the full-length porch and clapboard walls screaming for paint. It was hard to imagine a place could deteriorate so thoroughly in just a few years. It occurred to Peter that perhaps the remaining Dolans had simply pulled up stakes and moved on, their reclusive habits leaving their nearest neighbours none the wiser. There was no vehicle in the yard, no sign of life whatsoever.

Then Peter saw curtains in the dusty windows, and as he circled the turnaround, sheets fluttering in the breeze on a clothesline out back. He parked in front of the porch steps, slipped the boys' photos out of the folder on the seat beside him and emerged into the dusty heat. He started up the steps to the screen door and heard a muffled shout from deep inside the house, then footfalls, distant and heavy, followed by a muted slam.

He approached the screen hesitantly, feeling like a trespasser now, fearful of a barnyard dog or a jealous boyfriend, thinking this had been a dumb and impulsive idea. He could feel the words he'd rehearsed turning to ash in his mouth.

He knocked twice and stood with his nose to the rusty screen, the sun at his back printing a rectangle of glare onto the cracked linoleum in there, casting the hallway beyond into a well of darkness.

Fresh footfalls now, scuffing toward him out of the shadows of the hall. Common etiquette bade him step a few paces back—he had his face pressed to the screen like a kid at a glass candy counter—but Peter held his ground, watching a ghostly mass resolve into a large woman, the details vague at first, sharpening as light dissolved shadow.

Then she was bathed in the sun's glare, her dark eyes narrow in a face that was set in wariness, her body gliding toward him with a litheness Peter had seen in big people before. She had put on weight since that video was shot, but it wasn't fat, not the doughy variety he saw on more than half the patients who came through the OR back home. This woman was full-figured and robust. And she had to be six feet tall, her close-cropped hair peppered with gray.

"Mrs. Dolan," Peter said before she got to the door, the words rushing out of him. "My name is Peter Croft. I'm a doctor from Sudbury and I've got something I'd like to show you."

She stopped inside the screen and wiped her hands on her apron. "If you're selling something," she said, her voice huskier than he remembered it from the video, "I'm not interested. You didn't see the No Trespassing sign out there by the turnoff?"

He hadn't and he told her so, apologizing for the oversight, saying, "But I'm not here to sell you anything." He held up the two sheets of printer paper, the images turned discreetly away from her. Recalling Roger's reaction, he didn't want to blow it before he got started. He said, "I wonder if I could come inside? Or you could join me out here for a few minutes?"

"Listen, Mr....Croft, is it?" Peter nodded. "I'm busy and I don't appreciate people just wandering in here, ignoring the sign I nailed out there myself, in plain sight. Now if you don't mind—"

"It's about Clayton," Peter said, and saw her face clench like a fist, her dark eyes widening to look him up and down, gauging, Peter assumed, how little trouble she'd have tossing him off her porch. He took a step back from the screen.

Maggie Dolan said, "What about him?"

"If we could talk out here..."

Her hands dropped to her sides, her stance like that of a gunslinger. In a calm, modulated tone she said, "I'm about to walk away from this door, Mr. Croft, and go back inside to call the police. State your business, from where you're standing, and do it now. If you knew the first thing about me you'd know my boy was taken by a stranger, right here in this yard. For all I know it was you."

"Look," Peter said, "I'm sorry. This isn't going anything like I'd hoped. I didn't take your son, of course I didn't. But I have an interest in his disappearance that's difficult to explain."

"I suggest you give it a try."

Peter was beginning to feel intensely uncomfortable. "I have a friend whose son was taken, too. From his bed, three years ago. His resemblance to your son is amazing. Well, here, see for yourself..." He flipped Jason's picture around and held it up to the screen.

The woman's eyes widened slightly, then she said, "That's not my boy," and backed away, swinging the inner door shut.

"Please, Mrs. Dolan, I *know* it's not your son. That's why I'm here. I wanted to talk to you about—"

But the door continued through its arc until it latched. Peter heard it lock, then heard the woman's receding footfalls.

Tired, discouraged, no shred of the thin logic that had
brought him here in the first place remaining in his mind, he
turned toward the steps, thinking he'd spend the night in Ottawa, book himself into a nice hotel, the Lord Elgin maybe.
Thinking it was time to give up on all this lunacy.

He heard a sound then, a faint metallic jangle, like the rattle of keys only softer. He glanced along the length of the porch
and saw a tall, thin boy of perhaps eighteen standing on the
other side of the low railing, staring at him through crooked Buddy
Holly glasses, a John Deere cap perched ridiculously high on a
halo of curly dark hair, a set of dog tags—that jangling sound—
slung around his neck on a chain, one of them silver, the other
gold, the polished wafers setting off sunflares as the boy tapped
his ankle with the baseball bat that hung from his hand.

Startled, Peter said, "Aaron?" but the boy just stood there,
his mouth hanging open to show prominent teeth and a thick
tongue he ran out every few seconds to wet his lips.

Peter got back in the car and accelerated too quickly, raising a rooster tail of gravel as he blew past the tree line onto the
road. What he was leaving behind was a living tragedy, a once
strong woman and mother broken by suffering and loss, her
sanity fragile at best, its remaining shreds bound by depression,
isolation and paranoia, no one to keep her company but that
strange boy, his own mind stalled somewhere in early childhood. For Peter the experience underscored yet again the harrowing cost of the missing child, and as he turned left onto
route 22, heading east toward Ottawa now, he could hear
Roger's voice clearly in his mind, posing one of the most chill-
ing questions he'd ever heard.

"Now can you see how dead is better?"
And God help him, he could.

* * *

The Lord Elgin was booked solid, but Peter found a suite at the Chateau Laurier on Rideau Street. The place was a century-old landmark, its copper roofs and limestone walls mirroring the gothic style of the nearby Parliament Buildings. The interior was pure opulence, marble floors, high ceilings, brass bannisters and sparkling crystal chandeliers.

While he was waiting to register, Peter read an inscription on a plaque that said the man who'd commissioned the construction of the hotel in 1907, Charles Melville Hays, never made it to the grand opening in late April of 1912. Hays, a wealthy railway magnate, had been aboard the Titanic, accompanying a load of dining room furniture back from England.

Absorbing this information, Peter felt a stir in a forgotten part of himself, a part that had once reveled in facts like this, a part that would have felt an almost childlike excitement at the prospect of staying in a *place* like this, the privilege so costly it was pointless even to think about it. It made him feel young again, reminding him of the times before David was born that he and Dana had spoiled themselves, doing things that were reckless and spontaneous, spending money they didn't have, creating memories they'd cherish forever.

When he got to the check-in counter the uniformed clerk told him they were having a weekend promotion on some of their executive suites that included a lobster dinner catered in the suite, a double-decker bus tour of the downtown area and a ticket to a Blue Man Group concert at the old Rialto Theatre on Bank Street. Peter said, "Let's do it," and handed over his credit card.

He slept like a baby that night, cocooned in down and air-conditioned comfort, and in the shower next morning decided to treat himself to a nice long holiday as soon as the schedule at work would allow. Australia came immediately to mind, a place he'd always vowed to visit one day. And as ghoulish as it seemed, it occurred to him that Dana's death had left him more than able to afford such a whimsy, the various life insurance policies she'd insisted on having amounting to well over six hundred thousand dollars, money he hadn't touched a dime of yet, leaving its investment to the estate planner.

He pulled into Sudbury in mid afternoon and decided on a whim that enough time had gone by to drop in on Roger. The Suburban was parked in the driveway, but when Peter rang the bell there was no response. Standing on the porch, he called Roger's number on his cell phone and again got no response. He glanced back at the house as he pulled away and saw Roger standing in an undershirt in his son's bedroom window, staring out into space.

The message light on the answering machine was flashing when Peter got home. There were five messages, one from the Toyota dealership wanting to know if he was pleased with their service, one was a hang-up, and the other three were from Erika. She wanted him to call her back, wanted to discuss what happened the other night. She sounded upset, but Peter just didn't feel like getting into it with her. He erased the messages and went to bed.

He slept fitfully on that muggy July night, haunted again by his dreams, David's touch almost electric in its intensity now, his expression in the glare of the summer storm that flared up fretful and distressed. His image lingered tauntingly in the room this time, long enough for Peter to sit up in bed and reach out for him.

And when his son faded like a whisper Peter drove to the hospital and spent the balance of the night there, lying cramped on the couch in the deserted doctors' lounge, sleepless and numb.

Just before dawn someone crept in and started picking quietly through the shelves of scrub suits. Pushing up on one elbow under his thin blanket, Peter said, "It's okay, you can turn on the lights."

A woman's voice said, "Oh, okay, thanks," and the fluorescents ticked and shivered into life, making Peter blink. The woman said, "Sorry to wake you," and Peter saw that it was Lisa Black.

He said, "Lisa," and the word hung there. He sat up, running a hand through his hair, rubbing his aching eyes. "No bother," he said. "I wasn't really asleep. What are you doing here?"

"A cancer patient of mine is having surgery this morning. I promised her I'd go into the room with her. She's only four." She showed him a set of OR greens. "I was just looking for some scrubs."

Sighing, Peter said, "Lisa, I've been meaning to—"

"It's okay, Peter, I understand."

"Please, hear me out." He patted the couch beside him and Lisa glanced at the exit. He said, "I won't bite, I promise," and Lisa's shoulders relaxed. Smiling, she settled in next to him, her small hands fussing with the scrubs she'd chosen.

"I wanted to apologize," Peter said. "I've been meaning to come see you, it's just..."

She touched his hand and said, "Really, I understand."

"You did what you had to," Peter said. "I'd've done the same." He took her hand and squeezed it, gazing into her pale brown eyes. "And believe me, I'm glad you brought me back. There are things I need to do…for David."

Lisa tugged her hand away and stood. "I appreciate you bringing it up," she said, "but there's really nothing to forgive. I just hope you're moving on. I know it's hard, the hardest thing in the world. I see it all the time. But you've got to let him go, Peter. You really must let him go."

She left him then, almost running out the door, the scrubs she'd come in for forgotten on the couch beside him.

Peter lay curled on the couch again, pulling the blanket over his shoulders, staring at the clock on the wall. And when the first few staff members started filing in he trudged into the OR to face his day.

* * *

Over the course of the weeks that followed Peter Croft began to lose track of himself, any thought of Australia or companionship or healing laughter sinking into a kind of sucking black mud that filled his psyche.

* * *

At noon on Wednesday, July 30, Roger Mullen stood with his boss's nephew outside the cage, a narrow steel elevator that would carry them the last three thousand feet to the surface. Roger had spent the morning giving the seventeen year old a

VIP tour of the mine, taking him all the way down to 4700 Level, showing him the rich vein of ore they'd been working for the past several weeks.

Now he pointed at the green call button and the kid thumbed it, looking up with wide eyes as the cables in the open shaft shuddered and started rolling.

Roger said, "Won't be long now," and turned to see three miners walking toward them from an adjoining tunnel. One of them was Reggie Diggs, a mouthy asshole Roger had gotten into a scrape with about five years ago at a retirement party. The guy was constantly running his mouth and today was no exception, his pals flanking him like groupies, hanging on every word.

Roger heard him say, "I *told* the bitch to keep her brat quiet when I'm sleeping," and felt the muscles in his shoulders tense. "How hard is that? When I moved in I told her straight. I work shift, I put food on his plate, he's got to respect that."

One of the other guys said, "Right," and Roger turned his attention to the shaft, the lower half of the double decker cage dropping into view now. When the rig stopped he opened the outer gate, then the one to the personnel compartment. He put his hand on the kid's shoulder to lead him inside and Diggs said, "Hey, Mullen, who's your new girlfriend?" and his two buddies laughed.

Roger said, "We're heading up. You boys need a lift?"

Diggs said, "Jeeves, you're a good man," and brushed past him into the cage, his confederates right behind him.

The kid positioned himself at the back of the cramped compartment and stood mutely, avoiding eye contact with the men. Roger shut the gate and the cage started moving.

He thought, *Three more minutes*, and Diggs went back to his story.

"So Sunday morning I'm drifting off and the little peckerwood starts hollering at the top of his lungs. I yell at him to shut the hell up and the kid just *ignores* me." One of the lesser assholes said, "Whoa," like God himself had been provoked, and Diggs said, "So I get up and cuff him one in the ear. The kid starts bawling and now the bitch comes at me and I've got to belt her one, too. She threatens to call the cops and I tell her go ahead."

Without looking at Diggs, Roger said, "You don't deserve that kid."

Diggs said, "At least I can protect him," and Roger drove his fist into the man's face, shattering his nose, using his full weight to drag Diggs to the floor and piston a few more shots into his bloody beak, the thing already swelling under the vicious assault. Diggs spluttered, "Get this fucker *off* me," and his buddies dragged Roger to his feet, needing all of their strength to pin him to the wall. The cage was rocking in its shaft now, banging against the steel guides as it continued its unstoppable ascent, and the kid screamed, tears springing to his eyes.

Looking at the boy, Roger said, "Okay," and let the men subdue him. Diggs wobbled to his feet, picked up his helmet and slammed Roger in the side of the head with it. Roger saw a sliver of daylight as the cage glided to a stop at the surface, then sagged unconscious to the metal floor.

10.

Friday, August 29

The alarm on the anesthetic machine sounded again, and for the fifth time in as many minutes Peter silenced it, checking the monitor—again—for its source. He kept getting the same result, a flashing gray box identifying the problem as HIGH PEEP PRESSURE, which was odd because he wasn't using PEEP on this patient, an otherwise healthy fourteen year old with a fractured wrist.

He said, "Angie," and the circulating nurse looked up from her charting. "Call Biomed for me, would you? Tell them I've got a nuisance alarm."

The nurse made the call and Peter started backing off on the anesthetic, the surgeon almost finished closing the skin. The kid woke up promptly, a little combative as kids sometimes were, and Peter told him everything was fine, his surgery was over. Jake from Biomed came in as they were transferring the patient onto the stretcher. He hadn't seen Peter in a while and his face registered a faint horror when their eyes met. Peter was unfazed; he'd been getting a lot of that just lately.

He explained the alarm problem and Jake said he had an idea what it was, he'd be back in ten minutes to sort it out. Peter dropped the kid off in Recovery and returned to his room to prepare for the next case, an open femur fracture in a twenty year old girl who'd fallen off her mountain bike. He drew up the drugs he would need, then checked the integrity of his anesthetic circuit, making certain there were no leaks, something he'd done before every case since his first day of training.

As he completed his checks, a recovery room nurse hailed him from the doorway, waving an anesthetic record at him, telling him he'd forgotten to order something for pain. He did that now, scratching the order into the appropriate box, apologizing for the lapse. Then he went to the john in the change room, filled the sink with cold water and bent to douse his face in double handfuls, the water soothing against his throbbing eyeballs, his pounding forehead, his unshaven cheeks. He straightened to dry his face and caught his reflection in the mirror. A ghost stared back at him with skull eyes that registered the same faint horror he'd seen in Jake's eyes, in almost everyone's eyes over the past several days. It was no surprise, really. He hadn't slept more than two hours straight in weeks and had lost ten pounds from a frame that could have stood to gain twenty.

He went to the abandoned doctors' lounge and sat on one of the worn couches. A copy of *The Globe and Mail* lay strewn on the table in front of him, but it held no interest for him. He put his head back and fell asleep. A few minutes later a couple of anesthesia residents came through the door in animated conversation and startled him. Peter looked at them with red eyes, disoriented at first, then waved off their apologies. It was two-thirty in the afternoon.

He got up and started back to his room, meeting Jake in the hallway. The tech had a piece of equipment in his hand, which he held up for Peter's inspection.

"Condensation in the pressure sensors," he said, and Peter could see the droplets in the clear plastic valve ports. "You got a fresh one in there now."

Peter thanked him and continued along the hall, the nurses just wheeling his next patient into the room. Though he caught only a glimpse of the girl—blond, deeply tanned and slim—it was clear she was in a great deal of pain.

He took a deep breath and followed them inside. In the wake of his brief nap, which had seemed more like unconsciousness than sleep, the whole scene seemed faintly unreal to him: the lights too bright, creating shimmering auras around metal surfaces; the girl's moans and the nurses' murmured reassurances sounding somehow arcane, like a prelude to human sacrifice.

Peter grabbed the girl's chart and moved to the head of the operating table. After a quick scan of her lab results he prompted her through a brief medical history, then injected a potent narcotic into her IV. Within seconds the tight mask of pain on her face relaxed into blissful calm.

Now the nurse fitted an oxygen mask over the girl's nose and mouth and instructed her to take some deep breaths. Peter picked up the syringes containing his induction agents and glanced at the monitor. His patient's vital signs were stable, but her oxygen saturation—an indication of the adequacy of her respirations—was beginning to slip from its starting value of 100% into the middle 90's. The girl was sedated now, and Peter quite reasonably assumed that her desaturation was due to respiratory depression, a common side effect of narcotics. With a view to ventilating her manually, he injected his induction cocktail, rendering her paralyzed and unconscious. He then took the mask from the nurse, reached for the black rubber bag that acted as a reservoir of fresh gas flow and found it collapsed. He adjusted the fit of the mask on the girl's face, closed the pressure relief valve and increased the flow of oxygen, a series of maneuvers that predictably resulted in a fully inflated bag, the compression of which would then force oxygen into the patient's lungs.

But there was still no air in the bag; it hung there like a punctured beach ball. The girl's saturations were in the high 80's now and still falling.

Tendrils of panic tightened around Peter's heart. He said, "What the hell?" and turned to his machine.

The surgeon was in the room now, looking concerned. He approached the bed, saying, "What's going on?"

Peter said, "I've got no pressure in the circuit," and thumbed the oxygen flush button, opening a valve that purged the circuit with oxygen, a maneuver normally guaranteed to flood a closed circuit with fresh gas. The result was a loud *whoosh* of gas into the room through a huge leak Peter could not locate.

The surgeon said, "Pete, her saturation's seventy-nine."

Peter lifted the mask off the girl's face. Her lips were blue. "Fuck," he said, and punched the flush valve again, producing the same result.

All eyes were on him now, the room dead silent, everyone waiting for him to remedy the situation. He could feel the panic coursing through him like white water down a rocky chute.

The saturation monitor generated a musical note that registered the patient's heart rate, a finger probe sensing the pulse in concert with the oxygen saturation. When the saturation was normal—between about 96 and 100%—that note was high and cheerful, providing an auditory cue that all was well. But as the oxygen level fell, the note reflected its decline with an increasingly ominous descent into the lower registers. That was all Peter could hear now—that low, deathly note, sinking deeper with each subsequent heart beat—along with a growing shriek in the centre of his skull, the sound of a high wind over a seething gray tide.

The circulating nurse said, "Doctor Croft," and Peter said, "Get me an Ambu bag." The nurse dashed out of the room and now the surgeon came to the bedside. He said, "Shouldn't you do mouth to mouth or something?" and Peter said, *"Fuck,"* unable to free himself from this deadly inertia. The nurse was taking forever and Peter said, "Get me *something*," because his patient was dying and he couldn't think of what else to do.

Then the nurse was back with the Ambu bag, thrusting it at Peter, helping him tear it out of its plastic storage bag, and now Peter was pressing the mask to the girl's dusky face, squeezing air into her starving lungs with the self-inflating bag, trying not to black out as the nurse attached the feed line to an oxygen source and the saturation monitor quickly resumed its comforting pitch.

The surgeon said, "Jesus Christ," and gave a nervous laugh. People went back to their duties and Peter intubated the patient's trachea with shaky hands, feeling the hot flush of shame in his face, realizing he could have done this while he was waiting for the Ambu bag, could have stuck in the tube and forced air into it with his mouth. He attached the Ambu bag to the endotracheal tube and asked the circulating nurse to ventilate the patient while he turned his attention to the machine. He found the leak right away—the Biomed tech had removed the CO_2 absorber from its mount and forgotten to reattach it, leaving a gap in the circuit the diameter of a garden hose. Peter attached it now, then connected his patient to the mechanical ventilator. He dialed in an appropriate mix of gases and saw an Ambu bag hanging on the side of the machine, within easy reach. Every machine had one and he knew that.

He felt like an incompetent fool.

Once the patient was transferred onto the fracture table and the procedure got underway, Peter sat behind the drapes, out of view of the staff, and fought to suppress the well of tears that rose to his eyes. He spent the next hour and a half in the grip of the gnawing fear that he had harmed this innocent girl, though experience told him he hadn't. The entire event had lasted less than three minutes—he'd checked it on the monitor's data base—the period of critical desaturation no more than thirty seconds in duration. A young healthy patient could tolerate three times that degree of hypoxia and survive unharmed.

Still, he worried.

And when the case was done and the girl opened her eyes, responding appropriately to his commands, the relief he felt was indescribable.

He dropped the patient off in the recovery room, then told the desk clerk he'd be in Wendell Smith's office if they needed him.

* * *

Wendell was sitting at his desk when Peter came in, peering over the tops of his bifocals at something on his computer screen. He gave Peter a quick double take and hopped to his feet, as if afraid Peter might collapse.

"Jesus," Wendell said, "are you all right?"

Peter said, "Do you have a minute?" and leaned with both hands on the back of the stout leather chair facing Wendell's desk.

"Of course, sit."

Peter came around the chair and lowered himself into it, free falling the last few inches. His hands were still shaking.

Wendell removed his glasses, setting them on top of a stack of journals. He said, "What's going on?"

"I just came this close to killing a patient," Peter said, showing the department head a slip of space between his forefinger and thumb. Then he described the mishap in detail, shame making it impossible for him to meet Wendell's gaze.

When he was done Wendell said, "The girl's okay?"

"Yes, thank God."

"And you checked your machine before the case."

"Always do, but—"

"So it was Biomed's fault, plain and simple. Those guys are the mechanics, Peter, they know those machines better than you or I ever will. He should've known better." Wendell took out his pen and squared a small note pad on the desk in front of him. "Which tech was it?"

"That's not why I'm here," Peter said. "I'm not here to lay blame. And besides, you know full well that in a court of law a defense like that would be squashed in an instant by any even halfway competent prosecutor. The bottom line is, *I'm* responsible. I should have checked the circuit again. I knew the machine had just been serviced and—if it even occurred to me—I just assumed everything was okay." He waited for Wendell's concurrence, evident in the gradual softening of his posture. Then he said, "And even *that's* no big deal. It was how I handled it. That's why I'm here. If I'd handled it properly this would be a non-issue. But there was an Ambu bag right there on the machine, not two feet away, and I didn't even think of it. I froze, Wen. Just…froze."

"The nurse should have known that, too. Why'd she go running out of the room?"

"Please."

"Okay, okay," Wendell said. "Just my instincts coming through. It's my job to protect you guys, you know." He leaned back in his chair and smiled. "You think you're alone in this? Two weeks ago on call I switched a ventilator off to suction a guy's tube. I hooked him up to the circuit again but forgot to turn the ventilator back on. I didn't have a resident that night, but I did have the trots. I took a quick run out—three minutes tops—and when I came back the guy's sats were in his boots. I felt like an idiot, worried myself sick for the next four hours, but he was fine, too."

"I don't see your point."

"My point is, this is a dangerous, stressful job...and shit happens. We're human, we make mistakes. What matters is the outcome, right? Your patient's fine. And what better way to learn? If I live to be a hundred, I'll never make *that* little blunder again. I'm sure you won't either."

"I'm not talking about an isolated event here," Peter said. "Some days it's like I've never done the job before. I forget things...critical steps. The other day, instead of reversing a patient I paralyzed him again. Picked up the wrong syringe. The day before that I ran a Remifentanil infusion with no Remi in it, just saline. I drew the stuff up and forgot to put it in the syringe. If that patient doesn't have recall I don't know who will." He leaned forward in the chair, holding his shaking hands up for Wendell to see. "Look at me, Wen. What I'm telling you is, I'm unfit. I *froze* today and that kid almost paid the price. I want out. I can't do this anymore."

Wendell began to fidget. "Peter, if you need more time—"

"You're not listening," Peter said, getting to his feet. "I'm done, Wendell. Finished."

"Peter, please. I heard you out, now do the same for me."

Peter sank back into the chair, feeling breathless, trapped. He just wanted out.

Wendell said, "I can't even begin to imagine what you're going through, but you can't just throw your life away over this. You're a huge asset to this hospital, to this community. And you're still a young man. If you walk away now, what'll you do with yourself? How will you fill your time? Pay the bills? I know you like to keep your private life private, but what about counseling? Have you thought about that? I discussed it with the group while you were away, and if you needed more time for something like that, everyone's willing to give it to you, all the time you need. Maybe it'd help you get some perspective on things."

"I understand what you're saying, and I appreciate your concern," Peter said, standing again. "But it's over for me. If I hurt somebody here, through negligence or incompetence, I'd never be able to forgive myself."

Wendell stood now, too, his expression grim. He stuck out his hand and Peter shook it. "Sounds like your mind's made up."

"Thanks, Wendell. Thanks for everything."

"Can you finish out your day?"

Peter shook his head. "I'm sorry."

"Don't worry. Today's an admin day for me. I'll finish up for you."

"Thanks again."

At the office door the department head said, "Can I call you in a couple of weeks? See how you're making out?"

Peter said, "Sure."

Behind them Wendell's intercom buzzed, his secretary's voice coming through. "Sorry to interrupt," she said, "but there's a call for Doctor Croft."

Wendell said, "If it's the OR, tell them I'll be taking over."

"It's an outside call," the secretary said. "The OR transferred it down here. Apparently it's urgent."

Wendell said to Peter, "Want to take it?"

"Yeah, all right."

"Put it in here," Wendell said to his secretary. To Peter he said, "Go ahead, I'll wait for you outside." He pointed at the phone on his desk. "Just hit the flashing button."

Peter waited for the door to close behind Wendell before he picked up the receiver and said hello.

"Peter?"

At the sound of his name, it's frantic tone spoken by this man, Peter felt panic tighten around his heart all over again. "Roger?"

"Can you get to a television set? Right now?"

Peter thought quickly. There was one in the patient waiting area upstairs. "Yes, but it'll take a minute. Why?"

"Just do it. CTV, NewsNet. I'm taping it in case you miss it. I'm at home, call me right back."

The line went dead. Peter hung up and ran out of the office, past Wendell Smith and his wide-eyed secretary, the woman uttering a startled cry as he flew past her desk. He broke into the main hall on the admin level and veered into a stairwell on the opposite side, almost bowling over an elderly volunteer lugging a stack of charts. Propelled by a mix of emotions he had no time to define, he took the risers in reckless threes, slammed through the door on the second floor and skidded toward a surprised porter who yanked open the door to the waiting area for him. Out of breath, he waded into the midst of gray-haired patients in wheelchairs waiting for joint replacements, patients on stretchers with brain tumors and obstructed bowels, and snatched the remote off an end table cluttered with magazines. Under the collective gaze of patients and staff, he aimed the remote at the wall-mounted television and found CTV.

The program was already underway, and at first Peter couldn't figure out what Roger wanted him to see. Then the anchor said, "Back now to Angela Ling for more breaking news from the town of Oakville, thirty minutes east of downtown Toronto."

The scene changed to an attractive Asian reporter standing outside a cordon of police tape stretched between tree trunks in a sunny public park, the reporter raising the microphone to her lips now, pointing with her free hand into a broad expanse of tree-studded grounds.

"This peaceful urban setting was the scene not an hour ago of a brazen kidnapping attempt," Ling said, "the highlights of which were captured on film by this man—" the camera panned back to reveal an elderly gentleman standing next to the reporter, a silver video camera slung around his neck "—Donald Perfetto, who had been videotaping his granddaughter's seventh birthday party here in Warner Park."

Now the scene changed again, to Mr. Perfetto's amateur footage: a few seconds of kids swarming around a picnic table, lining up for slices of cake doled out by an old woman who could only be Mrs. Perfetto. In the midst of all the excited chatter came a distressed, "Grampa, look," and the video fell away from the scene, swaying above the old man's Hush Puppies for a beat as he lowered the camera to see what his granddaughter was upset about. Then Perfetto's voice, "Oh, Madonne," and the video flashed up and to the right, wavering into focus on a jittery scene, recorded from a long distance at first, then pulled in as tight as the camera's zoom lens would allow: grainy footage of a hunched figure wearing a black ski mask and dark, heavy clothing running toward the trees behind the play area, a span over flat ground of about three hundred feet. For the first few seconds only the figure was visible, then Peter saw a pair of small tanned legs dangling from the figure's off-camera side—and now a glimpse of blond hair, lit up by the sun as the kidnapper broke from the shadow of an enormous maple. Three shirtless young men who'd been playing Frisbee were converging on the kidnapper now, attempting to block his access to the dense stand of trees bordering the rear of the park; but the kidnapper kept running, straight-arming the first young man who got in his way, slashing at the second with what could only be a knife, its dull glint there and then gone. The third man, tall and heavily muscled, ran straight at the kidnapper as he passed a chain link fence enclosing what looked like a large power box. In the instant before impact the kidnapper sidestepped the young man, grabbed him by the hair and drove him head first into a fence post. With about a hundred feet left to the tree line now, two men on motorcycles roared into the space between the kidnapper and the trees and dismounted, dropping their bikes with the engines still running. The action vanished behind some bushes for a moment, then the kidnapper blurred into view again—without the ski mask this time—and made for the tree line unopposed, showing only his back to the camera. The kidnapper skidded to a stop at this point, the arm holding the child swinging wildly out in front of him, then the kid was on the ground and the bikers came into view, one of them limping, the kidnapper's mask in his hand, the other joining a trio of park workers rushing in on foot to join the action. Though seriously outnumbered, the kidnapper seemed ready to reach for the kid again. Then one of the park workers made a grab for him, the kidnapper spun defensively…and the footage broke up and ended.

Now the film reversed at high speed, the characters in this blurry drama backpedaling comically through space—then a freeze-frame of the kidnapper, a hunched behemoth in a long coat flared open like a cape, bald head bowed, powerful shoulders a streak of violent motion.

Then, with calculated deliberateness, the kidnapper's image clicked closer to the viewer, now closer again, each new frame centering on that gleaming head until it filled the screen in a kind of pixilated collage that was pure media art, a digital, impressionist's portrait of the dragon rampant, at once unforgettable and pointless, the details of the face obliterated by distance and shadow.

Now the spotlight returned to Angela Ling, Angela saying, "Exciting stuff. But despite the heroic efforts of almost a dozen people, this would-be kidnapper got away, fleeing the area in an escape vehicle police believe was waiting for him on a dirt service road behind the park. Numerous observers have reported seeing a white van peeling off recklessly down Shay Street, which intersects the service road, but apparently no one thought to record the license number.

"Two men were injured in the encounter, one of them seriously." A quick replay of the Frisbee player slamming into the fence post. "Twenty-one year old Samuel Basco was rushed by ambulance from the park. The other man—" a flash of the biker limping out from behind the trees "—thirty-two year old Clarence Hawes, is being treated at an Oakville clinic for a stab injury to his thigh, which apparently missed a major artery by less than an inch."

Angela Ling appeared again, closing in on a growing knot of reporters now, doing her best to clear a path for her cameraman. "Here they are now," she said, "six year old Graham Cade, the victim in this foiled abduction attempt, and his fifteen year old sister, Risa, who had been supervising Graham while he played in the park."

The girl, Risa, held her baby brother in her arms, the boy's back to the bobbing cameras, his thin chest heaving under a bright red T-shirt. The kid was clutching his sister for dear life, sturdy arms locked around her neck, bare legs clenching her hips. Risa was clearly distraught, her eyes streaming tears, her voice breaking as she described what had taken place.

"I was sitting on a bench reading a book and I heard Graham scream. When I looked up I saw this guy in a mask yanking him off the monkey bars over there—" she pointed to the play area behind her, to a set of igloo-shaped monkey bars surrounded by police tape "—then the guy was running away with him, heading for the trees. I tried to go after them, but I broke my foot last week and couldn't run." She pointed at the lime green cast on her foot, red-painted toe nails poking out the open end. "So I started screaming…"

The girl broke down now, unable to respond to the barked questions of the reporters. Then Angela Ling was there, comforting the girl, urging the others to give her some space. When the girl settled Ling was doing an exclusive, Risa Cade speaking only to her.

"Thank you," Risa said, taking the wad of tissue Ling offered, wiping her eyes with it.

"What happened then?" Ling said.

"I fell," Risa said, sobbing again. "Lost sight of them…"

"And where are your parents right now, Risa? Do they know about this yet?"

"They're at work." She looked around with frightened eyes. "Someone was supposed to call them."

"I'm sure they're on their way," Ling said. Then: "Can I ask Graham one quick question?"

Risa leaned her head back, trying to get a look at the boy's face buried in her neck. She said, "Gray? Can she ask you one little question? It might help them catch that bad man."

The boy's blond headed nodded once and Risa turned him to face the reporters, tucking his compact backside into the crook of her arm. The camera closed in on the boy's tear- and dirt-streaked face and Peter felt the floor tilt beneath his feet.

Graham Cade was the spitting image of Jason Mullen.

Ling tucked the microphone under the boy's chin, the other reporters silent now. Ling said, "Graham, how did you get away?"

Graham said, "I bit him," and managed a nervous smile. "On the arm." Now he pointed into the park, at the monkey bars, their summit just visible beyond his head as the camera shifted to include them in the shot. "Tommy Boy told me to."

As a wave of gray curled over Peter's eyes and he lost touch with the world, he saw the top of the monkey bars in the near distance. David was sitting up there with his back to the camera, turning now to look over his shoulder, his eyes as black as the hole Peter tumbled into.

11.

Peter regained consciousness as they lifted him onto a stretcher. Ironically, it was Lisa Black's voice he heard trying to reassure him, her cool hand tight around his forearm. "It's okay, Peter," she was saying. "You fainted and bumped your head. It doesn't look like you broke the skin but I think we should do a CAT scan and get some blood work done, look at your sugar and maybe your hemoglobin. You're white as a sheet."

Now he heard her say, "Take him down to the ER," and felt the stretcher move, angling out of the waiting area toward the orange exit doors. He waited until they were in the main hall and sat up, shaking his head against a swirl of dizziness. The porter said, "Maybe you should lie down," and Peter slid himself off the end of the stretcher, telling the porter he was fine.

He made his way down the hall without looking back, using a patient handrail for support. By the time he reached the locker room he felt better and changed quickly into his street clothes. Lisa intercepted him on his way out and followed him down to the lobby, doing her best to talk him into staying. Peter said he was fine, assured her that if he dropped dead in the parking lot he'd accept full responsibility, then hurried out the door. He called Roger on his way to the car, asking him if he'd gotten the entire newscast on tape.

"You bet I did," Roger said. "The son of a bitch is at it again. I can't believe they let him get away. Are you coming over?"

Peter said, "I'm on my way." The sun was bothering his eyes, the goose egg on his head beginning to throb. He wanted to ask Roger if he'd seen David on the monkey bars, but he knew how crazy that would sound and decided to wait, show it to him on the tape. He said, "See you soon."

"Make it quick. I'm going down there."

Peter said, "I'm coming with you," and signed off, climbing into the car. For a moment the muggy heat inside threatened to turn his stomach, but the feeling quickly passed. He sped out of the lot onto Paris Street, cranking the air conditioner to its highest setting, the image of his son's eyes, black in the sunlight, indelibly etched in his mind.

* * *

Sergeant Vickie Taylor, the lead investigator in the attempted kidnapping case, leaned against a picnic table in Warner Park with her cell phone pressed to her ear, waiting for the boy's father to come on the line. A curt sounding woman had told her Mr. Cade was out on a job site today and that it might take her a while to track him down. The woman offered to have Mr. Cade call Vickie back once she'd located him, but Vickie said thanks, she'd wait. That had been ten minutes ago. She was hoping to catch the man before he saw it all on TV.

According to Cade's daughter, Risa, Christopher Cade was a foreman for a Toronto-based construction company. Risa had given Vickie the mother's number, too—Angela Cade worked as a teller in a Mississauga branch of the Royal Bank—but from experience Vickie knew that if there was a dad in the picture, it was generally better to start with him. It lessened the hysteria factor. Where their children were concerned, even if the kid was fine, mother's tended to go off the deep end early, becoming liabilities to themselves and to the investigation. And in spite of what Vickie did for a living, she knew that if something like this ever happened to her daughter, Samantha—the world's most precocious three year old—she'd react in exactly the same way.

Cade came on the line now, his voice shaky with apprehension, saying, "This is Christopher Cade. What's this about?"

In calm, measured tones Vickie introduced herself and said, "I don't mean to alarm you, Mr. Cade, but there's been an incident involving your son. He's fine, he hasn't been injured, but he was the victim of an attempted kidnapping in the park near your home today."

"Oh my God. When did this happen?"

"About an hour ago."

"An *hour* ago. Why wasn't I notified sooner?"

"I've been having some trouble reaching you, sir."

"Has anyone spoken to my wife about this yet?"

"No, not yet. We were hoping you could handle that."

"Of course. I'll call her right away. And Graham is fine?"

"A little shaken up, but completely unharmed."

"My daughter...?"

"She's fine, too."

"Who was it? Did you catch the guy?"

"Unfortunately not, but we're in the process of accumulating evidence."

"What do you mean, evidence?"

"I'll explain it all to you when we meet, Mr. Cade. In the meantime I'd like you to contact your wife and have both of you meet me at the Oakville Regional Hospital. We're taking your son there now."

"I thought you said he was fine."

"He is, sir. It's just procedure. We'll get him cleared, then go to the station and take everyone's statements."

"Alright, Sergeant Taylor. And thanks, thanks very much. What about Risa?"

"Risa will come with us."

"Okay," Cade said. "We'll be there as soon as we can."

* * *

Roger opened the front door and said, "Peter, I..."

Peter said, "I know," and brushed past him into the house. He said, "I need to see that video," and sat on the couch in the family room.

Roger had the tape already cued up, paused at the beginning of the newscast. He got it rolling with the remote and sat next to Peter on the couch, reeking of stale booze and bitter sweat, his strappy undershirt and blue work pants stained and rumpled looking. Peter was sure he'd been sleeping in them. The man looked like shit.

Peter watched the parts he'd missed, teaser clips that included a shot of the boy crying, then a bunch of commercials Roger fast-forwarded through. When it got to the Angela Ling segment Peter took the remote and fast-forwarded through the bulk of the story, thumbing the PLAY button just as Graham Cade turned in his sister's arms to face the camera.

When the boy pointed at the monkey bars and said, "Tommy Boy told me to," Peter paused the tape and said, "Watch this." Then he hit PLAY and the camera made its subtle shift to include the top of the monkey bars in the shot.

David wasn't there.

The tape rolled on, Angela Ling doing a brisk wrap up before the broadcast returned to the studio and the anchor moved on to the next story.

Roger said, "What?"

Peter said "Hang on," rewound the tape and played it again, getting the same result. He said, "God *damn* it," and his hand tightened around the remote, his sudden, furious disappointment making him want to pitch the thing through the screen. The pressure of his hand activated the PAUSE function and the video froze on Graham's teary face.

With a stifled roar, Peter buried his face in his hands and wept, huge, wrenching sobs that convulsed his body. At this moment more than any other he felt critically unhinged, his connections with the world perilously frayed. He was so *sure* he'd seen David, and that kid had pointed right *at* him, calling him Tommy Boy...

Now he felt Roger's hand on his back, Roger saying, "Hey, hey, what's up? They're going to *get* this guy now, no matter how far he runs. And I want to be there when they take him down. They aired an update after you called, saying about a dozen people saw him, and they expect to get good DNA evidence off his mask. And somebody saw a white van they think he took off in. They're going after him, chum, big time, a huge dragnet. If Jason's still alive, this is the only way we're going to find out. So I need you to snap out of it, right now. We've got to get going—"

Peter stood up, *sprang* up, his wet eyes huge now, swallowing his face. He looked at Graham's image on the screen, then at Roger, an expression of sheer revelation on his face, the face of a man who has just seen God. He said, "He's not going to run. He's going to try for this kid again."

"How do you know that?"

Peter pointed at the Cade boy's image on the screen. "Look at him," he said. "He's perfect."

Roger stood now, too, his own eyes widening, his body seeming to harden and swell. He said, "Jesus Christ, you're right," and headed for the staircase, saying, "Just let me grab a few things." Then he stopped and said, "My truck's in the shop."

"No problem," Peter said. "We'll take the Corolla."

"What about work? Can you get some time off? I'll be staying down there till they nail this guy."

Peter said, "I'm retired."

"Are you serious?"

"That's what I was doing when you called. What about you?"

Roger said, "Suspended, without pay," and shrugged. "Got into it with an asshole in an elevator."

Peter blew air through his nose, the closest he could come to a laugh.

Roger put his hand on the newel post and gave Peter a huge, dimpled grin, the grin of a blue-eyed boy about to embark on the adventure of his life, a treasure hunt for a prize whose value defied estimation. And though the chances of actually finding that prize were incalculably minute—and this knowledge was there, too, in those smiling eyes—it was the hope that fueled Roger Mullen, the hope which, in this moment, made anything seem possible.

"Be right back," Roger said. Then he was gone, tramping barefoot up the stairs, and Peter rewound the tape, knowing it was pointless but powerless to prevent himself. And this time, when he got to the correct spot, he paused the tape and moved through the sequence one frame at a time, searching for even a glimpse of him.

But David just wasn't there.

He turned the TV off and set the remote on the coffee table. Roger came down a few minutes later in a blue T-shirt and a pair of faded jeans, a brown overnight bag in one hand. On the way out the front door Peter said he wanted to drop by his place to grab a few things, then they'd get underway. Roger said that was fine and locked the door behind them.

In the car Peter said, "Shouldn't we call the police?"

"And tell them what?"

"That we think he's going to try for this boy again. Have them beef up security around the kid until they either catch the guy or he makes his move again. You could call your friend Bernie, work it through him."

"I didn't want to tell you about this," Roger said, "but I talked to Bernie a few days after we met with him. He called me at the house."

"What did he say?"

"He asked if I was feeling better. Said I looked like shit that day in his office. Dazed, like a cult member or something. He wanted to know if I'd 'cut that nutcase loose', meaning you. Said he knew what I was going through was tough, but that I had to be careful, there was always some freak out there ready to take advantage of someone like me, the walking wounded. He reminded me of all the wingnuts that phoned or e-mailed me after Jason was taken." Roger sighed now, the sound impossibly weary. "That whole thing with the mug shots and the sketch artist? Bernie was just humoring me, because we're friends. He ran a check on you, you know. Called the chief of staff at the hospital."

"Why would he do that?"

"Because he thought you might be the one."

"Jesus, why?"

"Cop logic. Everyone's a suspect. And when you think about it, it's not that far-fetched. Maybe this guy, this kidnapper, maybe half his gig is outsmarting the cops. Showing his superiority. So when the heat dies down, maybe he feels neglected. Or just wants to put it in their face. So he studies me, finds out about the bereavement group and just shows up there one night with his own sad story. Nobody checks, you know, to see if group members are on the level. I mean, why would anyone lie about a thing like that? So for fun, he joins the group and starts spinning this weird tale about seeing the perp in his dreams. If he knows I've got a friend who's a cop, the rest is easy to figure out."

Peter said, "A bit of a stretch, don't you think?"

"Is it? Think about it for a minute. If you get off on showing people how smart you are, how cool would it be to walk right into the cop shop and start flipping through mug shots? When *you're* the guy."

As they turned into the Moonglow subdivision Peter said, "You don't think I had anything to do with it, do you?"

Roger smiled. "You think we'd be having this cozy little chat if I did? But I've got to tell you, after Bern brought up the possibility, I was glad to hear he'd cleared you."

Peter didn't reply. The information made him feel violated, betrayed, as if someone he trusted had rifled through his belongings without his permission.

They made the balance of the drive in silence. When they reached the house Peter parked in the laneway, told Roger he'd be just a minute and hurried inside.

The tomb-like silence of the house played on Peter's nerves as he stuffed fresh clothes into a carry-on bag, grabbing things at random, socks and shorts and T-shirts and jeans, stopping only when the bag was too full to hold anything more. Then he thought of toiletries and had to take a few things out, replacing them with a zippered, see-through sack that held his toothbrush, toothpaste, shaver and deodorant. On his way out of the bedroom he saw Jason Mullen's toy boxcar on the dresser and tucked it into his pocket, thinking that if an appropriate moment presented itself he'd give it back to Roger. If not, he'd just leave it at the house the next time he was over. He stuck the files he'd compiled on Jason and the Dolan boy into a black computer bag and stashed it all in the trunk of the car.

He paused for a moment after closing the trunk, looking up at the house Dana had been so in love with, thinking of all the wonderful times they'd shared here as a family, the love that had transformed this artful collection of bricks and boards into a home. Then he climbed in next to Roger and backed the car into the street.

* * *

Graham Cade held on to his sister's arm in the back seat of the police car. His two older brothers didn't like it when he touched them or tried to hug them, but they were away at music camp this week and Risa didn't mind. Sometimes she just grabbed him and hugged him like his mom did, giving him a big wet kiss on the neck. Mom said that was because girls were more affectionate than boys. He wasn't sure what that meant, but he was glad they were. Everyone was always telling him he was a real huggy-bear.

Risa was still very upset. She had her arm around his shoulders and her head resting against the police car window. She was looking outside, but Graham could tell she was crying. He'd been pretty afraid, too, when that man grabbed him and started running away with him, but he didn't cry until after, when he saw how scared his sister was. He wondered if he was going to get in trouble for biting the man, because he bit him really *hard*. Then Risa told him the man was bad and that biting him had been a smart thing to do. It was how he got away.

After the man dropped him and ran into the trees, Risa kept saying she was sorry, crying harder than he'd ever seen anyone cry, hugging him so tight he could hardly breathe. But he told her he was okay, just a little scrape on his elbow from when he landed on the ground. He looked at the scrape now and sucked air through his teeth. It was really starting to sting, and there was blood and some kind of juice leaking out of it, little drops that looked like the apple juice he had with his cereal this morning. Maybe it *was* apple juice. Curious, he rubbed off a bit with his finger and tasted it.

Nope. Too sour.

Now Graham patted his sister's arm, trying to make her feel better, but it just made her cry harder and squeeze him too tight again.

The mask, that was the scary part. Dark blue—like the sweater his Grandma made him for Christmas—with red stripes around the eyes and mouth. And the man was so *strong*. Graham had felt like an empty lunch bag flopping around under his arm. Graham even bit his own tongue once, when the man stopped too fast and Graham's teeth clicked together. While the man was running with him he kept saying, "Don't be afraid, baby, I got you now, I got you now," like he was saving Graham instead of taking him away. His clothes smelled bad, too, like the blankets at the summer camp Graham went to last August. *Musty*, that was what his mom called it. That was a cool word. *Musty*. Graham liked new words and tried to remember them, mostly to please his mom, who read a lot and called him her little genius.

Graham sighed and looked into the front seat. This was cool, too, riding in a police car. He sat inside one once when he was little and his JK class visited the police station on a field trip, but that one was parked and there were no guns in it. This one had a *huge* shotgun up there. He could see the driver's gun, too, sticking out of a brown holster. Graham liked the driver, a big guy with a bent nose, because when they were leaving the park he said, "Hey, little man, wanna hear the siren?" and Graham said *sure*. *That* was wicked cool, racing down the street with the siren going, everybody looking at them and getting out of their way.

Now they were turning into the hospital. Graham had been here once before, when he got stitches in his head. Risa was watching him that day, too. She made him go into a boring music store and started looking at CDs. He got mad because he wanted to go to Wal-Mart and Risa wouldn't let him, so he sat on the floor to wait for her. When she was finally done he stood up too fast and bumped his head on a shelf. It didn't hurt that much—not until later—but it bled a *lot* and Risa got all weak and fainted. That part was funny, and they both got a ride to the hospital in an ambulance, which was cool, but not as cool as riding in a police car.

Graham hoped they didn't use any of that stingy stuff on his elbow. He really didn't like hospitals.

The police car parked behind an ambulance and now Graham saw his mom and dad running toward them. His mom's face was all red and she was crying really hard, even his dad's eyes were wet, and when his mom opened the door and scooped him into her arms Graham started crying again, too.

On the way into the emergency department Graham saw the police lady who talked to him at the park. She said her name was Vickie and Graham thought she was too pretty to be a policeman. She smiled at him, then followed them through the automatic doors, saying something to his dad Graham couldn't hear.

* * *

They made a bathroom stop in Parry Sound, about a hundred and fifty miles north of Oakville, just before six that evening. Peter suggested they top up the tank, but Roger insisted they keep moving. The gas bar was lined up six cars deep at every bay, and Roger said that half a tank in a car like this was more than enough to get them where they were going.

When they were back on the road, Peter asked Roger what the plan was.

"Scope the place out," he said. "Who knows, maybe I can nab the son of a whore myself."

Peter glanced at Roger now, not liking what he saw in the man's face, the deadly intent. He said, "We don't even know where the Cade family lives. And even if we did, we can't just camp out on their doorstep. Shouldn't we just find a place to stay and let the police do their jobs?"

Roger said, "That news update I told you about? They showed an interview with one of the Cade's neighbours, an old guy mowing his lawn. He pointed across the street at their house. They blotted out the street number, but the front door's bright yellow and there's a fire hydrant at the curb. And I'm sure I heard one of the reporters say something about the park being just a couple of blocks from their home."

"What about letting the cops do their job?"

"Look at the wonderful job they did with Jason."

Peter had no reply.

They drove in silence for a while after that, until Roger found a rock station on the radio and started drumming on his legs. The man was a vat of raw adrenalin, exuding a caged, manic energy, and he was making Peter nervous. Peter had never been involved with such a volatile individual. He and Roger were completely different personalities, Roger a man of action, the kind of guy who threw the first punch in situations Peter had always done his best to avoid. And while that made them an unlikely team, Peter could understand how Roger felt. No matter how much an injustice affected an individual or his family, in many cases there was only so much the police could do. Only so many man-hours they could devote, only so much emotional investment they could provide. In many ways it paralleled the situation in medicine, even where the families of colleagues were concerned. How many late nights keeping vigil with David had he secretly cursed the nurses for taking so long to bring his son's pain medication or change his bed when he soiled it? And how thin had he judged their excuses about short staffing and impossible patient loads? But it was all true. In the majority of these situations, for physicians as well as the police, a point inevitably arrived at which priorities had to be shifted, hope tempered or even abandoned.

But there was no way he could talk to Roger about any of this now. The man was amped, three years' worth of dread, guilt and bottled fury suddenly given focus, however elusive the object of that focus might be. But the kidnapper—the faceless predator who had come into Roger's home and stolen the most precious thing in it—had just hours ago struck again in a place Roger could not only see, but could physically place himself in.

"The thing I can't understand," Roger said now, shouting over the music and giving Peter a start, "is why the guy keeps going after these look alikes. And why such huge gaps of time in between? The first one, what was his name?"

Peter turned the music down and said, "Clayton Dolan."

"That was six years ago, right? Then Jase, almost three years now. If it's some weird kink he's got and he…you know, kills them after, why wait so long in between?" Roger's face was brick red now, saying these things out loud clearly tearing him apart. "If it's a sexual thing, wouldn't he want it all the time?"

Peter didn't like the way the conversation was going. Over the summer he'd watched a documentary on a serial killer from Wichita or someplace like that, a man who had evaded capture for thirty years and left a string of corpses in his wake. What had struck Peter about this guy was the uneven periodicity of his crimes, the man going on savage binges for a while, then stopping all of a sudden, slipping into a period of dormancy that on one occasion lasted thirteen years. Watching the program, Peter had decided that in situations of extreme deviancy, the familiar parameters of reason simply could not be applied. These people just did what they did when they did it. And once they were captured, if they were willing to discuss their crimes at all, often seemed as baffled by their behavior as the rest of the world.

Cringing inside, Peter said the only thing he could think of: "It can't be easy finding kids who look so much alike."

"That's exactly my point, though. What's *with* that? If you're into blond, blue-eyed and dimpled, you could probably find three or four like that in every grade school in the country. An endless supply. I remember picking Jase up at school a few times and seeing these three little girls all about the same age who I thought must be sisters, but they were always picked up by different people. Why be so specific?"

Peter had no answer. He said, "Roger, I really don't know," and leaned a little harder on the accelerator, keeping his eyes aimed straight ahead now, the man beside him a coiled cobra, ready to strike.

* * *

The nurse at the hospital *did* use the stingy stuff, but she said it would only hurt for a minute and it would keep his scrape from getting infected. His brother Greg got an infection once from a bug bite and Graham remembered how nasty looking the pus was that Greg squeezed out of it. It looked like yellow mayonnaise and Graham knew he didn't want any of that in him. So he let the nurse use the stingy stuff, and it wasn't that bad. She put ointment on it after that, then a weird bandage that looked like an octopus with four legs. The doctor who checked him over said he was a hundred percent and he could go. The fun part was, he got to drive in the police car again, this time to the police station.

When they got there the police lady sent Risa away with another policeman, then took Graham and his parents into a special room called an interview room, though Graham couldn't see anything special about it. It was just a room, with a couch and a coffee table and a lamp and a big mirror on the wall. It reminded him of the family room at his friend Scott's place, except smaller and with no TV. There was a box of toys in the corner the police lady said he could check out while she went to her office to get a few things, but they were mostly just baby toys, big clunky trucks made of plastic and a few silly dolls.

The police lady asked Graham to sit on the couch between his parents, then sat in the big comfy chair across from him. Graham had kind of wanted that chair, but it was nice to sit with his mom and dad, except his mom kept squeezing his hand too hard. The police lady put something on the coffee table that looked like a radio, then pressed a button on it. A little red light came on and Graham saw that it was a tape recorder, like the one his uncle Brian used when he played his guitar, except smaller.

"So, Graham," the police lady said, looking right at him now. "My name's Vickie Taylor—remember?—and I was hoping you and I could have a little chat. My memory's not that great, so if it's all right with you I'm going to use this tape recorder. Would that be okay?"

Graham shrugged and said, "Can I hear it after?"

Vickie smiled. "Sure, if you'd like."

Graham said, "You want to talk about what happened in the park?"

"Yes, but not right away. I thought maybe you could tell me a bit about yourself first."

"Like what?"

"Like, how old are you?"

"Six, but I'm small for my age. Everybody always thinks I'm five or even four."

"What grade are you in?"

"Going into one."

"That's awesome. And what about your day today? What did you do before you went to the park? Did you sleep in late?"

Graham's mother, Angela, smiled nervously and said, "Not this guy. Gray's a real early bird—"

"I'm sorry, Mrs. Cade," Vickie said, "but I'd prefer if Graham answered my questions for now. I'll be talking to you and your husband individually later on."

Christopher Cade was rubbing Angela's back now, trying to help stave off a fresh wave of tears. When it came anyway he grabbed the kleenex box off the coffee table and handed it to his wife. Angela plucked out a handful and wiped her eyes with it, apologizing to Vickie for the lapse.

"Perfectly understandable," Vickie said. "It's been a trying day for all of you. But it's almost over."

Graham felt like crying again now, too, his bottom lip shivering, but he held it in, trying to be brave for his mom.

"Graham?" Vickie said. "Can you tell me about your morning? You got up early and then what?"

"Got a bowl of Cheerios and watched TV."

"What'd you watch?"

"*My Dad the Rock Star*, then *The Bugs Bunny and Tweety Show*."

"Yeah? My daughter Samantha loves Bugs Bunny. Then what did you do?"

Graham shot a quick look at his dad. "Played on my brother's X-Box."

"Would he thump you if he found out?"

Graham grinned and said, "Yup."

"Let's not tell him, then. When did you go to the park?"

"After lunch. Risa didn't want to because she broke her foot when she dropped her computer screen on it but mom said she had to because she's supposed to baby-sit me this summer.

For money. Her cast is green. I signed it. No *way* she can catch me now."

"Are you a fast runner?"

Graham nodded proudly. "My dad calls me 'The Flash.'"

"Do you go to the park a lot?"

"Every day. I like the monkey bars."

"How do you get there?"

"Walk. It's only two blocks. Risa's got a walking cast. It's got a rubber thingy on the bottom."

"And when you were walking today, did you notice anybody watching you or following you?"

"No."

"How about at the park?"

"Nope. If you mean the man who grabbed me, I've never seen him before. He had smelly winter clothes on and a blue ski mask. I didn't like that mask."

"His clothes were smelly?"

"Uh-huh."

"What did they smell like?"

Graham looked at his mom and said, "Musty."

"Good for you, Graham," Vickie said. "Did you notice anything else about him?"

"He was strong."

"Did he say anything to you?"

"Yes."

"What did he say?"

"He told me not to be afraid. He kept saying, 'I got you, I got you.'"

"Did he use your name?"

"No."

"Did he have an accent?"

Graham thought he knew what that meant but he wasn't sure. "You mean, like the Crocodile Hunter?"

"Yeah, but not just Australian. Any accent."

"I don't think so."

"Okay. Did he say anything else?"

Graham looked down at his feet. He didn't want to say the rest. He heard his dad say, "Graham?" and mumbled, "He called me a baby," without looking up.

Vickie said, "A baby? How did he say it?"

"I'm six. I'm not a baby."

"I know that, Graham, but maybe that's not what he meant. Do you remember how he said it?"

Graham looked at Vickie now. "He said, 'Don't be afraid, *baby*.'"

Vickie looked at Graham's mom and dad, then said, "And that was it?"

"Yes."

"Did you notice anything else about him?"

"His shoes were dirty. They had yellow laces."

"What about after the other man pulled his mask off? Did you see his face?"

"No. When he was carrying me I could only see the ground."

"What about after he dropped you?"

"The sun was burning my eyes, but I saw he had no hair."

"Did he have a moustache or anything?"

"I don't think so."

"Okay, kiddo. Do you remember all the people with cameras and microphones in the park?"

"The reporters?"

Vickie smiled. "That's right. Do you remember talking to them about how you got away?"

"Yes. I bit him."

"And you told them someone *told* you to bite the man?"

Graham looked at his dad and said, "Yeah. Tommy Boy."

Vickie said, "Tommy Boy?"

Graham didn't feel like talking anymore. He said, "Can I go to the bathroom?"

"Sure, sweetie," Vickie said. "I just need to know this one last thing."

Graham folded his arms and clenched his teeth. He didn't like talking about Tommy Boy because nobody believed him, especially his dad.

Now his dad said, "Tommy Boy's his imaginary friend."

The police lady looked at his dad and Graham could tell she was annoyed. She said, "Why don't we let Graham tell it?"

Graham said, "Just because you can't see him doesn't mean he's not there," and felt bad right away for getting angry at his dad. More quietly, he said, "His real name is David." Then he looked at Vickie and said, "Are we finished now? I *really* need to go to the bathroom."

"Okay, Graham," Vickie said. "That's enough for now." She stood and held out her hand. "Come on, I'll take you to the boy's room."

Graham stood up and took her hand, but it made him feel funny. He said, "Can my dad come too?" and felt better when the police lady said of course.

Dad held his other hand and they went out to find the bathroom.

* * *

By six o'clock that evening lead investigator Vickie Taylor felt she had a complete enough picture of the case to present it to her boss, Staff Sergeant Rob Laking, who headed up the Criminal Investigations Division. Laking was a firm but approachable guy in his mid forties who had played professional hockey in his early twenties, until a nasty knee injury cut that career path short. Laking had two kids of his own, teenage girls upon whom the sun rose and set—his office was cluttered with pictures of the two of them, filling every space that wasn't already occupied by hockey memorabilia or mug shots—and he took cases of this nature very personally.

Laking was on the phone with one of his daughters when Vickie came into his office. After giving her an acknowledging nod he pointed at the phone, winced and whispered, "Sit." Then, into the phone, he said, "Kel, this'll have to wait till I get home," and shook his head. Then, "But—"

Amused by the spectacle of this tough, ex-hockey-star cop being cowed by a teenage girl, Vickie sat in the chair facing his desk and waited.

A few seconds later Laking said, "Kelly, I have to go," and hung up the phone. Grinning, he looked at Vickie and said, "Car Wars." He saw the case folder in Vickie's lap and said, "What've you got for me?"

Vickie flipped the folder open and started peeling out documents, giving Laking a synopsis of each as she handed it over. "Thirteen eye-witness interviews, freshly transcribed. They all tell pretty much the same story as far as events are concerned. We've got the videotape anyway, so most of it's moot. Four composites, taken from the four guys who got close enough to get a look at him after the mask came off—the two bikers and a couple of park employees who were there weeding flower beds."

Laking arranged the computer generated sketches on the desk in front of him and shook his head, saying, "Great. The guy's bald. That much I got from the news." He picked up the third sketch in the group and showed it to Vickie. "This one looks like my mother-in-law, only cuter."

"You know what it's like, " Vickie said. "Heat of the moment, nobody ever really gets a good look. And the guy was waving a knife. We got great descriptions of it. Two of the witnesses thought the guy's head was shaved, though, as opposed to naturally bald. One of them said it was a real neat job, tight to the skull."

Laking said, "Interesting," and glanced again at the composites. "Which one are you going to run with?"

She pointed at the middle two sketches. "The artist said these two had the most points in common. Said she'd do a blend and let us go with that."

"Okay, what else you got?"

"Interviews with the kid, the older sister who was with him at the park, and the parents. Nothing much there, either. The guy was carrying the kid face down, and when he dropped him the sun was in the boy's eyes. The kidnapper called him 'Baby', though, as in, 'Don't be afraid, Baby.'"

"Like he knows the kid?"

"That's what I thought, but the parents couldn't think of anybody, family or otherwise, who'd be capable of an act like

188 · SEAN COSTELLO

this. Ditto for the sister. No weird friends who might've fixed on the brother, no jilted boyfriends. They're a pretty normal bunch. And as far as motive goes—outside of the obvious deviant stuff—ransom seems highly unlikely. Both parents work, but they've got four kids they're trying to build college funds for, two cars and a mortgage. I haven't seen the house yet, but it sounds like they live fairly modestly."

Laking glanced at one of the reports and said, "The kid's got two older brothers."

"Yeah, nine and eleven, both away for the week at a music camp near Parry Sound."

"What about forensics? You talk to Smitty yet?"

"Yeah, just before I came up here. He says the mask's a DNA gold mine. Sweat, saliva, skin cells. He said he'd put a rush on it, but even then it's going to take a couple of days."

"Alright. Let's hope our boy's in the data base. Anything from the neighbourhood yet?"

"Nada."

"And the white van?"

"No plates, thousands to choose from in the Greater Toronto area."

Laking pushed back in his chair and said, "So what now?"

"I'm going to escort the Cade's home, have a look around the premises."

"You think it was a random snatch?"

"Looks that way."

"That what you told the parents?"

Vickie nodded. "I said the guy's probably in another province by now."

"They happy with that?"

"Not really. The father wants extra protection until the perp is caught."

"And?"

"I told him we could probably have a squad car make hourly passes overnight. Maybe stick a surveillance camera on the pole across the street, if we can find a spare."

"Tell you what," Laking said. "Why don't you tell him we'll park a couple of plainclothes officers across the street from the house. See if that does it. With any luck, we'll have the prick in lockup by morning anyway."

Vickie said, "Shall do," and gathered up her files.

* * *

There was an accident on the 400 just north of Barrie that tied them up for almost an hour, traffic grinding to a standstill in the August heat. While they were waiting Roger found another news update on a Toronto FM station that said essentially nothing had changed. Police were still looking for a white van, a composite of the kidnapper was due for media release later today, and the six year old victim had been discharged from hospital with a clean bill of health.

When traffic finally started moving again, around eight-thirty, Roger said, "Back at the house, what were you looking for in that video?"

Peter looked at him and said, "I'm not sure you want to know."

"I'm asking."

He decided to just say it. "When I watched the newscast the first time, at the hospital, I saw David on the monkey bars."

"Could it have been a kid who looked like David?"

"When I watched it again at your place there was *no* kid on the monkey bars. I would've been prepared to believe I'd only imagined it if the Cade boy hadn't pointed right at him and called him Tommy Boy."

"Tommy Boy?" Roger said. "Like the movie?"

"Exactly. David loved that movie, and his mom used to call him Tommy Boy sometimes."

Surprising Peter, Roger said, "Makes sense. I read someplace that kids are more sensitive to things like that, seeing ghosts."

Peter said, "So suddenly you're a believer?"

"I'm not sure I'd go that far, chum. But everything you've told me so far has pretty much panned out, so either you're some weird kind of Sherlock Holmes or there's at least an element of truth to all of this."

Peter felt oddly comforted by this. Validated, less alone.

In a calm voice Roger said, "That's the real reason you figured the kidnapper'd go after this boy again, right? Because of the video?"

Peter nodded. "Even if I imagined seeing David in the newscast, the kid calling him Tommy Boy...I can't believe it's just a coincidence."

Roger nodded now, too.

They were coming up on a Barrie exit and Peter said, "We're down to less than a quarter tank and I'm starving. How about a pit stop?"

Roger agreed and they pulled into the next service centre. While Peter gassed up Roger ran into the Wendy's for burgers and drinks. Peter's cell phone rang while he was paying for the gas and he answered with a brusque hello.

It was Erika Meechum.

"Peter, hi."

Her voice was sombre, tentative somehow, and though Peter felt a vague guilt for not responding to her messages earlier in the summer, he said, "Erika, listen, I really can't talk to you right now. I'm sorry I haven't returned your calls, that was rude of me, since it was me who came to you in the first place, but—"

"Did you see the news?"

A chill surfaced at the back of Peter's neck and rippled down his spine. He said, "Yes. We're on our way there now."

"You and Roger?"

"Yes."

Silence. Then: "Tommy Boy. Is it David?"

"Yes."

"I saw something, Peter. On the monkey bars."

That chill again, coursing through him in quickening cycles. "You saw him too?"

"Not him. Just…energy. An aura, like a smudge of light."

Peter thought, *So maybe I'm not crazy* and said, "Roger wants to be close by when they catch him," because he had no idea what else to say.

"I'm sorry you were upset by what happened that night," Erika said. "With the toy train. But I stand by what I said."

Through the booth window Peter saw Roger coming out of Wendy's with a paper bag in one hand and a molded tray of

192 · SEAN COSTELLO

drinks in the other. He said, "I hope you're right, Erika, I really do, but I've got to let you go."

"I understand."

"Thanks for calling."

"Peter?"

"Yes?"

"Be careful."

Peter said, "I will," and signed off.

In the car Roger handed him a burger and a cold drink wrapped in yellow paper. Then he dug out one of his own. Peter stuck his meal on the dash and got them rolling again, his appetite gone.

12.

The Cades lived in a quaint, single-family dwelling on Cahill Street, two blocks south of Warner Park. In contrast to the cramped design of most suburban developments, the homes in this section of town had been built with a little breathing space between them, and the whole neighbourhood had obviously been cut from very old forest, the hundreds of trees left standing all huge and majestic, giving the area a shaded, rural feel. Compared to the townhouse Vickie and her husband shared in Mississauga, eight minutes east on the 401, Oakville seemed a paradise.

Christopher Cade took Vickie on a tour of the house. The first thing he pointed out was the alarm system. "State of the art," he told her. "Just had it installed last spring. So far we've only been using it when we're out, but you can bet I'll be arming it at night from now on."

On their way through the kitchen Cade asked Vickie if she wanted something to drink and Vickie politely declined. While Cade grabbed a glass of water for himself, Vickie scanned the sheaves of kids' artwork attached by magnets to the fridge. Interspersed with the artwork were a few newspaper clippings, one of which showed a smiling Graham Cade balancing a huge, cone-shaped piece of what looked like amethyst crystal. The caption read, YOUNG ROCKHOUND WINS MAN-SIZE DOOR PRIZE. Vickie started scanning the brief text and Cade said, "That was last month, at a gem show in Toronto we take him to every year. He was so proud of himself that day it was ridiculous." Cade set his empty glass on the counter and said, "Come on, I'll show you the rest of the place."

They did the upstairs next, four bedrooms up here, the master bedroom and Risa's room in the back, the oldest brother's room and the one Graham shared with the nine year old in the front. A second staircase serviced the back of the house and Vickie commented on it, saying how unusual it was to see something like this in a newer home.

Cade said, "Yeah, we thought it was neat. With a big family like this, it's kind of nice not having to hear the night owls thumping up stairs at all hours. It's not really that unique, though. Not in this neighbourhood. There's at least a dozen more like it in the Warner subdivision alone."

Graham was in his room playing checkers with his mom and Vickie traded smiles with him as she walked by his open door. The boy looked hollow-eyed and exhausted, but Vickie was betting he still wouldn't sleep all that well tonight.

They finished the tour with the basement. Cade had a gun safe down here and he showed it to Vickie now, saying, "And if the sick bastard is stupid enough to actually break into the house…" He patted the safe as one might the shoulder of a trusted friend.

Vickie said, "Mr. Cade, believe me, I understand how you feel; I've got a daughter of my own. But the worst thing you can do is start prowling around here at night with a loaded gun. People who do that end up shooting the wrong person almost one hundred percent of the time. And it's usually a family member."

Cade seemed disappointed by Vickie's response, but unswayed.

Vickie said, "I reviewed your case with my superior and he's in full agreement with what I told you and your wife earlier on. Given the evidence we've accumulated so far, the attempt on your son was almost certainly random. The mask, the heavy clothing, the fact that he was in the park, these things all strongly suggest that he *was* trolling; but it's highly unlikely that he'd actually targeted your boy in advance. Graham was just…handy."

"Be that as it may," Cade said, leading her back upstairs. "But if you've got a child of your own, Sergeant Taylor, I know you'll understand: I'll do *anything*—whatever it takes—to protect my family. You just get this son of a bitch behind bars, where he belongs, then we can discuss probability."

"We're doing our best, Mr. Cade. All I'm asking is that you try to stay calm." She led him to the living room window and pointed across the street. "See that gray Lumina over there?" Cade nodded. "In it are the two officers I told you about. They'll be there until eight in the morning." She handed him her card. "Our main number's on the front. I wrote my cell number on the back. If you have any concerns, please, feel free to give me a call."

Cade looked at her and smiled, and for the first time since meeting the man Vickie got the sense that he was starting to relax.

"Thanks, Sergeant Taylor," he said. "It's just...pretty terrifying, you know?"

"I understand," Vickie said. They were standing at the exit now. "If you don't mind, I'm going to take a quick look around the grounds before I leave."

"Of course, whatever you need. Want me to tag along?"

"No, thanks. I'll be fine."

Cade shook her hand, thanked her again, then let her out. On her way down the steps Vickie heard him run the deadbolt home behind her.

She turned left at the bottom of the steps and strode across the lawn, noting the narrow basement windows and thinking again about Cade's gun safe. She'd have to give her plainclothes guys a heads up on that. Citizens with guns made everyone nervous.

Now she turned left into the broad space between the Cade's home and the neighbours', a couple of those huge trees along here, an oak and what looked like a poplar. A pair of black squirrels were chasing each other around the oak, settling a dispute, Vickie assumed, over squatters' rights. Watching them, it occurred to her that in some ways animals were very much like human beings. The ground was littered with acorns, more than enough for fifty squirrels, and these two were fighting over who owned the tree.

The back yard was surprisingly large, a wide, sloping expanse of lawn bordered by lush flower beds edging a high cedar fence that enclosed the area in shaded privacy. What struck Vickie most were these fabulous trees, twisted, weather-beaten trunks sprouting thick branches that reached out as much as twenty feet in some instances, a few of them encroaching on the house itself, spanning high over the deck to brush the brick siding with their leaves. Her cop mind saw this as a liability, easy access to the upper windows for an agile cat burglar, but the little girl in her remembered wanting to live in a place like this when she grew up. The house was just a house, but this space was wonderful, a slice of Eden in the midst of endless suburban sprawl.

She strolled down the gentle incline to the rear of the property and unlatched the gate in the fence. It swung inward on oiled hinges to reveal a dirt alley that bisected the block, plastic garbage bins back here, wildflowers and scrub grass sprouting up between the ruts in the road, every yard on either side of the alley discretely fenced in.

Vickie swung the gate shut and secured the latch. After a last look around, she walked back to the street along the other side of the house and got into her car. On her way down the street, she pulled up along side the Lumina and told the officers about Christopher Cade's gun safe.

* * *

Graham heard his mother say, "Bedtime, sweetheart," and felt her cool hand on his forehead. Yawning, he opened his eyes. He was lying on the couch in front of the TV. He'd been watching *America's Funniest Home Videos*, but now something else was on. The news. He sat up, rubbed his eyes and saw *himself* on TV, in Risa's arms, talking to the reporter lady. Then the screen went dark, making that funny prickly sound. Graham looked at his mom and saw her aiming the remote at the TV. He said, "Mom, I was *watching* that," and gave her a grumpy look.

His mom put the remote on the table and lifted him off the couch, making a groaning sound and saying how heavy he was getting. She always did that. He put his arms around her neck, liking how her hair smelled, and heard her say, "You don't need to see that, sweetheart. I want you to forget about all that stuff now. You're home safe with us and tonight I'm going to thank God in my prayers for helping you get away."

He wanted to tell her it wasn't God who helped him get away but decided against it. His mom hugged him then put him down, asking him if he was hungry. Graham said he wasn't and his mom said, "Go brush your teeth, then. I'll be up in a minute to tuck you in." He looked out the window on his way up the stairs and saw his dad talking to two men in a car across the street. It was already dark outside.

He brushed his teeth with his electric toothbrush and got into his jammies. He heard his dad come back in the house, then heard him tell Mom he'd tuck Graham in.

Giggling quietly, Graham tiptoed into his bedroom and hid behind the clothes hamper. Sometimes it was fun being small, because you could scrunch into places people never thought to look.

His dad was in the back staircase now, the squeak of the second-last step telling Graham he was almost at the top. He heard his dad say, "Gray?" then heard him push open the bath-room door.

In the tight space behind the hamper Graham stifled a laugh. He liked hiding on his dad, then jumping out at him and yell-ing, *"Boo!"* because his dad always pretended he was having a heart attack, and when Graham went to save him his dad would tickle him until he laughed himself silly.

"Gray?"

His dad was in the room now, turning on the light, and now he shouted Graham's name—*"Gray"*—and Graham heard his mother's voice downstairs, "Chris, what's wrong?" His dad said, *"Graham?"* and Graham realized his dad was really afraid. He popped up from behind the hamper with tears in his eyes and said, "I'm right here, Dad," but his dad was in the hallway again saying, "Angie, are you sure he came up here?" to his mom, who was running up the stairs.

Afraid now himself, Graham ran into the hallway saying, "I'm right *here*, Dad, I was just hiding," and his dad lifted him up and hugged him and now his mom was there too, her arms around both of them and they were all crying, Graham saying, "I'm sorry, Dad," his mom and dad saying, "It's okay, sweetheart, it's okay."

After a minute his mom went into the bathroom and came back with a kleenex for each of them. Wiping his eyes, his dad said, "Wanna bunk in with us tonight, trooper?" and Graham said he did. He asked his dad where Risa was and his dad told him she was sleeping over at Sara's house tonight. Sara was Risa's best friend.

His dad took him into the bedroom and plunked him in the middle of the huge bed. Graham stood up and did a few bounces, touching the ceiling with his fingers, then crawled under the comforter and pulled it up to his chin. First his mom, then his dad kissed him on the forehead, saying they'd both be along in a minute. His dad turned off the main light, leaving the one on the dresser on. Graham didn't like that light—three metal monkeys with creepy faces using their hunched-over backs to balance a yellow bowl that had the light bulb inside it—but it was better than no light at all. Graham had a night-light beside his bed. He wasn't afraid of the dark, he just didn't like it.

His mom and dad went into the little bathroom his mother called an *on-sweet* and Graham heard them brushing their teeth in there, the water in the sink running hard. He could hear their voices over the hiss of the water, but couldn't make out what they were saying. Then the water stopped and he heard his mother say, "I don't want that gun up here, Christopher. You know how I feel about those damn things. I don't even want them in the house. You promised me six months ago you'd move them out to the garage."

In a low voice his dad said, "In case you've forgotten, Angie, some psycho tried to grab our son today, and he's still *out* there somewhere. A man has a right to defend his own family."

A shiver of fear stole through Graham. *He's still* out *there?*

His mom said, "There are two policemen parked right outside the house. The alarm system is on. Every cop in the city is watching for that man. Why can't we just get some sleep and let them take care of it?"

"Tell you what," his dad said now, and Graham could tell he was getting angry. "If the gun bothers you that much I'll sleep on the couch downstairs. But until this guy is locked up or dead, I'm not closing my eyes without a weapon beside me."

Graham glanced at the monkey lamp and felt cold under the down comforter.

His mother said, "All right, you win. You always do. Just try not to shoot one of us."

Then she was padding out of the bathroom, crawling in beside Graham. His dad came out next in his pajamas with the little golf clubs on them, one hand behind his back like he was hiding something. He sat on the other side of the bed and opened the night table drawer. Graham heard him put something hard inside, then push the drawer shut.

His dad got up and turned off the monkey lamp, the only light now a dim glow from the hallway. Tommy Boy was standing out there in his dark suit and Graham heard him say, *Hide*. Then his dad closed the door and the room was dark, his dad feeling his way back to the bed now, saying a bad word under his breath when his toe hit something hard along the way. It was funny but Graham didn't feel like laughing.

His dad climbed into bed, his weight making the mattress squeak. First his mom kissed Graham's cheek, then his dad, both of them saying goodnight.

Graham lay perfectly still for a minute, barely breathing, then said, "Is he really still out there?" and heard his mother say, "Happy now, Chris?"

His dad snugged an arm around him and said, "Sergeant Taylor told me he's probably in another province by now, sweetheart, and that's very far away. You don't need to worry."

202 · Sean Costello

Graham wanted to say, "Why do you have a gun, then?" but instead he said, "Okay, Dad."

"Don't worry," his dad said and this time Graham didn't say anything.

But he was worried. Very worried.

He pulled the covers over his eyes and vowed never to fall asleep again.

* * *

CID officer Frank McNamara glanced at his watch and cursed under his breath. Five minutes to eleven—nine god damn hours to go—and already his back was killing him. He'd been seriously injured eight years ago in a motor vehicle accident, an old broad tranked on valium rear-ending him with her Caddy doing eighty coming into a bottle neck on the 401, and for a while it had been touch and go as to whether he'd even walk again, never mind return to work. But after a year of grueling physio and pig-headed determination he'd come back on light duty, polishing a chair with his ass the first six months, then moving on to shit details like this one, staking out a private residence behind the wheel of this stuffy little car with the windows open, watching for a perp who was probably a hundred miles away by now.

They'd partnered him with Jack Bates, a skinny, beak-nosed guy in his fifties who couldn't keep his trap shut for more than a minute at a time. Frank had no idea how the man came up with so much horseshit to prattle on about. It was like listening to some lame talk show you couldn't turn off. In the past ten minutes alone Bates had delivered droning monologues on federal politics, SARS, insecticides, leaky pool liners and the pros and cons of legalized prostitution. When the little guy finally came up for air Frank said, "How 'bout some tunes?" and turned the radio on, hoping it would shut the man up.

No such luck. Eric Clapton's "Tears in Heaven" was playing and Bates said, "You know the story behind this one, Frank?" Frank did, but before he could say so Bates said, "Fucking tragedy. You never heard about that? Clapton's kid? Went out a tenth story window when he was only four."

Bates kept talking and Frank glanced out his window at a pop can the breeze had set rolling on a diagonal toward the gutter on the opposite side of the street. He heard Bates say "What the hell?" and realized there was no breeze. He glanced at Bates—the man staring at him quizzically now, his left hand pressed against the right side of his neck, something dark oozing out from between his fingers—and saw a husky woman with platinum blond hair coming around the hood from Bates's side of the car, coming fast. After eighteen years on vice Frank's first thought was, *What's a hooker doing in a neighbourhood like this?* then he glanced again at Bates, the man gurgling softly now, and realized the dark stuff oozing out of his neck was blood, lots of it.

Frank reached for his weapon and now the woman was leaning in through his window, her thick forearm pressed against his brow, forcing his head back. Frank said, *"Hey,"* and grabbed her by the hair, surprised when it came off in his hand. He had time to think, *Wig*, and realized his throat had been cut. He brought his service pistol up, shoved it out the window to fire at the fleeing figure—clearly a man now, *the* man, that bald head gleaming in the streetlight—and felt the gun slip out of his grasp to clatter onto the road beside the car. He turned to Bates, wanting to tell him to call it in, but Bates was slumped forward against the dash, blood-slicked hands limp in the V of his crotch.

Frank took a breath and felt his neck suck blood and air into his pipes and he started hacking, his lungs already shot from thirty years of smoking, a two-pack a day habit his wife had finally nagged him out of on New Year's Day.

The guy was heading for the Cade house, and though Frank knew he should call it in he wanted to get his gun first, maybe even go after the guy if he could still walk. He was bleeding, bleeding bad, but not as bad as Bates, and if he leaned his head to one side he could breathe better, the cough backing off a little.

He gave Bates a shake and tried to say his name, but only managed a wet croak. He thought, *Can't talk*, and opened his door, almost falling through it onto the street. He got himself turned around in his seat, both feet on the blacktop now, and saw the gun, just out of reach by the front tire.

Summoning all of his will, Frank McNamara pushed himself into a standing position, propped his way around the door to the hood and bent to retrieve his weapon.

* * *

They got directions from a teenage girl at a gas bar and found Warner Park easily enough, then began a systematic tour of the surrounding neighbourhood, hampered now by the dark. There were a lot of fire hydrants and even more yellow doors, and it wasn't until their second pass through a two block radius of the park that Roger noticed a street they'd missed. "Cahill," he said, "let's give this one a try," and Peter turned left onto the sleepy street, slowing the vehicle to a crawl.

About a third of the way down the block Peter thought he heard something and turned the air conditioner off. He listened a moment, then said, "Do you hear that?"

Roger said, "Yeah, sounds like a burglar alarm," and rolled down his window to lean his head out. Then he pointed up the street and said, "Step on it."

Peter tramped on the gas pedal, forcing Roger back in his seat.

Near the middle of the block on the right-hand side they saw a man in jeans and a white golf shirt staggering up the sloping lawn of a two story brick home with a yellow door and a hydrant at the curb. They saw the man from behind, saw his full head of wavy red hair and something else, something dangling from his right hand.

Roger said, "Is that a gun?"

"I think so," Peter said, angling the car toward the curb. The alarm was coming from that house, a few of the neighbour's lights coming on now. "Is he drunk?"

"What's that in his other hand?"

Peter said, "Looks like a wig," and Roger was out of the car before it stopped, charging up the driveway and across the lawn. It looked like he meant to tackle the guy.

Peter put the car in PARK and got out in time to see the man swing around with the gun and aim it at Roger's head, stopping him dead in his tracks. Roger raised his hands and started backing away.

That was when Peter saw the blood sheeted down the front of the man's shirt, turning it a soggy, glistening purple in the streetlight. Then he saw the gaping wound in his neck.

Now the man sagged to his knees, the gun still raised but aimed at Roger's legs. Roger closed in on him again, moving in a wide arc away from the gun, his demeanour no longer aggressive but concerned. He looked back at Peter and shouted, "You better get up here, man. He's a cop."

Peter ran up the lawn, watching Roger ease the man into a lying position on his side, then pry the gun from his hand. The man was spluttering weakly, his blood loss massive, puddles of it revealing his erratic course up the slope of the lawn. Peter knelt beside him and saw the gold badge on his belt.

Roger stood over them with the gun in his hand, looking up at the house, then down at Peter. He said, "Can you do anything for him?"

"He's lost so much blood," Peter said, rolling the man over to get a better look at the wound in his neck. "He needs a hospital, fast." He looked at Roger. "My cell's in the car. Call 911." He looked next at the number on the house, large black numerals under a bright porch sconce. "Twenty-six Cahill."

Roger ran the slide of the gun partway open, checking the load. "You do it," he said, his voice rising coolly above the apocalyptic wail of the alarm. "I'm going inside."

Before Peter could say anything more Roger was gone, running full bore up the walkway, taking the front steps in two quick bounds and now he was airborne, his body almost parallel with the porch, his feet striking the yellow door with explosive force. The frame splintered at the lock and the door flew inward on its hinges,

Roger rebounding from the impact to land hard on the porch. He was on his feet instantly, pushing his way through the debris of the Cade's front entrance, then vanishing into the darkness inside.

Peter looked at the dying man—his chest hitching now, his lungs sucking more blood than air—and started running back to the car. He heard a gunshot then—and now another—the muffled reports coming from inside the house. The sound startled him and he skidded on the damp grass, his legs opening into a painful split that pulled one of his hamstrings violently enough to make him cry out.

From a doorway across the street someone shouted, "What's going on over there?" and Peter couldn't summon the words to respond.

Moaning, breathing hard, he climbed to his feet and limped the rest of the way to the car. He had never been more terrified in his life.

* * *

Graham was almost asleep when the burglar alarm went off. The sound it made was high pitched and *loud*, rising and falling, and now his dad popped up beside him shouting, "What?" and flipped the covers off all three of them, scrambling in the dark to get the gun out of the night table drawer. His mom *screamed*, making a sound more terrifying than the alarm, a sound Graham had never heard come out of her before. She reached for him in the dark saying, "Graham? *Graham?*" and one of her fingers poked him in the eye. Then she had him in her arms, clutching him to her breast.

Graham saw the big red numbers on the alarm clock: 11:01, then heard his dad—on his feet now—saying, "Stay right here with him, Angie, and don't make another sound, do you hear me?"

His mom said, "Yes," and Graham felt her warm tears spilling on his neck. She said, "Be careful, Chris," and hugged Graham tight when his dad opened the bedroom door, holding the gun out in front of him. Graham blinked and saw something grab his dad's arm, then saw a flash of yellow light, the flash bringing a loud *bang* that hurt his ears and sent his dad flying backward against the foot of the bed, his weight driving the mattress against the wooden headboard.

Then the man from the park was *in* the room—Graham could smell him—stepping over his dad's legs to come around the bed to his mom's side, and now his mom *pushed* Graham away, pushed him hard across the bed, yelling, "Run, sweetheart, *hide*."

Graham spun off the bed to his feet on the cold hardwood floor, but he didn't *want* to run, he wanted to help his mom and dad. He looked at the man on the other side of the bed—a huge dark shape in the pale wash of light from the hallway—and heard an enormous crash downstairs.

Then he saw the man raise his arm, heard him say, "Bitch," and in the yellow flash that slammed that terrible *bang* into Graham's ears again he saw the mask, heard his mother's scream cut in half and understood that the man had hurt his mommy and daddy and Graham *hated* the man for that and now he launched himself across the bed in a fury that belied his years, his young mouth torn wide in a scream of his own, a scream he could barely hear over the whining drone in his ears. His tiny body struck the man's shoulder and Graham held on tight, clawing at that mask, slamming it with his fist, the hard skull underneath hurting his hand.

Then the man grabbed Graham's jammies at the back of his neck and peeled him off with one powerful hand. Graham came away with the mask in his hand and just dangled there, all the strength wrung out of him, staring into those dark eyes glinting back at him in the fuzzy light.

Now Graham felt himself crushed into those musty clothes and he shut his eyes tight, squeezing out hot tears, the man taking the mask away from him, then carrying him quickly out of the room. He could feel the man's heart beating hard against his cheek and now he heard someone shout "*Hey,*" from down-stairs—another gunshot—and his body flinched, his cold hands coming up to cover his ears. Then they were running fast down the hall into the stairs, the squeak of the second-last step tell-ing Graham they were using the back stairwell.

Limp with terror, Graham kept his eyes shut and prayed that when he opened them again this bad dream would be over forever.

* * *

The first gunshot froze Roger on the lower landing of the front stairwell and he brought the cop's weapon to bear, aiming it upward into the dim space ahead. The second shot was fol-lowed by heavy footfalls and Roger made a mistake, he shouted "*Hey,*" and felt a bullet whiz by his head, the buzzing heat of it creasing the air next to his ear. He flinched reflexively and his head struck the wall, the impact dazing him. He looked up and saw movement, dark against dark, heard footfalls receding

210 · Sean Costello

and started up the stairs with the gun at the ready, his legs unsteady now, the fact that he'd almost been shot in the face just beginning to register on his nervous system.

There was a second landing near the top bordered by a three foot wall and a run of four more steps to Roger's right. Using the wall as cover, he inched himself out of a crouch to peer between the balusters of a short section of oak railing, his gaze directed along a hallway now, the framed prints on the walls reflecting pale moonlight from the narrow window straight ahead. The window was only partially visible and Roger realized it was recessed into a second stairwell leading to the back of the house.

Cursing, he sprung to his full height, launched himself up the last four risers, pivoted on the newel post and charged along the ten feet of hall to leap onto the top landing of the back stairwell and press his forehead to the cool glass.

Through the still branches of the trees Roger saw a dark figure moving lithely across the back lawn toward the fence. The gate down there was open, and over the top of the fence Roger could see the roof of a van, a dirty white van…and as the figure darted through the gate, a glimpse of a tiny head, downy hair shock white in the moonlight.

Behind him Roger heard a moan, a sound laced with pain and fear.

Then he heard the slam of the van door, the gun of its engine, and he was bolting back along the hallway, spinning into the front stairwell to take the risers in heedless, free-falling bounds. In the foyer he clambered past the ruins of the front door and leaped off the porch onto the lawn, shouting,

"Get in the car, get in the fucking car," at Peter, Peter hunched over the motionless cop, the cell phone pressed to his ear.

* * *

Peter heard the third gunshot on his way back up the lawn, the 911 operator telling him to remain calm, coaxing the details out of him then telling him to hold, Peter's urgent, "Wait," greeted only with dead air. He said, "Hello, hello?" then bent to feel for a pulse in the crook of the cop's arm, finding none, the man exsanguinated now.

That was when Roger came flying off the porch like a man possessed, hollering at him to get in the car. The sight of him waving the cop's gun around made Peter freeze for an instant. Then Roger was tearing past him shouting, "Move it, man, the fucker's getting *away*," and Peter went after him, nothing he could do for the cop, the pain in his pulled hamstring flaring with each hobbled stride.

Roger got in on the driver's side and Peter barely made it in next to him, Roger cranking the vehicle into a screeching U-ie, pointing down the street at the van roaring through the intersection dead ahead. "There he is," he said, and gunned it.

Breathless, Peter said, "Did he get the boy?"

Roger said, "He got him alright," and swung hard right at the intersection, Peter almost dropping the phone. The van was a block ahead of them now, veering left through a red light. Roger said, "You on hold?"

Peter said, "Shit," and brought the phone to his ear, a tinny voice saying, "Mr. Croft? Mr. Croft, are you still there?"

Peter said, "Yes, I'm here," and looked at Roger.

"Tell them to look in the house," Roger said. "In the bed-rooms upstairs." He took the left without braking and Peter's shoulder slammed against the door.

Peter snugged the phone to his ear and said, "The officer's dead. Have the paramedics check the bedrooms upstairs. There were gunshots."

The operator said, "Where are you now, sir?" and Peter said, "I don't know the name of the street, but we're right be-hind the guy. He's driving a white van—"

Roger said, "We got him," and pointed up the street. The van had come to an angled stop behind a pair of city buses, a big yellow street sweeper blocking the opposite lane, the van's brake lights printing a bright red stain on the blacktop. The road at the intersection ahead was the one Peter and Roger had come in on. If the kidnapper made it onto that, he'd have ready access to at least a half dozen routes out of the area, including two major highways.

Roger said, "I'll box the fucker in," and floored it, but now the van's back up lights were on and Peter saw smoke roiling off the rear tires, the van reversing in a swerving S-shape, then braking again before turning right into the park-ing lot of a KFC.

Roger shouted, "Sonofa*bitch*," and wheeled into the same parking lot, right on top of them now, coming close enough for Peter to read off the license number to the 911 operator.

Then the van burst out of the L-shaped lot onto the main road, an eighteen wheeler braking hard to miss it, cutting Roger off as it hissed and juddered to a stop. Roger reversed in a tight curve, the rear bumper plowing into the side of a canary yellow Hummer, then dropped the shifter into DRIVE and roared across the sidewalk, going airborne briefly as the car left the curb. Roger accelerated around the transport and Peter lost his grip on the phone, the silver Samsung snapping shut and bouncing off his knee into the dark of the foot well.

Peter looked up and the van was gone.

Then Roger said, "I see him," and pointed across a field to their left.

There, blowing past a ragged tree line about a quarter mile away, was the van, its high beams playing off the trunks of the moonlit trees.

As Roger approached the turnoff Peter bent to feel for his phone and said, "Maybe we should take it easy, Roger. Just try to keep him in sight. I'll get the 911 operator again and we can lead the cops right to him."

Roger took the turn too fast and Peter felt the phone bump his heel. He picked it up and said, "Roger?" and Roger glanced at him, his eyes like stab wounds in the glow of the dash lights. "Did you hear what I said?"

Roger returned his gaze to the road without responding and Peter felt the car lunge ahead, its small engine shrieking in protest. In Roger's grim expression Peter read a desperate stubbornness, and understood that unless he could break through here, make the man see reason, they were both going to wind up dead.

He said, "Roger, listen. We've almost got him, but there's no way we can stop him with this car. If we try, we not only put ourselves at risk, we do the same to that little boy." Roger glanced at him, the tight set of his jaw beginning to slacken. "And if there's any hope at all of finding Jason alive," Peter said, "it resides with the man at the wheel of that van. At all costs, we need him alive. Let the cops do this, Roger. Please. Back off and let me tell them where we are."

Almost imperceptibly, Roger eased up on the accelerator. The van was still visible, still about a quarter mile ahead on this stretch of hilly road, its taillights appearing then disappearing. Roger said, "Okay, okay. Where are we now?"

"Radar Road," Peter said, flipping the phone open. "There was a sign at the turnoff." He looked at the dead keyboard and said, "Shit, I think it's broken."

"Check the battery, see if it got dislodged in the fall."

Peter ran a finger along the back of the phone and said, "Good call." The battery had popped loose but hadn't fallen off. He pressed it with his thumb, heard it click into place, then hit the POWER button.

While he waited for the phone to turn on Peter scanned the night for those taillights again, feeling a momentary start when he saw only darkness—but there they were now, cresting another of these low hills, still about a quarter mile ahead. He looked next to his right, at the bush that had sprung up without his noticing, a solid bank of trees cut only occasionally by a driveway or a dirt side road. Somehow in under five minutes they'd ended up in open countryside. He realized then that they'd come into the Oakville area from the opposite direction, and that the Cades lived on the very outskirts of town. In their haste to get down here neither of them had thought to buy a map. They'd just have to hope these back roads had signs.

The cell phone was on now but Peter got an idea. He flipped the glove box open and started rooting around inside.

Roger said, "What are you doing?"

Peter came out with a felt-tip pen and a plain white pad. Leaning the pad toward the dash lights, he jotted *left on radar road* and said, "In case we get lost."

"Smart."

Now Peter tucked the pad and pen under his thigh and keyed 911 into the cell phone. The signal indicator was down to only two vertical bars, but it was ringing.

The operator picked up and said, "911 emergency," and Peter could barely hear her through the crackle of static. He said, "This is Peter Croft. Are you the operator I was just speaking to?" The woman said no, but told him she knew who he was and asked him to hold, she was going to connect him directly to the officer in charge.

* * *

By the time Vickie Taylor got to the scene S.W.A.T. had already cleared the dwelling. Both plainclothes officers were deceased and Vickie felt numb watching Forensics prep their bodies for removal. The Cades had been more fortunate, though in Christopher Cade's case, only marginally so. EMS had just wheeled him out intubated and unconscious, an IV running full bore in each arm. Mrs. Cade had been the luckiest, the single shot she'd taken shattering her clavicle but missing anything vital. She was conscious and exceedingly distraught, her fury aimed briefly at Vickie as the paramedics loaded her into the ambulance. "You," she spat, her head coming up off the pillow, the cords in her neck straining against the skin. "You said it was *random*. You said we didn't need to worry and now my boy is *gone*."

Vickie felt sick to her stomach.

A few minutes later she was trying to piece together a statement from one of the neighbours when her cell phone rang. It was the 911 operator, telling her she had someone on the line who claimed not only to have witnessed the crime, but to be currently in pursuit of the getaway vehicle.

Feeling a cold excitement, Vickie waved an officer over and told him to finish questioning the neighbour. Then she saw Staff Sergeant Laking arriving on the scene and hurried over to greet him, the phone still pressed to her ear. She was about to fill him in when the operator came back on and apologized, saying she'd lost the call.

"Alright," Vickie said. "Get back to me immediately if they call again."

The operator said, "I will, Ma'am," and broke the connection.

* * *

Graham was going to be sick. Not right now, but he knew it was coming. He always got car sick, sometimes even when his mom gave him Gravol first, and it was always worse if he closed his eyes. And his eyes were still closed, as tight as he could make them; his head was starting to ache from doing it.

The bad man had put him in this smelly van, then done up his seat belt and said, "Don't worry, sweetheart," in a different voice, a *nice* voice, "we'll be home soon," and Graham kept thinking about that, about being home soon. He thought about it while they were driving fast and he was bouncing around in his seat and he never once opened his eyes because if he did the dream might not be over yet and the bad man would see him. If he kept his eyes closed, nothing could hurt him.

He hoped his dad would wake up soon and come get him.

They were still driving fast, but not so crazy now. The bad man hadn't said anything else to him yet, just made a few grunts and said some bad words when they were driving *really* fast. Graham could hear him doing things now though, shuffling stuff around, opening something that sounded like a cardboard box, and now a bright light came on in the vehicle, making Graham flinch.

Curious, he turned his head very slowly and let his eyes open just a crack...and through the fuzz of his eyelashes saw a big woman with long, jet black hair driving with one hand and putting lipstick on with the other, leaning forward to watch herself in the mirror. Graham was so surprised he let his eyes come all the way open and the woman looked at him and smiled.

"*There*. you are, honey," she said in that nice voice and dropped the lipstick into a big floppy purse. "I'm so glad you decided to join me."

She reached over to touch his face and Graham let her, his young mind stalled for a beat, trying to fit this new information into what had just happened at home. The woman was wearing a nice frilly blouse with black pants, but there was still that musty smell around her and Graham saw that heavy coat scrunched into the seat behind her. It made him feel confused, but a little less afraid. She didn't seem so bad. Her voice was deep, but not as deep as the bad man's. Not as scary.

Very quietly, Graham said, "Where's the bad man?"

The woman smiled and said, "He's gone, sweetie. I made him go away. You don't have to be afraid anymore."

"Are you going to take me home now?"

"You bet I am. You just sit tight." She reached behind her seat and brought out a big fluffy pillow. Resting it on Graham's lap, she said, "It's a pretty long drive, though, so you might want to catch a few winks."

Graham hugged the pillow to his face. It smelled good, clean and fresh, like when his mom did the laundry. He was glad to hear they were going home, but he didn't think it was *that* far away. He looked at the woman and said, "Your hair's crooked," then saw her do the strangest thing. She reached up and *moved* her hair, then smiled at him and said, "Better?" and Graham said, "I'm gonna—"

But that was all he got out, his body jackknifing as his dinner and the bottle of apple juice he'd had watching AFV came sluicing up his throat, gobs of it hitting the dashboard, the floor and his tiny bare feet. It felt warm on his skin and smelled really bad.

He took a deep breath, let out a moan and threw up again, the smell of it reaching down his throat and squeezing his tummy hard. He was afraid the woman would be mad, but she said, "Oh, you poor thing," and tore some paper towels off a roll she had beside her seat and wiped his face with them, then got some more and did his feet. Leaning closer, she gave the dash a quick rub then threw the dirty paper towels over the mess on the floor. She said, "Just open your window a crack, sweetie." Saying, "Like this, see?" then grabbing the handle on her door and opening her own window a bit.

Graham did as he was told and felt the night breeze cool on his forehead, whisking some of that smell away. Shivering, he said, "Can I have one of those?" and pointed at the paper towels. The woman told him to help himself and Graham leaned over to pick up the roll. He tore one off and wiped his mouth with it, trying to get rid of that awful taste.

The woman said, "Yucky, huh."

Graham made a face and nodded.

Now she said, "I've got just the thing," and opened the lid of a small cooler that was tucked in the space between the seats. "I've got raspberry juice, bottled water, Coke, ginger ale and cherry Gator Aid."

Graham said, "Coke, please," because he loved Coke and wasn't allowed to drink it at home.

The woman pulled one out for him and Graham heard the chatter of ice in the cooler, a sound that reminded him of the camping trips his family sometimes took in the summer; a comforting sound. She reached over with the can but instead of giving it to him held it to his forehead, saying, "Feels good, huh?" and it did. Then she put it in his hand and he pulled the tab, liking the sound it made. He took a long swallow, rinsing that taste out of his mouth, then he burped and the woman laughed, saying, "Good one," and Graham laughed a bit too.

They made a lot of turns while Graham was drinking his pop, and the woman kept looking at something on the dash, something Graham couldn't quite see. All he knew was that it looked like his dad's pocket computer with the screen lit up, casting its pale blue glow. He pointed at it and said, "What's that?"

The woman said, "This?" and turned it toward him. "This is a GPS system." She pointed at a little blue arrow that was moving along a curvy red line.

"Oh, yeah," Graham said, "my uncle Jim's got one of those on his boat."

The woman looked at him funny and Graham thought she was going to be angry; but she pointed at the screen and said, "The little arrow tells me where I am, and the words on top tell me where to go next. I got it all mapped out, lots of twists and turns to make the drive more fun."

Graham scooched over for a closer look and saw his father's gun lying on the dash. The woman saw him looking and picked the gun up by the barrel.

"I hate these things," she said. "You too, huh?"

Graham nodded. The bad man had used that gun to hurt his mommy and daddy.

"Tell you what," the woman said. She rolled her window all the way down, the wind getting in to stir things up in the van, and tossed the gun out into the dark. "There," she said, smiling. "Better?"

Graham said, "Yes."

Then she looked in the rearview and said, "Looks like we still got company," and Graham heard the engine roar, the sudden lurch of the vehicle making his tummy feel icky again.

He said, "What's wrong?"

"It's the bad man, honey," the woman said, the light from the mirror printing a silver Zorro mask across her eyes. "But don't worry your sweet little head. There's no way he's ever gonna catch us."

* * *

Peter said, "Roger, we're too close," but it was too late. The van was picking up speed now, widening the distance between them at an alarming rate. They'd lost sight of it for a solid minute on this fresh stretch of road, each new curve and switchback blinding them, creating the very real worry that the kidnapper would slip unnoticed down some unmarked side road and disappear for good. It made Peter wonder if the guy was from around here—it would explain why he seemed to know these roads so well—or if he was simply tearing around at random, attempting to throw off pursuit.

Either way, it looked like Roger was losing it again. That crazed gleam was back in his eyes, and he was pushing the car dangerously hard on this loose gravel surface. To make matters worse, the cell phone had lost its signal while the 911 operator had Peter on hold and he hadn't been able to get her back yet. On the upside, he'd managed to record all of the turns they'd made and knew the road they were on now was called Uplands.

Bracing himself with his feet, Peter dialed 911 and this time got through to the operator. He identified himself and the woman said, "I've got Sergeant Taylor holding for you, Mr. Croft," then set him adrift on dead air again.

* * *

"Is your seatbelt on good and tight, sweetie?"

Graham checked it and said that it was.

"That's good, because we're going to go really fast again for a minute, then you're going to see some things that might scare you." Driving with one hand now, she dragged the smelly coat over her shoulders and pulled it on, first one arm, then the other. Doing up the buttons, she said, "But I want you to remember that I am *not* going to hurt you. I would *never* hurt you."

Graham looked out the windshield and saw that the road they were on was about to end, a big yellow sign up there showing a black arrow with a point on either end. The woman slammed on the brakes and Graham felt his seatbelt dig into his shoulder, then they were turning, bouncing off this rough road onto smooth pavement. Graham saw the headlights of another car coming toward them and thought of driving home from his Grandma's place late at night.

The woman said, "Okay, baby, here comes the fast part I told you about," and Graham heard the engine roar, its vibration making things rattle inside the van. She said, "We're going to go like crazy for a bit, then we're going to play a trick on the bad man. Ready?"

Graham nodded.

Then the woman took her hair off and dropped it into the space between the seats. It landed upside down and Graham stared at it in horror. When he looked up he saw the bad man sitting where the woman had been, rubbing red lipstick off his mouth with a paper towel. Graham felt something tighten inside him and he closed his eyes again, closed them hard.

"Here we go," the bad man said in the woman's voice, and now Graham covered his ears, too.

* * *

"This is Sergeant Taylor." A woman's voice, cool, official.

Peter said, "My name is Peter Croft," and braced himself against the door jamb, Roger correcting for a skid that brought them perilously close to the gravel embankment. "I'm with a friend by the name of Roger Mullen. We witnessed some of the events at the Cade home and we are now following the kidnapper's van. I gave the operator the license number a while ago—"

"Yes, I know," Sergeant Taylor said, "the plates were stolen. Where are you now?"

"On a road called Uplands, maybe twenty minutes from town."

Peter heard her repeat the name to someone on her end, then heard her say, "Okay, listen. I do not want you to engage this man in any way. Don't challenge him, don't try to cut him off, don't even let him know you're there."

"I'm afraid it's too late for that."

"Alright, then just try to keep him in sight and *stay* on the line. We're going to send some cars into the area and try to seal it off. In the meantime—"

Peter said, "Hold on."

They'd just crested a steep hill and Peter saw that the road was about to end—but there was no sign of the van.

224 · SEAN COSTELLO

Roger said, *"Fuck,"* and slammed on the brakes, the vehicle skidding and twisting toward the intersecting blacktop. He said, "Which way?" and Peter said, "Go left," pointing at the fresh looking skid marks that veered off in that direction. Roger tramped on the gas and had to brake again for a staggered line of cars approaching from the left. Barely avoiding a collision, he shouted something unintelligible and yanked so furiously on the wheel Peter thought it was going to come off in his hands.

Then the cars were gone and they were making the turn, accelerating up a long incline on this narrow highway. When they reached the summit there was still no sign of the van, but Roger kept going anyway.

Breathing hard now, Peter said, "Uplands just ended," into the phone. "I don't know the name of this new road, but it's paved and we just turned left. Right now we're not even sure if this is the way he went."

"Okay," Sergeant Taylor said. "Are you the one driving?"

"No."

"Then tell your friend to calm down. You're no help to us dead."

Peter wanted to explain to her the depth of Roger's commitment to catching this man, but this was not the time. He said, "I will."

"Can you see the van?"

"Not yet."

"That's okay, I'll stay on the line with you. Cars are already on their way and we're in the process of arranging a helicopter."

Peter said "Okay," and kept the phone pressed to his ear, as if this slim link with authority might somehow extricate him from this insane situation.

The road leveled out for about half a mile, then banked sharply around an outcrop of rock. Roger took the curve too fast, and when they barreled out the other side the van was stopped in the middle of the road, angled across both lanes with the rear doors gaping open. The kidnapper was standing on the road in the V of the open doors, a black ski mask on his head and the Cade boy clutched in one arm. The boy was in his pajamas, his blond hair a luminous halo in the glare of the headlights, and as the Corolla bore down on him his eyes popped open flashing red and Roger said, "Jase?" and cranked the wheel hard right, the car going airborne as it left the road to splash nose first into the swamp that bordered the highway. Peter struck his head on something and saw black water explode over the hood to splatter the windshield. The airbags deployed as they ploughed deeper into the swamp, the front bumper shearing off bulrushes and whippy saplings.

Then the car jerked to a stop. The engine stuttered and died and Peter saw blood trickling out of Roger's scalp, Roger leaning limp against the door.

Fighting panic, Peter collapsed his airbag with both hands, then dug the Leatherman tool Dana had given him as an anniversary present out of the glove box, flipping it open and finding the knife blade, using it to puncture Roger's airbag. As the bag collapsed Roger struck out with both fists shouting, "Did I hit him? Did I hit Jason?" and Peter grabbed him hard saying, "That wasn't Jason, Roger, it was the Cade boy, and we've got to get out of here *now*."

He dug his flashlight out of the glove box and shoved the door open with his knee, foul water sheeting in over the running board. He saw the phone on the floor mat, glinting silver under two inches of algae-clotted water, and plucked it out, then slopped his way around the hood to help Roger out of the car.

But Roger was already out, slogging back toward the road as fast as his legs would carry him, first his left shoe, then his right oozing to the surface in the beam of Peter's flashlight.

Peter picked up the shoes on his way to the road, a distance of about thirty feet through broken scrub, soggy hillocks and muddy sinkholes. When he got there he found Roger standing on the soft shoulder covered in muck, breathing hard in the wash of a transport's high beams, blood still streaming from his scalp.

The van was gone.

13.

Peter led Roger away from the roadside to a flat boulder at the edge of the swamp. Using the flashlight, he sat the man down and examined the laceration in his scalp. It was about a half inch long but superficial, and Peter doubted it would require stitches. He asked Roger if he was hurt anywhere else and got only a vacant stare. Gingerly touching the bump on his own head, he sat next to Roger and turned the flashlight off.

They sat in silence for a while, nothing left to say, watching the occasional vehicle speed by on the roadway, listening to the lively chatter of insects and night birds in the swamp. The air was cool and Peter started shivering in his wet clothes, the ebbing rush of adrenalin making him feel ill. The whole thing seemed unreal to him now, sitting here at the side of a road he'd never been on before, miles from home, alone under a starlit sky with a man he barely knew, a man driven by an obsession Peter not only understood but had freely adopted as his own. The quiet was maddening; in it, all Peter could hear was the kidnapper getting farther away.

It wasn't long before he heard the sound of sirens approaching fast, and he got up to flag down the first police car. Roger didn't move, just sat there with his elbows on his knees, staring at his hands. Peter told the officer what had happened, saying he couldn't be sure in which direction the van had fled after their vehicle left the road, assuring him that neither of them had been seriously injured. The officer said he'd have an ambulance dispatched anyway, then repeated into his radio exactly what Peter had told him.

Another police car appeared now, slowed, then kept on going. Within seconds an unmarked car ground to a halt behind the first cruiser. The driver introduced himself as Staff Sergeant Laking, his handshake firm, his expression grim in the glare of head lights. The tall, freckled woman who got out on the passenger side said her name was Sergeant Taylor and identified herself as the lead investigator. Peter shook her hand too, saying he was pleased to meet her, apologizing for his filthy clothes. She told him not to worry, then glanced at the Corolla in the swamp and asked the officer to call for a tow truck.

Peter led the investigators over to Roger and made the introductions, but Roger only grunted, not responding when Laking held his hand out to be shaken. Sergeant Taylor asked Peter if he was sure his friend hadn't been seriously injured and Peter said, "I'm a doctor," and told her he was confident Roger was fine. Then he led them a discrete distance away and said,

"I think I should explain how we came to be involved in this thing."

Sergeant Taylor said, "Are you telling us it's more than coincidence?"

"Much more," Peter said, glancing back at Roger, who was staring at them now. "To do it properly, though, I'm going to need a computer."

* * *

Graham felt the van come to a stop and let his eyes open halfway, hoping he was finally back home. But they were parked in a row of cars behind a long brick building with a bunch of red doors. The ceiling light came on now, making Graham squint, and he heard the man say, "Okay, kiddo, we have to change cars." Then he felt a sting in his leg and saw a *needle* stuck in him, right through his jammies, and now the man was squeezing something into him with his thumb, saying, "Sorry, little man, but we've got a long drive ahead of us and you're going to have a nice little nap." The man pulled the needle out and Graham started to cry, hiding his quiet sobs in his pillow.

The light went off and the man got out of the van with his hair on, locking the door behind him. Graham watched him go to the small silver car parked next to them on Graham's side and take something out of his coat...a set of keys. Then he turned his back to Graham and unlocked the car door. Graham rubbed his eyes and saw the man get in behind the wheel. He wanted to see what the man was doing in there, thinking maybe he could climb out the other side and run away, but his head

230 · SEAN COSTELLO

felt funny now, heavy, like his neck couldn't remember how to hold it up anymore.

Graham lost track of things for a while, then he heard the man's voice, the man saying something that didn't make sense. It was hot in the van and Graham was very sleepy. When the man picked him up and Graham felt the cool night air on his skin, he curled his hands under his chin and rested his head against the man's chest, thinking his daddy had him now and he'd fallen asleep again on the drive home from Grandma's.

A little smile found his lips and he knew that in a couple of minutes he'd be safe in his own bed.

* * *

After performing a cursory neurological assessment, the paramedic closed the wound in Roger's scalp with a butterfly bandage and suggested he see a doctor should he experience any dizziness or headache over the next twenty four hours. The tow truck, Jonesy's Towing, arrived as Peter and Roger climbed into the back seat of the unmarked car.

Both men were quiet during the half hour drive to the Oakville police station, Peter at one point almost falling asleep in the quiet hum of motion. When they arrived Sergeant Laking showed them to a staff restroom, suggesting they take a few minutes to clean themselves up. He returned a short time later with some bright orange prison fatigues, saying that if they didn't mind they could pull these on over their dirty clothes. Peter thanked the Sergeant, agreeing that it was a good idea.

Surprising Peter as they were pulling on the fatigues, Roger said, "You look right at home in those," and grinned.

Peter felt a knot loosen in his chest. No artist at quick comebacks he said, "I'm sorry he got away, Roger."

"Yeah, me too."

Lowering his voice, Peter said, "They're probably going to interview us separately."

"Why do you say that?"

Peter said, "C.S.I.," and both men chuckled. Then, more soberly, Peter said, "I thought I might just...leave out the stuff about David. You know. Keep it simple."

Roger said, "You and I met four years ago at the boys' daycare. You saw that Missing Person photo of the Dolan kid at work and brought the resemblance to my attention, but after discussing it we decided it was probably just a coincidence. When I saw the news about the Cade boy on TV I got in touch with you right away and asked you to make the trip to Oakville with me. I wanted to be there when they caught the guy but I didn't want to do it alone. It was simple curiosity that took us into the Cade's neighbourhood."

"What if they ask us why we didn't notify the police the instant we made the connection? If it was the resemblance of these other kids to Jason that brought us down here, why didn't we speak up right away?"

"Because we could hardly believe it ourselves."

Peter said, "I suppose," but he was worried.

Laking came back a few minutes later and led them through a big room partitioned into work stations, most of them abandoned at this hour. Sergeant Taylor got up from one of the desks

232 · SEAN COSTELLO

and fell in step with the men, following them along a narrow corridor to a series of offices with plain gray doors. Laking held the door to the first one open and said, "Mr. Mullen, why don't you come ahead in here with me."

Roger glanced at Peter, then did as he was told.

Peter followed Sergeant Taylor through the next door and, at her polite invitation, sat at the desk in the corner of the room, facing a flat screen computer monitor.

There was a tape recorder on the desk and the police-woman turned it on, telling it the date and time, then saying that she, Sergeant Vickie Taylor, was the interviewing officer and that he, Peter Croft, was the interviewee.

Then she pulled up a chair and sat next to Peter saying, "Okay, show me."

Peter said, "I need the Internet," and Vickie took over the keyboard, logging in and getting him online. Peter brought up the *Child Find* site and clicked on the letter D. When he scrolled down to Clayton Dolan's photograph and enlarged it he heard Vickie Taylor draw a sharp breath.

Now he said, "Do you have a printer?" and Vickie took over the keyboard again. A printer on a side table hummed to life and spat out a colour copy. Vickie picked it up and said, "Who—?" and Peter said, "Wait," clicking on the M now, click-ing again to bring Jason Mullen's smiling face into centre screen. He said, "This is Roger's son."

Vickie said, "Oh, my God," and printed this one out too.

* * *

Staff Sergeant Laking sat at his desk with the pictures of the three kids lined up on the blotter in front of him. He said, "Unbelievable," and looked at Vickie, seated in the chair across from him. "Pretty clear we've got a serial on our hands."

Vickie said, "Looks that way."

"What did you make of the doctor?"

"I think there's more to his story than he's admitting," Vickie said, "but I don't think there's anything criminal going on. I don't believe he's involved. It got a little weird when I told him his name popped up on CPIC, though. Turns out he 'saw' the face of the Mullen boy's kidnapper in a dream or a vision of some kind. Mullen was desperate, so he talked a cop friend of his into letting Croft go through some photo line-ups. I got the copper on the horn a few minutes ago, staff Sergeant by the name of Bernie Eklund up in Sudbury. Said he checked Croft out and the man came up clean. Croft's own son died recently and he and Mullen attended the same bereavement group."

"Strange, but benign."

"That's how I felt," Vickie said. "What was your impression of Mullen?"

"About the same, though he didn't mention anything about visions."

"I can understand his reluctance. So how do you want to proceed?"

"We'll need copies of the case files on these other abductions," Laking said, "but I'm not sure it's going to make much difference." He pointed at the data under the photos. "I mean, look at his intervals here. If we can't pick this guy up on the evidence we've already got—or get just plain lucky—how long

before he surfaces again? Three years? Longer?" Laking shook
his head. "If we don't nail him now, before he holes up for good,
we're going to have to hope for a DNA match. And if he's not in
the system…"

Vickie nodded. She was dog tired and felt a migraine
coming on.

Laking said, "Did you hear we got the van?"

"No, where?"

"Stashed behind a motel, five miles down the road. Guy doubled back after he lost our two friends. Must have had a second
vehicle waiting, or an accomplice. Nobody saw anything."

"I take it the van was stolen?"

Laking nodded. "Off a long term lot at Pearson International.
Lifted the plates off an SUV in the parking lot of a strip mall right
here in town, *after* he tried to grab the kid in the park."

Vickie thought of Cade's wife screaming blame at her and
felt a fresh stab of guilt. "I really believed he'd rabbit."

Laking said, "Me too, Vick, me too." He reached across
the desk and patted her hand. "But you've got to let it go. It's
not your fault and I'm going to need you sharp."

Vickie nodded. "What are your thoughts about motive?"

"Outside of the usual? Nothing yet."

"What about the wig?"

"What about it?"

"Disguise or part of his kink?"

"I think it was just a disguise. We were looking for a bald
guy, not a big frumpy broad with a bad dye job. Bates and
McNamara had no idea what hit them, so I'd say the ruse
worked rather well."

Vickie checked her watch. It was almost five-thirty. She said, "What do you want to do with Mullen and Croft?"

"Let them go. I don't imagine they'll stray very far, not for the time being at least. Any word on their car?"

"Jonesy towed it to the Esso on Elgin; says it's wet and smelly, but it runs. He found Frank's gun in it. I'll have someone drop them off there now."

"Sounds good. See you back here in ten? We've got a press conference at seven. It's gonna be a long day."

Vickie stood. "Okay, Rob, see you in ten."

* * *

Peter fed some more quarters into the big Esso station vacuum cleaner and got busy on the slop in the back seat. The rug was soaked with the stuff, rancid water mixed with dark ropes of algae. Fortunately, since they'd gone into the swamp nose first, the trunk wasn't so bad, the mat back there just a little damp. Their luggage had been spared too, and Peter couldn't wait to find a hotel and get out of these foul clothes.

Roger was sitting on the curb by the car wash, drinking a Swiss cream soda and staring at his feet. Peter was worried about him, this brooding silence he kept lapsing into. Since they left the police station, every attempt Peter had made at conversation had been met with either a blank stare or a dismissive grunt. Part of him wanted to just drive home now and be done with it; but it was almost dawn, the eastern skyline a pale sapphire, and he was bone tired. And though his gut told him the kidnapper had gotten away, he couldn't let go of the hope that something still might break in the case, some fresh piece of evidence surface that would finally lead to closure for Roger.

The vacuum cycled down and Peter thought, *Good enough.* The car was going to need body work and a professional cleaning anyway; right now he just wanted to make it halfway tolerable to drive.

He put the rubber mats back in and told Roger he was done. Roger tossed his empty pop can into the garbage and got in the car. Peter drove the short distance to the pumps and topped up the tank, then merged into morning traffic. Sergeant Taylor had told him there was a hotel about a mile east of the Esso station and Peter found it without difficulty. He got them registered in a room with two double beds and Roger followed him along the carpeted hall.

At the door to the room, as Peter fiddled with the card key, Roger put a warm hand on his shoulder and said, "Thanks, man."

Peter faced him. "For what?"

"For everything. Hanging in. Being a friend."

Peter felt himself blushing. "Glad to do it, Roger. And for what it's worth, I still think they're going to catch this guy."

Roger said, "I hope you're right," and Peter unlocked the door, holding it open for Roger.

Brushing past him, Roger said, "Dibs on the shower," and Peter felt the tension break like spring ice. Feeling giddy from fatigue, he tossed his bag on the bed closest to the door and said, "You got it. But this puppy's mine."

Roger dropped his bag on the other bed and started peeling off his clothes. Peter dug a T-shirt and a pair of scrub pants out of his bag and went into the bathroom to change. When he was done he came out to find Roger sitting on the foot of the bed in his shorts and undershirt with the TV on, flipping through the channels with the remote. He stopped at a news update on the kidnapping, the reporter saying that police were no longer looking for the white van, which had been found abandoned behind a local motel, and that an Amber Alert was now in effect.

Without looking at Peter, Roger hit the mute button and said, "I can't believe he got away."

"Me neither," Peter said, sitting on the edge of his bed. "We were so close."

Roger looked at him now, his eyes darker somehow, discs of blue steel. "I wanted to beat it out of him, you know? Make him tell me what he did to Jason. Then I wanted to kill him."

Peter had to look away from the savage intensity of that gaze. At different times in his life he'd wondered about people who killed; wondered what it took and whether he would have it should a situation demand it of him: wartime, protecting his family, defending himself. When it came to protecting his family he'd always believed that he could. But in Roger's eyes he saw no trace of doubt; if Roger got his hands on this man, he would kill him if he could, without qualm or hesitation.

Peter glanced at the silent television and saw a composite of the kidnapper, obviously computer generated, the lines smoother than those created by the sketch artist in Sudbury. The sight of it startled him, that rigid, emotionless face, and for an instant he flashed on the face in his dream.

Now he heard Roger get to his feet. Heard him say, "Guess I'll grab that shower," then heard his undershirt coming off over the chain that was always around his neck. There was a jingling sound and Peter turned to see a pair of dog tags tumble out of Roger's undershirt as he pulled it over his head, one of them silver, the other gold. Lamp light flared off the thin metal wafers and Peter felt a click in his throat—for a moment, he couldn't breathe—then he gasped and wobbled to his feet, his heart beating so hard he could feel its frantic bound in his skull. Startling Roger, he plucked the dog tags off his chest, almost breaking the heavy ball-chain. He saw Jason's name engraved on one of the tags and said, "Where did you get these?"

Roger frowned. "Summerfest, five years ago. It was Jason's idea. He got a pair exactly the same, except his say 'Dad'." He tugged the tags out of Peter's hand, letting them fall back to his chest. "Why?"

Peter's gaze rose to meet Roger's. His mouth was as dry as dirt. "I know who took Jason," he said. "I know where she lives."

* * *

Just before dawn—around the time Peter and Roger were leaving the police station in Oakville to retrieve Peter's car—Graham Cade awoke in a strange bed with a terrible, aching fog in his head. He said, "Oh," and lifted his head off the pillow, surprised at its leaden weight. The light on the ceiling was off, but Graham could see pretty well in the pale morning glow that shone through the window beside the bed.

He was in a child's room, faded Batman wallpaper and a bunch of old toys on wooden shelves, some of them spooky-looking in the purple shadows. His memory was fuzzy, and for a moment he had no idea where he was or how he came to be here.

Then he remembered and his eyes filled with tears.

A familiar voice said, "Don't cry," and Graham saw his kidnapper sitting on a chair at the foot of the bed. She was a woman now, wearing a dress and her long black hair but with no lipstick, her dark eyes soft and moist-looking as she rose from the chair to sit next to him on the bed. She reached out to touch his face and Graham stiffened, the woman saying, "That's okay, sweetheart, the scary part's over now. You're safe. Safe here with me." Now she did touch his face, her big hand warm and soft against his cheek, and Graham let her, the feeling somehow comforting in this creepy room. She said, "I've got some clean clothes laid out for you on the dresser over there." She pointed and Graham saw a brown shirt folded neatly on top of a brand new pair of jeans, the paper tags still on them. He didn't like blue jeans when they were new, that stiff feeling against his skin, but he didn't complain.

Now she tousled his hair and rose to her feet beside the bed. She said, "Do you remember where the bathroom is?" and Graham shrugged. Wherever he was, he didn't remember ever going to the bathroom here. The woman said, "That's okay, it'll all come back to you soon," and walked to the door, turning to face him as she pushed the door open. "Why don't you get dressed," she said, smiling now, tilting her head to look at him with her wet eyes. "The bathroom's right at the end of the hall if you need it. When you're ready, come ahead downstairs and I'll make your favourite breakfast. Then I'll explain everything."

Wiggling her fingers at him, she said, "It's so nice to have you home, honey."

Then she was gone.

Graham pulled the covers over his head and wept, hoping his mommy and daddy were okay, praying they would come for him soon.

* * *

Peter unzipped his computer bag and dug out the material he'd compiled on the Dolan boy. With trembling hands he spread the various printouts on the thin bedspread, Roger watching in stony silence over his shoulder. Peter found a still he'd copied from the video of Margaret Dolan's media appeal and held it up for Roger to see.

Roger said, "Yeah, so?"

"It's *her*," Peter said, the truth of it buzzing through his bloodstream like an amphetamine. "I didn't tell you about this, but I went to see her over the summer, thinking…I don't know, I just got this idea it might help, you know, find Jason. And she's different now, Roger, much heavier, built like a man." He glanced at the TV but the composite was gone, the anchor detailing another story on the muted set. Peter said, "With her head shaved, heavy like she is now…"

Roger gave him a skeptical look. "Listen," he said, "calm down, okay? The last thing I want to do right now is go running off on a wild goose chase."

Peter said, "I'm calm," and handed him the grainy still. "Her name is Margaret Dolan. She has another son named

Aaron. He's around eighteen, mentally challenged. I saw him when I was there." Now he pointed at the dog tags on Roger's chest, saying, "May I?" Roger nodded and Peter scooped the tags into his palm, raising them up for Roger to see. "Aaron had a pair of these around his neck, one silver, one gold. The same kind of chain."

Roger slipped the tags out of Peter's hand into his own. "Are you sure?"

"I've never been more certain of anything in my life. It's her, Roger. It's her."

"But why?"

And even as Roger posed the question it all came together in Peter's mind, the sad, twisted logic of it. "The loss of her son shattered her mind. I saw it in her eyes the day I talked to her." He told Roger about her attempt on her husband's life and her prolonged incarceration, saying that at the end of it she came out permanently scarred. "By the time she got back home, the desire to find her son had already become an obsession."

Roger was nodding and Peter could see that he understood.

"Then, somehow," Peter said, "probably just dumb luck—she sees Jason."

"And thinks he's her son."

"Exactly. So she grabs him and disappears."

"Jesus Christ. But why not stop after Jason?"

"Remember what you told me about the times you thought you'd seen Jason? Like that day in the mall. He's still only six when you see him, right? Even though he'd be almost ten now?"

"That's right."

"So this woman, all she's got left is a mental image of the kid at six—or a photograph she carries with her everywhere—and she becomes fixated on that. She sees Jason and grabs him, believing she's found her son. But time goes by and Jason starts growing up. After three years he looks almost nothing like the kid in the photograph anymore." He found the age-enhanced shot of Clayton Dolan and showed it to Roger. "See? Even her own son looks different after a few years. So she wakes up one day, looks at Jason and thinks, 'This isn't my kid,' and starts looking for the next six year old.

Pale as a ghost now, Roger said, "So what does she do with Jason?"

Peter just shook his head. He had no answer.

Roger's hands closed into fists. "Where does she live?"

"On a farm about thirty minutes west of Ottawa," Peter said. Then he was reaching for the phone saying, "We've got to tell Sergeant Taylor—" and Roger caught him by the wrist, squeezing so hard Peter's fingers sprang apart and the handset clattered to the floor. He tried to pull away and couldn't.

Roger glanced at the fallen handset and released Peter's wrist. The veins in his neck were fiercely engorged and Peter realized the man wasn't breathing, his skin an unhealthy plum colour, the capillaries in his eyes magnified behind a film of raging tears. Then he let out the breath he'd been holding and sank to the edge of the bed gasping for air, his body shuddering, the tears falling freely now. He looked at Peter and said, "I'm sorry, man, I'm sorry," and Peter sat next to him on the bed, slinging an awkward arm around his shoulders, saying, "Jesus, Roger, what's wrong?"

Roger buried his face in his hands, scrubbing away the tears. So many tears. He said, "The night Jason was taken…" but he shook his head, the words refusing to come. Now he cursed bitterly and said, "The night Jason was taken…I was drunk. I was mad at Ellen, that stupid argument we had over the phone, and after I tucked Jase in I sat in front of the tube and got plastered. Fucking idiot." He faced Peter now, the tears getting away on him again. "Usually I'm a light sleeper, you know? The neighbour's dog farts and I'm awake. But that night I was full of booze…and I *slept* through my son's abduction. The fucker came right into my *house* and I slept through the whole thing. When I think of what must have been going through Jason's mind that night—some stranger taking him out of his bed with a smelly hand pressed over his mouth to keep him from screaming—I want to put a bullet in my brain so I can't hear his voice anymore. Peter, they had to go right past my bedroom door to get out of the house. The damn thing was open. I could have seen them go by…"

Peter felt the weight of this confession slam into his chest like a drop kick. Self loathing was coming off Roger now in waves as he cursed and damned himself to hell, the heat of his anguish palpable in the room, a thrumming turbine eating the air.

Then he was on his feet, replacing the handset in its cradle, fixing Peter with an expression that was at once beseeching and coolly menacing. He said, "I need you to tell me exactly where this woman lives. Then I need you to make a decision. Either you're coming with me—because I'm going there, right now—or you're not, in which case I'm going to have to borrow your car. If you decide not to come, I need you to give me enough lead time to get there and find out about my son before you call the police. This is my last chance, Peter. I don't want a bunch of cops busting in with their guns blazing before I get a chance to talk to that woman."

"Talk to her?"

"That's all I want to do. Just find out what she did to Jason."

"A while ago you wanted to kill her."

"That was before I understood."

"And what if you find out she, you know, did something bad to Jason?"

"I don't know. I can't say."

"What about the Cade boy?"

"I don't think she'd hurt him."

"What about back there on the highway? If you hadn't taken the ditch we'd probably all be dead."

"Nobody wants to harm a child, Peter. No sane person, anyway. I believe she was counting on that. And she was right."

Peter turned away from him and sat on the foot of the bed, trying to clear his mind. His first instinct was to call the police; it was the obvious—and sane—thing to do. Let them handle it. There was more at stake here than Roger's son, who, as much as Peter hated to admit it, was probably already dead. There was also Graham Cade, another innocent child who was almost certainly still alive. And Peter's take on the stunt Maggie Dolan had pulled with the boy on the highway was very different from Roger's. It was his belief that in that moment, the woman's feelings had been much like his own on the day David died, the woman thinking, *If we can't live together then we'll die together*, her love for her son that deep. And he was far more worried about Roger going in there hotheaded than he was about the police. If Graham Cade ended up hurt or dead because of any action Peter was responsible for or condoned, he would never be able to forgive himself.

He looked at Roger and said, "Can you give me a few minutes?"

Roger was actually vibrating, his knuckles bone white, his nostrils flaring like those of a race horse. He looked at his watch. "What for?"

"To decide," Peter said, standing. "I'm going to go outside, sit somewhere quiet for a few minutes and think this all through, okay? I want to do what's best for everyone. Maybe it's the nature of the work I do, but I can't rush into things, Roger, not when they matter this much."

The man looked ready to explode; but he said, "Alright," and his shoulders sagged a little, some of the tension leaking out of him. He said, "I'll wait for you here." But something had changed in his eyes: the beseeching in them had vanished; now there was only menace. He said, "But I'm asking you, Peter—as a friend—don't call the cops without talking to me first."

Peter said, "I won't," and opened the door. As he closed it behind him, he saw Roger pick up the map off the bed, the one he'd used to find the Dolan farm.

* * *

Graham smelled bacon cooking and his tummy groaned under the covers, that empty feeling squirming around inside him. He sat up in bed and swung his legs over the side, sliding off the edge to the cool linoleum floor. He took a step toward the dresser, but he felt dizzy and had to lean against the bed until the sensation passed. He had a headache now and his ribs hurt from throwing up.

When his head stopped spinning he slipped out of his jammies and put on the clothes the woman had left for him, the stiff new jeans hurting as he slid them over the needle hole in his leg. There were no sock or shoes, so he folded his jammies on the pillow and pulled the covers up, making the bed the way his mother had taught him.

Then he went into the hall in his bare feet, following that sweet smell of bacon. The floor out here was made of wood, smooth gray boards that squeaked when he stepped on them, and the raw plaster walls were painted yellow. The sun was coming up now, its warm light spilling into the room next to Graham's, making the big wooden dresser in there seem to glow.

Graham thought, *Her room*, and hurried past.

He had to pee really bad, but there was a third room beside the bathroom at the end of the hall. The door to that room was closed and Graham heard a sound in there, a cough maybe…or a growl. The sound frightened him and he kept on walking until he got to the top of the stairs. Then he paused, gazing down the steep gray steps to another linoleum floor and a door beyond that, thinking about something he'd half-seen on the dresser in the woman's room. He froze there a moment, torn between his curiosity and his desire to get away from whatever was behind that closed door, whatever had made that sound.

Then, very quietly, he tip-toed back along the hall, past the bathroom and that scary closed door—no sound from in there now—to the woman's room.

Standing in the doorway with the staircase railing behind him, he thought he could hear the bacon sizzling in its pan down there, and the woman softly singing, a happy sound, a harmless sound.

He took a breath and scooted into the room, his feet all sweaty, leaving shiny footprints on the floor. There was an oval-shaped mat beside the bed and he stopped for a moment to stand on it, rubbing the soles of his feet on its nubby surface. His eyes found the thing on the dresser he'd noticed before— a picture in a wooden frame the same brown colour as the dresser—and what really confused him about the picture was that *he* was in it, smiling in the arms of the woman down-stairs, his curly blond hair lit up by the sun, a band-aid on one bare knee. The woman was thin in the picture and her dark hair was short, almost like a man's...but it was her. Those were *her* eyes.

Graham felt dizzy again, his heart thumping hard in his chest. Going on tip-toes, he moved closer to the picture and picked it up, looking closely at it now, wondering why he couldn't remember. He knew about twins, knew he didn't have one, so the boy in the picture *must* be him.

So why couldn't he remember?

A raised voice behind him said, "Ma?" and Graham spun to face its source, the picture slipping through his fingers to the floor, the glass shattering at his feet.

There was a tall, skinny boy standing in the doorway, nearly naked in a pair of baggy underwear that looked dirty, a grubby fist screwed into one sleepy eye. He had a chain around his neck with two shiny pieces of metal on it Graham knew were dog tags, like the ones on the soldiers in his brother's X-Box games.

Now the boy hollered, "Ma, Clayton busted your pitcher," and Graham heard the woman coming up the stairs, her feet making loud booms against the risers, and Graham felt something warm spill out of him. He heard the woman say, "For God's sake, Aaron, go put some clothes on," then she was staring in at Graham, her eyes as round as saucers, and now she turned on the boy and slapped him on the back of the head. "See what you did?" she said, slapping him again. "You *scared* your baby brother and he wet himself. Now go on, get yourself dressed and stay in your room till I tell you, hear?"

The boy said, "Yes, Ma," and thumped off down the hall.

Graham looked down at himself and saw that he really *had* peed his pants. His eyes filled with tears and now the woman was coming toward him. Afraid she was going to slap him too, he cringed and said he was sorry; but then she lifted him up and hugged him, not minding that his new jeans were all wet. "Thank God you didn't cut your precious little feet," she said, carrying him into the bathroom now, saying, "Let's get you all cleaned up." Saying, "You saw the picture, huh," then sitting him on the toilet seat and turning on the water in the tub, testing it with her fingers the way his mommy did. "I wanted to wait till later to talk to you about this," she said, "but I guess now's as good a time as any." She knelt in front of him on the bathroom floor and unbuttoned his shirt. "You go ahead and get yourself in the tub like a good big boy," she said. Then she was standing, telling him she'd be right back.

She went out the door, closing it behind her, and Graham did as he was told, taking off his shirt and his soggy pants and climbing into the tub, a deep one with feet shaped like claws clutching smoky crystal balls.

The water was perfect and Graham leaned back against the sloping wall of the tub, swishing his legs back and forth to get the pee off them.

* * *

There was a picnic table under a shade tree behind the hotel and Peter sat on it now, watching sunbeams spill through the foliage to dapple the lawn. There was a breeze working back here with a breath of fall in it—that damp, sweet smell of golden rod and rot—and it sent a chill through him, pebbling his arms with gooseflesh. It was going to be a beautiful day...but not for the Cades, both of them shot and without their boy; not for the families of those two policemen. Maggie Dolan had crossed the line, all the way over this time, compounding her kidnappings with murder.

And yet, God help him, Peter understood. The woman was acting out of the deepest, most fierce breed of love. The tragedy was that she was wrong. Had either child actually been her own, no parent in the world would have faulted her actions. As it stood, only her fractured state of mind made what she'd done even remotely defensible. Either way, once caught, she'd be facing a lifetime of incarceration.

Which brought him back to that single, nagging worry: out there on the highway, the woman had been prepared to die and take the child with her, anything to avoid having him 'stolen' from her again. If threatened again, might she not choose a similar path? Murder-suicides were frighteningly common; in Maggie Dolan's mind, what better motive than this?

But did this strengthen the argument for letting the police handle the situation? Or weaken it? Maggie Dolan had murdered two police officers in cold blood, dispatching them execution style in the front seat of their own car. How much sympathy would the cops have for a person who could do a thing like that, insane or otherwise?

The trick was to diffuse the situation without setting the woman off, this exceedingly dangerous woman who would clearly do anything to protect the child she believed was her own.

The more Peter thought about it, the more he realized he would have to do this on his own. Approach the woman not with aggression but compassion, try to break through the barrier of her delusions. And even as the thought came to him he felt that rush of love he'd always felt in David's presence, the same fleeting feeling that had haunted him over his long summer weeks of inaction.

He thought, *Okay, sweet boy*, and felt a simple, blissful peace he hadn't experienced in months. He basked in it a moment, this contented, almost childlike sense that everything was as it should be, then he made his way back inside.

* * *

There was a bar of soap in a wire dish and Graham used it to wash himself off. He didn't want anyone to see him with no clothes on so he bathed quickly and climbed out of the tub, using a big white bath towel to dry himself off. He put the brown shirt back on, then wrapped the towel around his waist and hurried back along the hall to the room he'd slept in. His jammies were still on the pillow and he grabbed the bottoms, pulling them on as the woman came back upstairs. He heard her push the bathroom door open, then heard her say, "Sweetie?" with the same raw fear in her voice he'd heard in his father's voice last night, when he hid behind the hamper.

Something jarred uncomfortably in his young mind as he realized home was only one sleep behind him; it seemed like a very long time ago.

Then the woman was coming down the hall, her footfalls heavy on the floorboards. Graham said, "I'm in here," because he didn't want to make her mad, and she smiled coming through the doorway, carrying a plate of bacon and eggs in one hand and a couple of big books in the other. She said, "*There* you are," set the plate on the dresser and dropped the books onto the end of the bed. Opening the closet now, she said, "You scared me, you little scamp," and brought out a Batman dinner tray. Then she plumped his pillow against the middle of the headboard and lifted him up to lean against it on the bed. She set the tray across his knees and put the plate on it, a kid's fork already tucked under the eggs. Graham wasn't hungry anymore—and he was allergic to eggs—but he picked up a piece of toast to nibble on. The woman said, "There," picked up the books and sat down beside him, her hands resting on the books that Graham now saw were photo albums. She took a big breath and blew it out; it smelled like Listerine, the burny kind his Grandma always used. Graham munched his toast, waiting.

Now she opened the top album and looked inside. Graham heard her say, "Aw, look at you. Sweet baby boy." He tried to see what she was looking at but couldn't, the big brown album cover blocking his view. He leaned his head back to try again and she let the cover fall closed.

Turning to look at him, she said, "There's some things I have to tell you, sweetheart. Things you might have a hard time believing." She patted the photo albums on her lap. "But I can prove them to you, if you'll give me the chance. Will you do that for me?"

Graham nodded. He had no spit in his mouth now and couldn't swallow his toast, a dry ball of it stuck to the inside of his cheek. He put the rest on the plate, away from the runny eggs.

She said, "Oh, this is so hard," and Graham realized she was crying. He watched her bring a knot of kleenex out of a pocket in her dress and use it to wipe her eyes. "It seems like such a long time ago now," she said, "but it really isn't. I mean, look at you. You're still the same. I couldn't believe it when I came home from work that day and they told me you were gone. Do you remember that day, baby? The day the bad man took you?"

Graham was confused. *She* was the bad man and *of course* he remembered. It happened just last night. But he didn't think she was talking about that so he said, "No."

"No, I didn't think you would. Do you know what brain-washing is?"

Graham believed he did. His brother Greg explained it to him once when they were watching a cartoon movie that had brainwashing in it. He said, "Is that when someone tells you so many fibs about something you end up believing them?"

She tousled his hair again, saying, "My, aren't you the clever one. That's exactly what it is." Now she looked right at him, using her fingers to tilt his chin so he had to look right back at her. "Well, that's what they did to you."

Graham said, "Who?" continuing to look up at her after she took her fingers away.

"The people who stole you from me."

Now Graham was totally lost. He said, "But...*you* stole me, from my mommy and daddy."

"See, honey? *That's* the brainwashing part."

She opened the top album again, angling it so Graham could see inside. The first page had four baby pictures on it, the baby a boy in a blue plastic bathtub, grown up hands Graham knew were the woman's supporting his blond head, washing his plump little body with a face cloth.

Pointing at the first picture, the woman said, "I know it's hard to believe, honey, but this is you. You were born at Mercy Hospital in Arnprior one minute before midnight, Christmas Eve nineteen ninety-five, just like the baby Jesus, practically."

Graham peeled the dry ball of bread out of his mouth and set it on the tray, rolling it out of sight under the edge of the plate. His stomach felt sick again.

She said, "Your real name is Clayton Dolan, after my daddy, Clayton Barr." She took his hand in hers and squeezed it. Then she said, "And I'm your ma," and Graham could barely hear her after that, a dull buzz starting up inside his head. Far away, he heard her say, "That boy you saw prancing around in his drawers this morning is your big brother, Aaron. He was a difficult birth, got stuck coming out and the lack of oxygen made him slow. But he's a good boy and he loves you to death. I know he's glad to have you back."

She turned some more pages in the album now, mostly baby pictures in this one, and Graham watched without seeing, knowing that what she was saying couldn't be true. His mommy was always telling him what a terrific memory he had. He even remembered his second birthday party, when his daddy brought a pony home in a trailer and Graham rode it around in the back yard, his daddy walking along beside him, holding him tight so he couldn't fall off. Sometimes out of the blue he would say, "Remember when the pony pooed on the grass?" and his mommy and daddy would laugh, telling him they couldn't believe he remembered that. But he did.

The woman moved the top album to the bottom and flipped the second one open, the pictures in this one harder for Graham to dismiss. Here was one of a blond boy climbing onto a school bus, the woman saying, "Here you are on your first day of school, such a brave little boy, not a peep coming out of you," and it was *him*. And there were so many others—even one of him riding a pony, except in this one the woman was holding him so he wouldn't fall and there was a barn in the background, not his yard at home.

"You don't have to call me Ma right away," the woman was saying, "but I'd like it if you did. Because these people you've been living with stole you from me, baby, and put all this stuff in your head about being someone else. About being their boy instead of mine. I bet they treated you nice, huh. Gave you whatever you wanted?"

Graham didn't get everything he wanted, but he nodded.

"You see, Clayton, *that's* how they trick you. You're just a kid, you don't know any better. And maybe they drug you at first, I don't know. I've read about how it's done but I can't say how they did it to you. But they did."

She took his face in her hands, the tray almost spilling when his knees came up, and kissed him softly on the forehead. And though Graham understood none of this, he felt only love coming from this woman and he thought that if he just did what he was told his mommy and daddy would find him soon and take him back home.

He just had to do what he was told.

She said, "Is there anything you'd like to ask me?"

Graham thought for a moment and said, "Where's your real hair?" and the woman laughed.

She said, "I had to shave it all off so they'd think I was a man. People are easy to fool, Clayton. They believe what they want to believe. On the news they're saying *I'm* the kidnapper, can you believe that? But they're looking for a man." She slipped the wig off her head and Graham shivered looking up at her. "A bald man."

She rested the clump of black hair on top of the photo albums; it looked like a dead animal and Graham shivered again, his tummy doing sick little flip flops now. She said, "They're never going to find us," and Graham lurched off the bed and ran to the bathroom, just making it to the toilet before his stomach turned.

But there was nothing left inside him.

* * *

They were on the road by 7:15, heading east on the 401 doing the speed limit, Saturday morning traffic rolling along smoothly at this hour. On the way out of Oakville Peter had pulled into a McDonald's and ordered Egg McMuffins to go and they'd eaten them in silence, not tasting the food, just filling the hole. Peter had estimated the trip at about five hours and, since neither of them had slept in the past twenty-four, suggested they split the drive into shifts, giving the free man a chance to rest. Incredibly, as soon as he was done eating, Roger tilted his seat back, closed his eyes and fell asleep. Peter's mother had always told him that was a sign of a clear conscience, being able to just pop off like that, and in his scattered musings as he drove Peter thought, *Here's the exception that proves the rule.*

He couldn't begin to fathom the depth of Roger's guilt. It made him think of a patient he'd had recently, a courageous old girl in her seventies with rheumatoid arthritis that had plagued her since her teens. She was having a knee replacement done and Peter elected to do her awake, under spinal anesthesia. Every movement the woman made caused her pain, and Peter did his best to get her positioned without hurting her too much. It was like handling balsawood, her frailty that extreme, her twisted hands and misshapen feet looking as if someone had flattened them with a hammer, the knee they were replacing swollen to the size of a melon. Peter had to struggle to get the spinal, the soft-tissue spaces in her back narrow and ossified, and the woman sat stoically through it, never complaining as he poked and prodded with the three-and-a-half inch needle. And when he finally found the spot and injected the drug Peter heard her sigh, a sound of immeasurable relief, a sixty year burden of suffering suddenly, gloriously lifted. And though they both knew the respite was only a temporary one, the two of them revelled in it, spending the next couple of hours chatting and telling jokes.

Peter imagined that Roger's guilt must be something akin to this old woman's pain, a pitiless, unflagging presence that coloured every aspect of life until, like some insatiable parasite, it sucked its victim dry, leaving only a husk. The tragedy was that in Roger's case, should his son never be found alive, the only effective anesthetic for his suffering would be death. And perhaps not even then.

He took the Lindsay-Peterborough exit off the 401 and followed 115 north to the Trans Canada, Roger snoring restlessly beside him, talking occasionally in his sleep, abrupt, unintelligible bursts that sounded angry and made Peter's skin crawl. The Trans Canada would take them right past the town of Arnprior. From there it was only a twenty minute drive to the Dolan farm.

Following a brief discussion in the hotel room earlier this morning, the two of them had agreed upon the ground rules, at least in principle, Peter insisting that he approach Maggie Dolan alone, Roger conceding only reluctantly—and with the proviso that he be in the car while Peter made his bid, out of sight in the back seat or even the trunk if need be. "If she goes ballistic on you," Roger had said, "you'll be glad we did it this way." Considering the damage the woman had already done, Peter was inclined to agree. Still, he was counting on a civil response to a civil approach.

And yet, the more he thought about it on this balmy, late-summer morning, the more unnerved he became. Maggie Dolan had already demonstrated her willingness to do whatever it took to protect what she believed was her own. Pondering it now, Peter was hard pressed to imagine why she would see him as anything other than a threat.

It was madness, all of it. And all he had for counsel was this crazed, volatile man—Maggie Dolan's first victim—and the vague, possibly imaginary nudgings of his own dead son.

Peter shifted uncomfortably in his seat, an ache awakening in the centre of his skull, the nidus of a dark and growing foreboding.

14.

When his tummy settled, the woman showed Graham the rest of the house, telling him it had been built by his great grandparents more than a hundred years ago and had been in the family ever since. She said it hadn't been a working farm since his grandparents, her parents, retired in the eighties, when she was still just a girl. She said his grandparents were both dead now, telling him, "Your Grandpa went first. The cancer got him. Grandma died a year later of a broken heart."

She showed him the summer kitchen first, telling him that in the winter they used to close off this part of the house and not heat it. There was an old wood stove out here, a table with four chairs, and a steel door with a big padlock on it, the door facing the back of the house. On the other side of the room a screen door led outside to the long front porch.

She took him into the main part of the house next, the dining room and winter kitchen in one big space with a small room next to the fridge she called 'the pantry', and a family room at the back of the house with a TV and windows that looked out over acres of open field. "You got lost in the corn out there once when you were four and had nightmares for weeks after. Remember that?"

Graham said no and she told him not to worry, it would all come back in time. There was a window on the far side of the kitchen-dining room, and she picked him up to show him a homemade swing outside, the swing an old single bedspring with rusty legs, the metal frame nestled next to a bush with tiny red berries. She said, "There's a vegetable garden behind the 'suckle—cabbage, potatoes, cucumbers and such—and a raspberry patch, your favourite berries."

Graham's favourite was blueberries, and yet this woman had confused him with her pictures and her stories and he felt himself going numb inside, like the time he bumped his head in the music store and the world got all fuzzy for a while. She led him around by the hand, talking away, and Graham let her, hearing only half of what she was telling him now, thinking only about finding his way home. The stuff about brainwashing frightened him, because this woman really *believed* it and she had all those pictures of him, doing all those things he couldn't remember, some of them things he *could* remember doing but with his real mommy and daddy, and it made him afraid that maybe she was right, maybe he really *had* been stolen from her and he just couldn't remember.

She walked him through the summer kitchen again, across the hilly linoleum to a door that opened onto a narrow porch with no railing. There was a clothes line out here, the double line drooping through space to a small building made of rough gray boards Graham could tell had never been painted. She told him the building was the woodshed, saying, "When us girls were bad Pa'd take us out here to paddle our behinds, winter or summer, didn't matter, you crossed the line, it was out to the woodshed with you." This memory seemed to please her and she smiled, saying, "Come on," leading him down the creaky steps now to a path that sloped downhill through the weeds to a pair of big apple trees. "Macs," the woman said, stooping to pick one up off the ground. The trees were laden with them, the ground littered with the bright red fruit. She polished the apple in a fold of her dress and handed it to him. "Go ahead, Clay, honey," she said, "they're sweet and good as gold for you." Graham took a bite and his mouth filled with spit, the taste bitter at first, then turning sweet. He chewed hungrily and took another bite, his empty tummy wanting more.

The woman said, "Your Aunt Marie and I used to—" and a voice rang out behind them. Graham turned to see Aaron with his head out the door, his glasses crooked on his face, Aaron shouting, "Ma. Car."

Then Graham was in the woman's arms and she was running like she did in the park, running up the hill to the house, and Graham's apple fell in the weeds and his heart started racing in his chest. Aaron met them at the door and the woman handed Graham to him, saying, "In the root cellar now," her spit speckling Aaron's glasses, making him blink his magnified eyes. The woman kept running, turning left through the screen door to the front porch, and now Aaron was running too, his wiry arms wrapped too tight around Graham's chest, making it hard for him to breathe. As they ran past the door to the porch Graham saw a car roll into the yard out there, the woman walking now, moving across the dead grass to meet the car, smoothing the front of her dress with her hands.

There was a half step down into the winter kitchen and Aaron stumbled and almost fell. Startled, Graham cried out and Aaron clapped a hand over his mouth, covering his nose too, and now Graham couldn't breathe at all. He started to squirm and Aaron rushed him into the pantry and put him down, holding a finger to his lips to tell him to be quiet. Then he opened a trap door in the pantry floor and said, "Get in."

Graham saw a ladder leading down into darkness and shook his head. Aaron said, "Get in *now* or Ma's gonna be furious," except the way Aaron said it, it sounded like *furr*-ious, but Graham knew what he meant. "Go," Aaron said, "I'm comin' in witcha an' turn on the light." Graham heard the clunk of a car door outside and Aaron said, "Now or I'm gonna hafta push ya," his dark eyes round and afraid behind his glasses.

Graham got down on his hands and knees, slipped one foot over the edge to find the top rung and started down, stopping partway to make sure Aaron was coming too. Then Aaron was on the ladder, looking down at Graham, saying, "Keep goin' so I don't squish your fingers." Graham did as he was told, not stopping until his bare foot touched the hard-packed earth and he noticed the smell down here, black and damp and rotten.

Aaron stopped on the ladder and reached into the dark above Graham's head. Graham heard a tinkling sound, then a soft *click* and a light came on, blinding him at first, a bare bulb hanging from the ceiling by its cord, swaying to fill this cold space with shadows like roving phantoms.

Aaron reached up to pull the trap door shut, looked at Graham and said, "Shh." He brought the door down and let it rest on the top of his head, leaving a crack to peek through.

Graham heard a man's voice now, the man saying, "Myrt's expecting me back any minute," and Aaron whispered, "It's Mr. Muldoon from across the field. Ma says he's a snoop gonna get his nose chopped off one day," and Graham touched his nose, not liking the sound of that. He wanted out of this smelly hole in the ground.

Very quietly, Aaron said, "Wanna see?"

He squeezed to one side, giving Graham enough room to climb up the ladder. Scared but curious, Graham hesitated a moment, then climbed up beside the boy to peek through the crack in the trap door.

He could see the dining room table from here, and now an old man in a straw hat coming in from the summer kitchen to sit in the chair the woman pulled out for him, asking him if he'd like something to drink. The old man said, "Thanks for asking, Maggie, but this ain't exactly a social visit."

Graham thought, *Maggie*.

The woman, Maggie, stood over the old man now, saying, "What kind of visit is it then, Albert?"

The old man took his hat off, set it on the table and said, "You mind sitting, Mag? It's hard on the ol' neck, staring up at you like this."

Maggie pulled out the chair next to Albert's and sat down. She said, "What kind of visit is it?" and Aaron whispered, "Uh-oh."

Albert said, "Myrt and me, we seen the news this morning. We know what you been up to, Maggie."

Maggie said, "And what is it you believe I've been up to?"

"You know what I'm talking about," Albert said. "It was you killed them two coppers down in Oakville and kidnapped that kid. And the other one, three years back. I remember that one, too. Even remember thinking, Goddam, don't he look like Maggie's boy? But I never made the connection. Neither did the cops, till now, except they think you're just one of the victims. They're calling them the Triplet Kidnappings now, saying it's some freak collecting look alikes. But when I seen that video from the park, when you tried to grab the boy off them monkey bars?" He touched the side of his head with a bent finger. "It clicked. I said to Myrt, 'That's Maggie Dolan,' and she said sure as hell it is."

Maggie said, "What else do you think you know?"

"I'm not here to play games with you," the old man said. "I knew your daddy and his daddy before him. And even though we've lost touch over the years, you and me, I know deep down you're a good person. Myrt wanted me to just call the cops but I said no, I'm gonna drive up there and give her the chance to do the right thing."

Maggie said, "Do the right thing?" and Graham started shaking, the woman's voice growing deeper with her anger. She was turning into the bad man again. "You think taking my boy back from the animals that stole him is *wrong*?" Graham wished the old man would just leave, but he wasn't backing down.

"That boy isn't yours, Maggie," he said. "His name's Graham Cade. He's six years old and he's got two brothers and a sister. You put his parents in the hospital. You—"

Maggie said, *"That's what they want you to believe,"* screaming the words. Then she was out of her chair, heading for the
pantry, and Aaron said, "Jump," and let the trap door snick
shut, grabbing Graham by the shirt and pulling him off the ladder to land on the dirt floor. Graham could still hear Maggie's
voice— "That's what they want *everybody* to believe"—and now
the trap door flew open and her face was up there over the
hole. "Aaron," she said in that deep voice, "bring your brother up
out of there." Aaron didn't move and Maggie said, "This instant."

Then Aaron was pushing him up the ladder and the woman
had him by the wrist, pulling him the rest of the way out. She
said, "Come on, sweetheart," and led him into the main room,
tugging him over to stand in front of the old man sitting in the
chair. She said, "Okay, Albert, you tell me. Who does this look
like to you?"

The old man looked at Graham with twinkling eyes, winked
at him and said, "Granted, the boy's the spitting image of Clayton." He shook his head. "It's downright spooky, really. But Mag,
think about this a spell, would you? When was Clayton born?"

Her brow tightening, Maggie said, "Christmas Eve, nineteen ninety-five. A minute before midnight."

Looking at Graham now, the old man said, "Tell me, son,
what year is it?"

Graham looked at Maggie and saw a funny glaze in her
eyes. He said, "Two thousand and eight?"

"See?" Albert said. "Clayton would be twelve now. Not six.
He was six when he was taken."

Maggie was starting to tremble, her hand squeezing Graham's
wrist too tight.

Albert said, "Son, what's your name?"

Wincing, Graham said, "Graham," and the old man lifted his gaze to Maggie. "Maggie," he said. "I want you to tell me what you did with that other boy. The Mullen kid. Did you hurt him? Where—?"

Graham heard that word—*Where*—then he saw a streak of motion as the woman let go of his wrist, her fist slicing through the air to strike the old man in the throat. Whatever the man meant to say was lost in the wet *snap* Graham heard and now the man was gurgling, clutching his broken throat.

Maggie said, "Aaron, take your brother upstairs," and he was in Aaron's strong arms again, not breathing, his ankles banging the steps as Aaron dragged him up as fast as he could go.

On the first landing Graham looked back to see the old man slump off his chair, blue eyes bugging, the woman just standing there watching him.

At the top of the stairs Aaron put him down, grabbed his hand and tugged him along the hall to the room at the front of the house, the room Graham had slept in. He stood Graham on a wooden chair in front of the window and squeezed in beside him, tugging the sheers aside so both of them could see into the yard below.

A couple of minutes later they saw Maggie marching toward the Muldoons' big red car with the old man slung over one shoulder, his hat and car keys in her free hand. Graham couldn't be sure, but he thought he could hear her singing.

She used the keys to open the trunk, bent to dump the old man inside, then threw his hat in after him. The old man's eyes were still open, and Graham got the feeling they were looking right at him.

Maggie closed the trunk and climbed into the car on the driver's side, blue smoke issuing from the tailpipe as she gunned the engine and accelerated out of the yard.

* * *

Peter pulled into the Shell station in Arnprior a few minutes after noon, the gentle bump of the access ramp waking Roger up.

"Jesus," Roger said, squinting at the digital clock. "You didn't wake me. Where the hell are we?"

"Arnprior," Peter said. He parked next to an open pump and killed the engine. "I didn't have the heart to wake you." He opened his door, being careful not to ram it against the cement island. "I've really got to pee," he said, "and I thought we should top up the tank."

Roger was shaking his head, clearing the cobwebs. "Go ahead and pee," he said. "I'll take care of the gas." As Peter got out Roger said, "How much farther?"

"Twenty minutes, maybe less."

Roger nodded and got out on his side.

Ten minutes later they were rolling again, Peter driving in rigid silence, Roger hunched forward in his seat like a sprinter waiting for the *crack* of the starter pistol. Peter could feel him winding tighter with each passing mile and wished there was something he could say to calm the man down.

And the closer they got to their destination, the more Peter feared his plan was a flawed and dangerous one. This woman was like a grizzly protecting its young, her fury indiscriminate, unbounded by truth or reason. During the long drive up here an image had played on a continuous loop in his mind, one of himself mounting Maggie Dolan's porch steps in August sunshine, pressing his face to the screen as he had before, except this time it wasn't a woman that emerged from the gloom in there but the unwavering barrel of a shotgun, its terrible blast shattering the afternoon stillness, the fire it spat bowling him off the porch to bleed to death in the dirt.

To break the silence he told Roger about the old farmer he'd sat with that day in July, suggesting that perhaps they should stop at the man's place before going on to the Dolans'. "We could borrow his phone, call Sergeant Taylor and let her know what's going on. She could send in the local police and we'd still have plenty of time to talk to the woman."

Roger agreed it was a good idea, and when the Muldoon homestead appeared Peter pulled into the gravel driveway, parking behind an old red Chrysler with its trunk open.

Peter said, "Be right back," and got out, closing the door behind him. On his way around the hood he saw Albert's straw hat lying on its side in the Chrysler's trunk, the leather head band stained black from years of dirt and sweat. The sight of it struck a chord of alarm in Peter. On his first visit here he remembered thinking the old guy probably slept in that hat. It was part of what he'd liked about the man. Why would he leave it in the trunk, just tossed aside like that?

He glanced at Roger staring at him from the passenger seat, then went up the porch steps. The inner door was open and Peter called through the screen, "Albert? Myrt? Anybody home?" When he got no reply, he opened the screen door wide enough to hammer the brass knocker on the inner door. He shouted, "Mr. Muldoon?" and stepped inside, the kitchen right there, a pot of water boiling over on the stove.

Feeling like a trespasser, Peter crept over to the stove and turned the element off. Then he caught a whiff of something foul and moved through an archway into a sitting room steeped in shadow, heavy curtains drawn against the daylight. The smell was worse in here, and as his eyes adjusted Peter stumbled over something by the coffee table—Albert's feet, shod in work boots, the old man laid out on his back on an oval area rug, his big hands folded across his chest. In the man's stillness Peter recognized death without the need for further verification, and now he saw Myrt on the other side of the table, posed in exactly the same manner. The smell was coming from her, the impossible angle of her head telling Peter her neck had been broken, her bowels letting go in the cataclysm of spinal shock.

There was a phone in the kitchen and Peter ran to it now, an old wall-mounted rotary by the fridge. He grabbed the handset and almost fumbled it, then brought it to his ear to find only dead air, as dead as the Muldoons laid out on the rug in their sitting room. He jiggled the U-shaped plunger, listening for a dial tone, then ran out to the porch to tell Roger.

But Roger wasn't there.

Peter ran down the steps into the yard, looking up the road in time to see his car turning left at the top of the hill, raising a cloud of dust, Maggie Dolan's farmhouse less than a mile away.

He came back to the Chrysler, saw the empty ignition and ran into the house. There was a staircase to his right and he bolted to the top, entered a room on his left—Myrt's sewing room—and strode to the window facing the back of the house.

Out there, hazy across a rolling field of corn, stood the Dolan place, only its gray shingled roof visible through the surrounding trees.

Peter ran down the stairs as fast as his legs would carry him. There was a back door off the kitchen and he pushed through it onto a wooden stoop. There was a brand new maple axe handle leaning against the railing, the price sticker still on it, and Peter picked it up, testing its heft.

Then he started out across the field of corn, sprinting through the buzz of insects and the dry rustle of leaves, the tall stalks swallowing him whole.

* * *

Graham sat stock still in a rocking chair on the porch, his slender arms folded across his chest, watching Maggie back a big motor home out of the high garage and park it in front of the house.

After she drove away in the old man's car, he and Aaron had looked at comic books until she got back, sweaty from hiking through the corn. She came straight upstairs and told Aaron to get busy, it was time to hit the road. Then she carried Graham out to the porch and said, "Don't move from this spot, okay? Your brother and I've got some things to do, then we're going for a nice long drive." Graham asked where and she said, "You'll see."

Now Aaron came out lugging a suitcase, breathing hard through his open mouth, a worried look on his face. He glanced at Graham, then wrestled the suitcase down the steps and across the yard to the motor home, his mother helping him lift it up through the narrow entrance. Aaron came back then, going inside again, and now Maggie came back too. "Come on, sweetheart," she said, taking Graham's hand. "I want to show you something."

She led him to the motor home and lifted him inside. Graham had never been in one of these. It was like his school bus except with a miniature house inside: a kitchen with a fridge and stove and a table with booth seats, a comfy looking couch behind the driver's seat, a little TV and a carpeted hall-way that led to a bed in the back.

"Hot as the dickens in here right now," Maggie said, "but just wait till we get the A/C fired up, we'll all be cool as cucumbers." She opened a skinny door in the hallway and said, "The bathroom's in here," and Graham saw a funny little toilet in there and a sink made of chrome, a medicine chest and a shower with glass doors. She said, "Neat, huh? This is going to be our home for a while. I thought maybe we could head north. Plenty of places to hide up there."

Graham didn't want to hide. He wanted his mommy and daddy, his sister Risa and his two big brothers. He thought of his daddy telling him to be brave when he had something hard to do, like going to the dentist or getting a booster shot, but he was *tired* of being brave. He looked up at Maggie, showing him the bedroom now, telling him he'd be sleeping back here with her, and said, "I want to go home," and the tears came again, gushing out of his eyes to dribble onto his shirt.

He thought Maggie would be angry, but she said, "Aw, honey," and sat him on the foot of the bed, kneeling in front of him, brushing the hair off his hot forehead. "I know this is hard for you," she said, her own eyes filling with water. "It's all so new. But sweetie, this *is* your home." She squeezed his hand. "You need to just give things time. You'll see, everything's—"

There was a clattering noise and Aaron appeared in the doorway. He said, "Ma, another car," and Maggie got to her feet, telling Graham to stay put.

She said, "Close the door," to Aaron, shuttered all the windows on her way to the front of the motor home then told Aaron to go sit with his brother. She opened a cupboard under the sink and brought out a pair of short brown sticks made of wood, then went down on one knee behind the driver's seat, watching out the big front window.

Graham shifted to let Aaron sit beside him and now he could see through the front window, too. For a moment there was nothing.

Then a small gray car zoomed into the yard, skidding in the dirt as it ground to a halt between the motor home and the house. A big man got out without closing the door, stared at the motor home for a moment, then ran up the porch steps to the screen door, his hands balled into fists. He banged hard on the door and Graham could hear him shouting the woman's name, "Margaret Dolan?" then banging again on the door. "I know you're in there," he said. "You need to come out here *right now. You need to tell me what you've done with my son.*"

Peeling off her wig and tossing it onto the table, Maggie opened the motor home door and stepped through it into brilliant sunlight. The instant she was gone Aaron scooted around the bed to the small window facing the house, spreading the slats in the Venetian blind with grubby fingers to see what was going on.

Curious and afraid, Graham crawled across the bed to join him. He couldn't see Maggie at first, just the man on the porch shading his eyes to look in through the screen, then pulling the door open to go inside.

Now he heard Maggie say, *"Hey,"* and saw her step into the yard facing the porch, the sun beating down on her shaved head, one of those brown sticks in each hand. The man turned to face her, letting the door swing shut behind him. Pointing one of the sticks at him, Maggie said, "This is private property. *You* need to leave right now."

Graham saw the man smile, but it wasn't a happy smile. It made him think of a nature program he'd seen, a big snake slithering up behind a tiny bird with flickering wings, the bird still drinking from a puddle when the smiling snake plucked it off its feet with its fangs.

The man said, "I'm not going anywhere," and started down the steps, that cold smile still on his face. "Not until you tell me what you've done with my boy."

Maggie said, "Have it your way," and moved forward to meet the man, coming across the yard now with fury in his eyes. Graham felt a funny sickness inside him watching this happen, and a part of him was afraid the big man was going to hurt Maggie; but another part was *glad*, thinking the man was going to save him, take him back to his family.

Now the man was running, his hands twisted into claws. Maggie kept moving, and when the man was almost on top of her she leaned away from him and jabbed a stick into his belly, spinning to drive the other one into the back of his neck. The man cried out and fell, landing hard on his face in the dirt, Maggie circling him now with those sticks, and when he tried to get up she kicked him in the face with her heavy boot and the man stopped moving, his breath raising dry puffs of dirt off the ground, the blood on his lips turning gray.

When Maggie bent over the man's head Graham pushed away from the window, his tiny body shaking in the explosive heat of the motor home. Aaron stayed where he was, watching out the window, whispering, "Uh-oh. Uh-oh. Uh-oh."

Graham scurried into the small bathroom and locked the door. Sobbing, he sat on the toilet lid, closed his eyes and pressed his hands over his ears. He stayed that way, gently rocking, until he felt the motor home shift under Maggie's weight.

Then she was tapping on the door, saying, "Clayton, honey, open the door for your ma," and Graham started screaming, screaming as hard as he could.

* * *

Peter slowed coming up a rise toward the back of the house, the gray roof visible now through the corn stalks swaying in the breeze. Crouching, he continued at a brisk walk, the axe handle slippery in his palm. The rise crested and he started down the other side, his lungs searing from the quick mile run.

The corn field ended at a barbed wire fence and Peter miscalculated ducking underneath, one of the rusty barbs hooking his shirt, tearing into the skin of his back. He opened his mouth to cry out and caught himself just in time, knowing that if he screamed he wouldn't be able to stop and the woman would find him and kill him.

He heard a door slam at the front of the house and went down on his haunches in the weeds, winded and terrified, no idea how to proceed. Should he sneak in through the back of the house somehow? Threaten her with the axe handle? Or find the Cade boy and get him out, let Roger take care of himself? Where *was* Roger anyway? Maybe it was all over and all he had to do was walk around to the front of the house. Unless she'd shot him on sight—and Peter hadn't heard any gunfire on his way across the field—the woman would be no match for Roger, not in his current state of mind. If he hadn't killed her already, surely he'd subdued her.

Peter knew he had to move. He couldn't see a thing from back here, just this overgrown yard, a jumbled pile of scrap lumber and an old wooden rain barrel under a downspout at the right hand corner of the house. There was a newer addition on the left with a satellite dish on the wall, an unpainted, tin-roofed structure that looked like a garage but with no windows or doors, the only access, Peter assumed, from inside the house. The blinds were down in the two ground-level windows in the main part of the house, and a patch of honeysuckle blocked his view of the roadway and those three barracks-like outbuildings.

Feeling dangerously exposed, he made a dash for the back of the house, the weather-worn clapboards hot as he pressed his back to them. He edged along the space between the windows, moving in quick side steps with the axe handle at the ready, stopping when he got to the window to duck under-

neath, his view of the room inside blocked by the blind. The
axe handle felt awkward in his hand, the idea of using it as a
weapon utterly foreign to him. In his whole life he'd never even
been in a shoving match, never mind a fist fight, and he had no
idea whether he could actually strike the woman with the thing
or not. Hopefully threatening her with it would be enough. His
only advantage here was surprise.

He came to the corner with the rain barrel, brimful from a
recent rain, and dipped his hands into the cool water, leaning
forward to scrub his face. He had a bad moment standing over
the barrel, the water dark and impossibly deep-looking in the
sunshine, the illusion giving him a feeling of suffocation until
he turned away. Then he heard the slam of that door again,
the sound louder now, reminding him of the Muldoon's screen
door clapping shut on that balmy July afternoon they sat together eating biscuits. All he had to do now was turn the corner and walk the last twenty feet to the front of the house.

But he couldn't. He'd been afraid before, but never like
this. The fear he felt now was like a drug, a potent paralytic,
and he just...couldn't...move.

A voice now, muffled but filled with anger, and Peter flinched
at the sound of it: "Aaron, get out here and give me a hand."

Then he heard footfalls, a kid's runners scuffing fast through
hard-packed dirt, and he turned the corner gripping the axe
handle, ducked under another shaded window and stopped in
a crouch at the front corner of the house. He saw the Corolla
in the yard with the door open, and beyond that a tan
Winnebago, the Corolla partially blocking his view, and as he
rose to look past the hood he saw Roger's legs hanging out the

motor home door, his lifeless legs, then his shoes as someone dragged him roughly inside.

Peter recoiled from the scene, sinking on boneless legs against the side of the house, his lungs starving for air, the world spinning around him in the cloying sweetness of honeysuckle. The axe handle slid from his grip and he brought his hands up to clutch the collar of his T-shirt, its soggy proximity to his throat strangling him.

Then he was running, back through the overgrown yard to the barbed wire fence, catching a toe leaping over it to slam to the ground in the corn, felling the stalks in his path. He rolled to his feet and ran through the slashing leaves, thinking he'd go back to the Muldoon's place and call the police, but *fuck* the line was out, and as he stumbled to a stop and looked back at the house he knew he couldn't leave his friend like this, dead or alive. He had to go back.

Seconds later he was peeking around the front corner of the house again, watching Maggie Dolan with her head shaved stepping out of the Winnebago to cross the yard toward the house. She glanced his way and Peter was sure he was caught. Then she was scraping up the porch steps and he looked through the railing to see her go inside, the impact of the screen door against its frame echoing back at him from the distant barn.

Finding an unexpected calm, Peter bent to retrieve the axe handle, strode the three quick paces to the porch and climbed over the railing. Dropping to his hands and knees, he crawled under the front windows to the door and got to his feet at its edge, pressing his back to the peeling clapboards. He took a breath, his legs steady now, and brought the axe handle up like a baseball bat.

He glanced at the Winnebago and saw Roger staring out at him through the open door, wedged like a plank into the booth seat with blood in his eyes and a strip of duct tape over his mouth. His hands were taped together behind him, his neck raked back at a vicious angle, duct-taped to the chrome faucet behind him. He was trying to signal Peter with his eyes and Peter tensed, hearing footfalls in the hallway now, coming his way.

* * *

Roger saw Peter scuttling on his hands and knees across the porch, then rising by the door with the axe handle ready. He'd regained consciousness only moments ago, and now he strained against the duct tape with everything he had, bucking like a landed fish, trying to rip the faucet from its base with the muscles of his neck; but he was caught, his struggles serving only to tighten his bonds, making it harder for him to breathe. It was as hot as an oven in here and he could feel himself wanting to black out again, the knockout kick she'd delivered still ringing in his ears.

The slow kid Peter had told him about was sitting in front of him not six feet away with Jason's dog tags around his neck, still as a statue on the couch behind the driver's seat, whispering, "Uh-oh, uh-oh," over and over, paying no attention to Roger. The woman had told the kid to stay put and keep an eye on him, saying, "They're coming out of the goddam woodwork." And in a single instant of righteous misjudgment he'd gone from raging avenger to helpless hostage. He'd underestimated this woman and it had cost him.

He looked across the yard and saw her through the screen door, coming out of the hall toward the porch. He tried to warn Peter with his eyes and felt a tug at the back of his neck. Turning as much as he could, he saw the Cade boy trying to tear through the tape with his fingers...but God, he could be Jason. It was like seeing an angel, a frightened, helpless angel, and now the boy said, "It's too thick, I can't tear it," and Roger tried to say something through the gag in his mouth. The boy seemed to understand and came around in front of him, tugging the tape off his face, pulling the oily rag out of his mouth.

Roger said, "Look for something sharp," and glanced at Aaron, the kid still repeating his terrified chant.

As the Cade boy ran to the kitchen area Roger saw the screen door swing open out there. Saw Peter tighten his grip on the axe handle, showing his teeth in a snarl.

* * *

The door creaked open on dry hinges and Peter saw her fingers, long and curiously elegant, pushing against the frame, and now her arm, tan and smooth, the forearm ropy with muscle. His body tensed and reflex almost brought the axe handle around too soon—then she was *right there*, her dark eyes widening, her hands coming up too late to block his attack.

The flat part of the handle struck her above the left eye as she looked at him, recognition replaced by fury and then, as she toppled to the porch with her dress hiked up over bare white legs, no expression at all but the slack mask of unconsciousness.

Shifting from foot to foot, blood roaring in his ears, Peter bent to feel for a pulse, certain he'd killed her, seeing the empty leather scabbard laced to her thigh and thinking, *Oh, no,* even as Roger screamed, "*Stay away from her,*" and her eyes clicked open.

Something stung Peter Croft under the rib cage. His body recoiled from the force of it and his back struck the wall, his legs going boneless on him again, his body sagging into a sitting position on the porch. He looked at his belly and saw a wet red circle on his shirt, a growing bloom tacky and hot against his skin.

The world slipped out of focus. In the blur Peter saw Maggie Dolan roll to her hands and knees in front of him, her breath a wheezing engine, a wicked upcurving blade in her hand, honed steel stained crimson with his blood. Her free hand went to the railing and she pulled herself up, grunting like an animal, a mother grizzly, wounded but unstoppable. She paused a moment to steady herself, glancing back at him dazed through a veil of blood, then hobbled down the steps to the yard.

* * *

When Roger saw the knife go into his friend every muscle in his body clenched in fury. Struggling against his restraints, he screamed, "*Fucking bitch,*" and saw Graham Cade standing beside him with a butter knife in his hand, his blue eyes round with fear. Roger said, "Sorry, son. Go ahead, try to cut it."

Then Maggie Dolan was there, grunting her way up the stairs, her glazed eyes taking in the scene, the gash in her forehead bleeding freely. She took the knife from Graham saying, "Careful, sweetie, that's not a toy," then picked him up and belted him in across from Aaron, the kid silent now, staring at the floor through his glasses. Cuffing blood from her eyes, Maggie pulled the door shut and secured it, glanced out the porthole window at the house for a moment, then picked Roger's gag up off the floor.

Roger said, "Please, just tell me what you did with my son," and she stuffed the gag back in his mouth, silencing him. Now she moved toward the front of the motor home, setting the blood-stained knife on a counter next to a roll of duct tape. There was a paper towel dispenser mounted over the counter and she spun off a handful, then sat in the driver's seat with the wadded towels pressed to her wound and keyed the ignition, the big engine rumbling to life.

As Maggie fastened her seatbelt and the ponderous vehicle lurched forward, Roger looked out the window to see Peter still propped against the wall on the porch, pale as a ghost. His eyes were open, staring off into the field beyond the road, and though he appeared barely conscious Roger could swear the man was smiling.

* * *

Graham had passed through terror into a state of passive observation, his ability to comprehend or react to the events unfolding around him short-circuited in the moment the woman strapped him into his seat. In that moment he understood that he would never see his family again and the prospect shut his young mind down.

Now, as the motor home roared past the outbuildings toward the road, Graham barely flinched when Aaron took off
his frayed leather belt, looped it around his mother's neck from
behind and pulled it taut with both hands, the veins in his
skinny arms popping with the strain. Reaching for the strangling belt, Maggie slammed on the brakes and Aaron almost
tumbled off the couch; but he didn't let go of the belt.

Weeping now, his voice a mournful wail, Aaron said, "No
more hurting," and stretched lengthwise on the couch behind
his mother, bracing his feet against the back of her chair, reefing
on the belt with all of his might. Maggie was choking, her face
turning purple, and Aaron said, "It's not their *fault*," in that
awful barking voice, "It's *my* fault, I done it." Maggie reached
for her seatbelt lock and Aaron kicked her hand away. "I didn't
mean to, we was just playin' and it happened, just…happened.
Clay wanted to win so bad and I was helpin' him…"

Maggie was still struggling but not as much now, her hands
rising to her throat then slipping away. The man with the tape
on him was trying to talk again, and when Graham looked at
him something woke up in his head and he undid his seat belt,
grabbed the bloody knife off the counter and cut the man loose.
The man got his hands free, spat the rag out of his mouth and
took the knife from him, hacking the tape off his ankles, shouting
at Aaron now, saying, "Aaron, *Aaron*, let her go, don't kill her."

Aaron kept yanking on the belt, his words turning into
wretched sobs Graham couldn't understand. Maggie wasn't moving at all anymore, her arms dangling at her sides, and now the
man was up, grabbing Aaron's wrists, prying the belt out of his
hands. The man stood for a moment with the knife aimed at

Maggie's head, as if afraid she might leap up and grab him. When she didn't move, he did a curious thing. After using the duct tape to quickly tie her to the chair, he filled his chest with air and kissed her, blowing the air into her mouth, then he did it again, and again. Now he stopped to look at her saying, "Come on, god damn it, don't you dare die on me," and gave her that blowing kiss again. This time her body jerked in the chair, her hands bouncing up, and the man backed away from her, aiming the knife at her again. She started coughing, big throaty hacks, spraying the windshield with spittle, and now her eyes rolled open, blood red and leaking tears. The man called her a bad name and pushed her head back, holding the knife to her neck. "Tell me what you did with my son," he said, "right now, or I'll bleed you where you sit."

Grinning at him with blood on her teeth, Maggie said, "I stuck your friend out there in the spleen. You might want to tend to him."

The man looked over his shoulder at the house, then taped her wrists to the steering wheel and her neck tight to the head rest. She said something to the man Graham couldn't quite hear and Graham was sure the man was going to hit her; but he slid the keys out of the ignition and took Graham's hand, tugging him to his feet. Waving the knife at Aaron, he said, "You too, kid," and Aaron got up, knuckling his glasses higher on his nose, going out the door ahead of them.

Behind them Maggie rasped, "Clayton, honey, come back here to your ma," and Graham hesitated, looking back at her. But the man tightened his grip on Graham's hand, telling him not to worry, it was over now, he was going to see his mommy and daddy soon. Then he went back to Maggie, stuffed the same oily rag in her mouth that had been in his own and duct-taped it into place.

On the way across the yard the man asked Aaron if he knew where the other boy was, the other boy that looked like Clayton, the one who owned the dog tags around his neck, and Aaron started shaking his head, his gaze aimed at the ground. Grabbing Aaron's arm, the man took the dog tags off him and put them in his pocket, then told Aaron to go sit in the gray car and close the door. Then Graham went up the porch steps with the man, almost running to keep up, the man sinking to his knees beside his friend with the blood on his shirt.

* * *

Peter's eyes were closed now and he didn't seem to be aware of Roger's presence. Roger touched his arm, alarmed at the amount of blood he'd lost, and Peter's eyes fluttered open. He said, "Did you get her?" in a voice that rose barely above a whisper and Roger told him that he did.

Roger looked at Graham now, the poor kid leaning against a porch beam with his fingers in his mouth, fat tears standing in those blue eyes that were so much like Jason's. Getting to his feet, Roger said, "Is there a phone around here, kiddo?" and the boy pointed through the screen. Roger took his hand again and said, "Show me." To Peter he said, "I'm going to call 911, then I'll be right back. What can I get for that wound?"

Peter smiled, his eyes dazed, dreamy. "Pressure," he said, lifting his hand off his soggy shirt, blood gouting from the wound. He put his hand back and Roger went inside, the boy hustling along behind him. More than anything he wanted to search this place for his son, ransack it for the slightest sign of him; but his friend needed him now. The woman said she'd got him in the spleen and Roger had no reason to doubt her. One of the members of his group had lost a child to a ruptured spleen and Roger was determined not to lose Peter Croft the same way.

Graham showed him the phone on the wall in the winter kitchen. Roger said, "Thanks, son," and cupped the boy's flushed face in his palm. He said, "I need your help now, okay?" and Graham nodded. "Go find a towel and take it out to my friend. His name is Peter." The kid ran off and Roger called 911, telling the operator a man had been stabbed in the spleen, giving her directions to the farm. The operator said she had a unit doing a drop off in Galetta and could have it there in fifteen minutes, twenty tops. Roger asked to be put through to the nearest police station and she got him an O. P. P. desk sergeant in Arnprior. As briefly as possible Roger told the man what had transpired, telling him the Cade boy was fine, then asking him to get in touch with Sergeant Vickie Taylor of the Oakville police. The officer said there was a cruiser ten minutes away in the village of Fitzroy that was being dispatched as they spoke. Roger said, "Please hurry."

Then he hung up and shouted, "Jason? *Jason?*"

But he got no reply.

15.

Vickie Taylor stood at the counter in the Tim Horton's across the street from headquarters, watching a teenage girl in a two-tone brown uniform put a lid on her large double-double. The clock on the wall above the coffee machine said ten minutes to two and when the teenager said, "A dollar-sixty," Vickie was thinking, *Thirteen hours*, knowing that the majority of child abductees who didn't turn up within the first three were usually found dead or not at all. She was thinking of the boy's mother screaming blame at her when the teenager planted a ring-laden fist on one cocked hip, gave her that *Duh* look her niece sometimes gave her and said it again: "A dollar-sixty?" Returning the kid's dull stare, Vickie handed over the exact change, resisting the urge to reach across the counter and bust the little creep in the chops.

She took the coffee to a table for two in the sunny front window and sat alone, sipping the soothing brew and staring out at headquarters, thinking of the reasons she had wanted to become a police officer in the first place, the gloss worn off most of them now. She'd come on board at a time when the resistance to the notion of women on the force in any capacity other than secretarial was at its peak, and had put up with immeasurable quantities of bullshit because she had believed it was worth it, had believed she could make a difference. Now, with Graham Cade already a grim statistic and his parents seriously injured, one of them critically, Vickie was left to wonder if they'd been right about her all along. Maybe she should have gone into nursing like her sisters or become the happy little homemaker her mother had worked so hard to shape her into.

When her cell phone rang she was sipping her coffee, silently rehearsing her resignation speech to Rob Laking. She flipped the phone open, saw Laking's number on caller ID and said, "I was just thinking about you."

Laking said, "The Cade boy, we got him," and Vickie was sprinting for the exit, any thought of tendering her resignation dripping to the restaurant floor with her spilled coffee. She said, "Alive?" and Laking said, "Alive."

Crossing the busy street, Vickie said, "Where?"

"About three hundred miles northeast, a farm near a village called Fitzroy."

"Never heard of it."

"Me neither."

"What's the plan?"

Laking said, "Look to your right."

Vickie stopped on the sidewalk in front of headquarters and saw Laking in his car on the parking ramp, wearing his amber aviator shades, the blue dash light already strobing. "Get in," he said. "We're going for a helicopter ride."

* * *

Roger knew he should check on Peter, but once he'd uttered Jason's name he could contain himself no longer. His son had *been* in this house, and the possibility, however slight, that he might still be here was too compelling to ignore. He had to act on it.

He started with the upstairs, dashing from room to room calling Jason's name, looking under beds, in closets, clothes hampers, a big cedar chest in the master bedroom, anything that might conceal a small boy. In the child's room at the front of the house he found something that simultaneously set his heart soaring and tipped it into a tailspin, something he might have missed had he not dragged the bed away from the wall.

There, behind the headboard, carved through the Batman wallpaper into the plaster underneath, were the initials JM, *Jason Mullen*, the J flipped around backwards in a reflection of the mild dyslexia that had revealed itself in Jason in the first grade.

Staring at his son's work, the plaster almost black now with age and mold, Roger imagined him alone in this strange room, his young head filled with the bullshit that crazy bitch must have fed him. Imagined him finding an old nail or a stiff scrap of wire and carving his initials into the wall, the act symbolizing his efforts to preserve who he was under a constant assault of lies, loneliness and fear.

Intent on beating it out of her now, Roger headed for the stairs. Halfway down he changed his mind, deciding to check the rest of the house first, knowing the woman was as tough as any man and crazy as hell and would almost certainly lie to him no matter what he said or did to her.

He turned right at the bottom of the stairs, into the winter kitchen again, opening every cupboard in the place, then checking the family room at the back of the house, finding no trace of his son. On his way out to the summer kitchen he noticed the pantry next to the fridge and entered the narrow alcove stocked with canned goods and preserves. It was dark in here and when he reached for the light switch his foot made a hollow sound against the floor. When the light came on he saw the trap door and bent to open it, hope warring with apprehension in his thundering heart.

He raked the door open and bellowed Jason's name into the earthen pit. Calling out again, he scrambled down the ladder, feeling a chain brush his face as his feet touched the dirt floor. He gave the chain a tug and the light came on, stirring restless ghosts, the stench of mold and decay making him want to gag. There were more preserves down here, arranged on crude shelves, and two raised storage compartments like shallow grottos stocked with drifts of turnips and potatoes. It occurred to him that Jason at six might have fit into one of these damp bunkers but not Jason at nine. The realization raised another possibility, one he'd shunned since the day Jason went missing, and he turned his gaze to the floor, searching for a soft spot in the hard-pack, a rectangle of loose earth tamped firm with the back of a spade. Tears of relief burned his eyes when he found none.

He went up the ladder fast and out the door to the summer kitchen, his wild eyes taking in the table and chairs, the old wood stove, the screen door leading to the porch—and now the padlocked steel door facing the back of the house. He looked around for a key, thinking, *This is it, this is where I'll find him*, but there *was* no key and he started pounding on the door with his fists, screaming Jason's name, the rage in his heart reaching a detonation point.

There was a hatchet leaning against the wall behind the stove and Roger brought it to the steel door, striking the padlock with it now, sparks flying with each savage blow; but the lock wouldn't give.

Gripping the hatchet in frustration, he turned toward the front door.

* * *

Graham was kneeling next to Peter on the porch, leaning with both hands on the towel bunched over the hole in his tummy, the man too weak now to do it on his own. Graham's friend Emily got a nose bleed once at school and it bled a lot, but not as much as this. Graham had never seen so much blood, could hardly believe a person had that much inside him. And it was still leaking out. He pressed down harder and Peter's eyes flickered open in his white face, then drooped shut again.

Graham could hear the other man, Roger, screaming someone's name in the summer kitchen, pounding on that big steel door in there, and now something else—a car coming in from the highway, raising a high plume of dust. Graham saw it turn toward the house, saw the rack of flashing lights on the roof and said, "Police car," to Peter, getting no response.

The police car was halfway to the house when Roger came through the door, his fierce eyes fixed on the Winnebago, a small axe in his hand. Graham said it again—"Police car"— but Roger didn't hear him either. Graham watched him walk past the hood of the gray car, Aaron still sitting in there shaking his head, then step up into the Winnebago, pulling the door shut behind him.

The police car stopped behind the gray car and the officer at the wheel looked at Graham with round eyes, then at his partner climbing out the other side. Now he got out too, leaving his cap in the car, his hand going to his gun. Both officers started running toward the porch, freezing when they heard the terrible scream from the Winnebago.

* * *

Roger ripped the tape off Maggie's mouth, the gag coming out with it, slapping her hard when she glared at him and said, "I want my boy back *right now*."

Roger grabbed her blood-slicked face, pressed his nose against hers and said, "You're going to tell me where my son is. You stole him out of his bed three years ago. His name is Jason Mullen. He was six and a half when you took him. He was in the first grade." The woman jerked her eyes away and didn't say anything, just kept breathing her stale breath at him, and

Roger said, "I understand why you did it, I really do. But it's over now. Jason's not your son. He's mine. And that other kid out there? He's not your son either. His name is Graham Cade. End this now, tell me where my son is, and I swear, I'll do everything in my power to help you."

Hissing at him, Maggie said, "Get your hands off me. You took *my* son from *me*. But I've got him back now and you have no *right* to keep him from me." She lunged in an attempt to head butt him, but her bonds prevented it, and when Roger backed away she spat in his face.

Roger wiped the spit away, seized the woman's right wrist and brought the hatchet down against the steering wheel, lopping the ends off her pinky and fourth finger.

Maggie Dolan screamed.

* * *

Graham watched as the officer who'd been driving strode toward the porch and his partner ran to the motor home door, pulling it open and climbing inside with his gun out. Graham heard the officer shout, *"Put it down,"* then a gust swung the door shut.

The other officer ran up the steps and knelt beside Graham, moving his hands away to look at Peter's wound under the towel. Peter's eyes came partway open and the officer said, "Hang in there, okay? There's an ambulance on its way." Peter gave the man a little nod. The officer said, "It's probably better if you lie flat," and took his jacket off, folding it into a pillow for Peter's head, then helping him lie on his side facing the yard.

Now Roger came out of the Winnebago with his hands on his head, the policeman stepping out behind him, putting his gun away, saying something into the radio on his lapel. He walked Roger to the gray car and told him to put his hands on the hood, then quickly frisked him, glancing at Aaron in the driver's seat as he did, Aaron sitting still now, his shaggy head bent forward. The policeman signaled the officer on the porch, thrusting his chin at the Winnebago, then went back inside.

The officer with Graham stood up, telling him to press on the towel again, it was almost over. Then he went down the steps to help his partner and Graham saw something at the end of the road, something that made him smile.

* * *

There was no pain, no fear, just this glorious glow to every-thing and a dreamy feeling of peace. He knew he'd been badly hurt, realized he was slipping into shock, but it didn't seem to matter. The Cade boy was with him, a worried little angel do-ing his best to help, and Peter was glad it was over for him. He saw Roger down there with his hands on the car, looking back at the cop going into the Winnebago, and now he felt Graham's warm hand on his arm.

The boy said, "Look," and pointed at the No Trespassing sign out there at the T in the road. He said, "It's Tommy Boy," and Peter saw David standing by the sign, his hand raised in a little wave.

Smiling, Peter said, "I know." He dug something out his pocket, then said, "Go get Roger," and Graham scooted off down the steps.

* * *

Graham said, "Peter wants you."

Through the fading crimson of his rage Roger stared at Graham Cade in awe. Right down to the sound of his voice the kid was so much like Jason it was frightening. He could see how the mother in Maggie Dolan got confused, crazy or not. Part of him wanted to pick the boy up and drive away with him right now.

Instead, he tousled the kid's hair and said, "Okay, chum. You want to wait here?"

The boy pointed at Aaron in the car. "Can I wait with him?"

Roger looked at Aaron staring at his feet in there and said, "Tell you what." He opened the passenger door, rolled down the window, then swung the door shut, saying, "Stand over here, okay? You can talk to him through the window."

Shuffling to the window, Graham said, "He won't hurt me."

Roger said, "I'm sure you're right, son. Just do it this way for me, okay?"

"Okay."

The two cops were leading Maggie Dolan out of the Winnebago in handcuffs now, her right hand wrapped in a towel, and what Roger wanted to do was go over there and knock her down and make her talk; but that part of it was out of his hands now. He watched the cops march her to the squad car and put her inside, her eyes never leaving Graham's. When they closed the door on her Roger saw her mouth the words *I love you* to Graham and Roger saw tears in the boy's eyes. Shaking his head, he told the cops his son was still missing and they were going to need a search party right away. He told them to question the woman and they told him not to worry, they'd take care of it.

Exhausted, frustrated, feeling cheated, Roger went up the steps to Peter. Despite the amount of blood he'd lost and the deathly pale of his skin Peter was smiling, his eyes exuding a warmth and peace that spooked Roger a little. He told Peter an ambulance was on its way then sat by his head on the porch, resting his back against the wall.

Pointing to the end of the road, Peter said, "See him?"

Roger looked and saw nothing. He said, "Who?"

"David. See him? By the sign."

Roger looked again, seeing only heat shimmer out there, the sun parching the dirt road. "You should rest," he said. "The ambulance is coming. They'll have you fixed up in no time."

Peter was handing him something now. Roger put his hand out and Peter dropped one of Jason's toy boxcars into his palm. He looked at Peter and Peter said, "Don't ask." Then he was holding Roger's hand around the boxcar, his skin tacky with blood, saying, "I need you to do something for me."

Roger said, "Anything."

"Tell Erika I'm sorry."

"For what?"

"She'll know."

Roger said, "Consider it done. You can do it yourself once they patch that hole in your belly."

Squeezing Roger's hand, Peter pointed again, saying, "See him now?" and Roger did, a tiny figure in a dark suit and white tie, looking almost solid in the heat shimmer at the T in the road. The instant Roger saw him the boy turned to stride on wavering legs into the tall grass over there, moving away from the road, looking back over his shoulder in a way that made Roger feel like the boy was looking directly at *him*.

He said, "My God."

"Isn't he beautiful?" Peter said, squeezing Roger's hand again. Their eyes met then, and Peter said, "Go to him, Roger. For me. Tell him I love him."

Roger started to say he should wait here until the ambulance arrived; but there was a siren now, and a dust trail billowing in from the highway.

"Go," Peter said. "I'll be fine."

Roger got to his feet, squinting to see David Croft still out there, five hundred yards down the road, still moving slowly away from him yet seeming no smaller for the distance, no less real or unreal.

Frightened, his entire world view crumbling in this strange, suspended moment, Roger looked at Peter and said, "I'll be right back." But Peter's eyes were closed, his drained face expressionless. Had Roger not been able to see the shallow excursions of his chest he would have thought the man dead.

He started down the steps, moving slowly at first, almost reluctantly; passing the Corolla now, feeling Graham's eyes on him, then the squad car as if wading upstream through water up to his waist.

By the time he reached the road he was running.

* * *

The LE class 427 Bell Helicopter cut through space at its maximum cruising speed of 160 miles per hour, the sleek eight seater much quieter with its doors closed than Vickie had imagined. Though she'd been a cop for nine years, this was her first ride in a chopper and the experience was making her giddy; or maybe it was just the fatigue.

They'd already been in contact with one of the officers at the scene and had learned that the Dolan woman had been arrested and that their friend Roger Mullen had called it in. Apparently Mullen had injured the woman in an attempt to glean information from her, an attempt that had failed. Vickie couldn't wait to hear how those two had figured out Margaret Dolan was the kidnapper.

She also learned that Peter Croft had been seriously injured trying to subdue the woman and that Roger Mullen was demanding a search party for his son. The prospect gave Vickie a sinking feeling in her stomach. Mullen's boy had been missing for three years. Statistically, he was long dead.

The pilot said their ETA was forty minutes and Vickie looked out the window at a sloping patchwork of farmland, adrenalin erasing her fatigue.

* * *

The paramedics gave Roger a curious look through the windshield, slowing as they approached him, Roger running along the side of the road toward the T, but Roger waved them on and the ambulance accelerated away from him. He lost sight of David after that, David or whatever it was, and slowed to a walk when he reached the No Trespassing sign, already coming up with rational explanations for what he'd seen—a shared hallucination, induced by desire and dread coupled with extreme fatigue; a good old-fashioned mirage.

Then he saw the boy again, standing amongst the remains of the farmhouse that had burned to the ground, David Croft a hundred feet away in the shade of a butternut tree, tiny hands folded in front of him, knowing eyes bluer than the August sky. Roger called out to him and started running again, closing the distance in frantic strides, thinking with each blink of his eyes this ghost or illusion or hallucination, whatever it was, would vanish. Then it did, there and then gone, persisting in Roger's vision until he was ten feet away and his foot struck something hollow on the charred wooden floor of the burnout, making a sound Roger had heard before, in Maggie Dolan's pantry, a sound dampened by soil and encrusted moss but utterly unmistakable.

He looked down at his feet, at the raw boards scabbed over with vegetation, the earth pulling them under in its own good time, and found himself standing in the centre of a perfect square crudely disguised by fallen leaves. He lifted his foot and stamped it down, hearing that hollow sound again.

Roger's heart pounded as he stepped off the square in the earth, sank to one knee and swept aside the dead leaves. He saw a rusted ring recessed into a rotting board and looped his finger through it.

Then he pulled the trap door open, the world around him starting to spin, sunlight spilling like something molten into the root cellar beneath him.

* * *

Peter was aware of being lifted, the sensation stirring memories of his father lifting him up, that feeling of weightlessness and safety he'd cherished so much as a boy. He felt the hard surface of the stretcher under his back, then a snug sensation across his thighs and chest, the attendants securing him with velcro straps.

The sun was in his eyes now, the tilt of his body telling him they were carrying him down the steps…then he was lost for a while in a tranquil lightness and the sun's glorious heat, though he could smell autumn in it, anticipate its coming chill.

A sharp pain in his arm brought him back, and he opened his eyes to see the inside of the ambulance and a frightened girl, a young paramedic, taping his IV into place. He wanted to tell her not to worry, but couldn't seem to shape the words.

He drifted off again as the vehicle started moving, hearing the urgent chatter around him, someone saying, "I'm going to have to intubate him."

And as his eyelids slid shut he saw David smiling at him from the foot of the stretcher, his touch against Peter's ankle like the quivering wings of a butterfly.

He slipped instantly into the most vivid dream, shimmering sunlight and the sounds of surf and laughter, the laughter broken and distant, only its tinkling high notes reaching him on a breeze that smelled of tidal flats. Reluctant to emerge from this blissful state, he kept his eyes closed, enjoying the dancing interplay of light and shadow against his eyelids. For a moment he had to think about where he was, so deep and peaceful was the plane he'd drifted into. Then the coarse feel of terrycloth and the dry rustle of fronds overhead told him he was on a beach towel in the shade of a cluster of palms, his favourite siesta spot on the beach in Barbados.

He heard footfalls now, sifting toward him through the sand, and brought his hand up to shade his eyes, seeing David in his baggy Homer Simpson trunks, grinning down at him with a piece of driftwood in his hand.

"Come on, Dad," David said, hopping with excitement, "It's a dead *octopus*."

Peter gazed up at his son, the boy's skin bronzed by the tropical sun, his young eyes twinkling, and thought how beautiful he was.

David said, "Dad, come *on*," and took off down the beach.

With what seemed a huge effort Peter sat up, squinting after David to see him slam on the brakes fifty yards down the beach, his lean body partially blocking Peter's view of a tanned woman kneeling in the sand in a burgundy bikini and a big floppy sunhat, poking something at the tide line with a stick. Now David hunkered down beside her and Peter thought, *Dana*.

He stood up and started down the beach, the white sand hot under his feet, his stride clumsy and uncertain. Dana glanced up at him and waved, making a face at the dead thing on the beach.

Peter smiled and waved back, his stride growing stronger with each quickening step.

* * *

Garbage, that was all Roger could see down there. A cereal box lying empty on its side, assorted cellophane wrappers, a crumpled cookie bag, a few crushed juice boxes. A dead garter snake in the midst of it all with its guts gnawed out.

There was no ladder, the drop about eight feet, and when Roger tilted his head to look deeper under the floor he saw something so white he thought at first it was a scrap of paper; but it was skin, a human heel intruding on the crisp line between light and dark.

He said, "Jason?" and the heel slithered into the dark.

Roger dropped into the reeking hole without touching the sides, landing hard in a puddle of muck, crouching to sweep the dark with both hands. His fingers touched a cold foot and he said, "Jason, is that you?"

There was no answer, only dry breath, a whisking sound of sickness and fear. Roger leaned into the dark and felt more cold skin, hard bone just beneath the surface, and lifted a body that weighed almost nothing, and when he shifted it into the light he saw that it was his son, "Oh, God, Jason, it's you," the boy wasted almost beyond recognition, naked but for a tattered pair of boxers, his body caked with mud, his bloodless skin covered with insect bites.

Roger held his son limp in his arms in an oblong of sunlight and screamed his thanks to the heavens, feeling the boy's breath on his neck, the weak flutter of his heart against his palm.

* * *

The helicopter touched down in the yard between the barn and the house, its rotors spawning dry twisters. Vickie ducked her head climbing out, getting grit in her teeth, turning to see Laking hop out behind her. They hurried together out of the dusty maelstrom, moving toward a group of O. P. P. officers gathered in front of the house, six of them now, clutching their caps in a circle by their cruisers.

Vickie saw a bald head bowed in the back seat of one of the cruisers and thought, *There she is*, with a kind of cold reverence. The feeling surprised Vickie. The woman was a cop killer, deserving of little but her contempt. Yet as a mother Vickie understood, and in a strange way admired the woman's courage and resourcefulness in achieving—not once one but twice—what she clearly believed was the discovery and rescue of her abducted child. That part of it broke Vickie's heart.

Peter Croft's car was parked near the porch, Graham Cade sitting in the passenger seat, an older boy hunched behind the wheel. The older boy was talking to Graham, constantly pushing his thick glasses up on his nose, and Vickie assumed the kid was the Dolan woman's other son. She'd had the Dolan file faxed to the station early that morning and had reviewed it with Laking during the quick flight here.

Graham was looking at her now and Vickie smiled, the boy wiggling his fingers at her in a little wave. He looked exhausted. Walking to the car, Vickie leaned on the sill and ran her fingers through the boy's blond hair, feeling the sweaty heat of his scalp. The older kid, Aaron, looked away, his respirations quick and noisy through his open mouth. The interior of the car was blistering, but when Vickie suggested Graham get out for some fresh air the boy refused. Seeing no harm in it, she told him she had good news, his parents were both going to make it. She didn't tell him his father was on a ventilator in ICU after almost eleven hours of surgery and would probably end up paralyzed from the waist down. Instead, she told him she and the other officers had some work to do here, but someone would be taking him home soon. Graham said, "Can you take me?" and Vickie said sure, if he didn't mind waiting a little longer. In a very adult manner, Graham said that would be fine.

She joined Laking and the milling cops, Laking getting the lowdown from the officers first on the scene. Vickie glanced at Maggie Dolan sweating in the back seat of the cruiser and saw her staring at Graham twenty feet away in the Corolla, a terrible longing in her eyes. Vickie heard one of the arresting officers say Peter Croft had been stabbed and taken by ambulance to the hospital in Arnprior, no word yet on his condition. He said the paramedics told him the other man had run off down the road maybe forty minutes ago and no one had see him since.

Laking said, "Okay, Vickie and I'll take the house." He pointed to the others in pairs, telling the first two to take the barn, the second pair the outbuildings, then split the arresting officers up, assigning the grounds to one and asking the other to go look for Roger Mullen. He said, "We're looking for a nine year old boy. Pray he's still alive," and the teams went their separate ways.

The helicopter was idle now, the pilot standing by the open door smoking a cigarette, his face raised to the westering sun.

* * *

Aaron said, "You sure look like 'im."

Graham said, "Your little brother?"

"Uh huh. More'n the other one."

"There was another one?"

"Uh huh."

"What was his name?"

"Clay...I mean, uh, Jason. Yeah, Jason. He didn' talk much."

"What happened to him?"

"Ma thought he was Clay, like you. Pretty soon he got too big an' she tol' me to put him in the hole. Sometimes I brought him stuff. Sometimes I forgot. I liked him. We had fun." He pushed his glasses up on his nose and said, "I like you, too."

Graham said, "Me too," and saw Aaron's big eyes fill with tears. He touched the boy's arm and said, "What's wrong?"

"That day...we was just playin'. Clay was good at makin' up games'n' I like to let him win 'cause he's so little. I wanted to tell Ma what happen' but Pa tol' me don' do it, don' you *dare* do it 'cause Ma'll kill us dead. Pa's gone now. Got drunked an' smacked a bridge. He bonked me on the head with his big ashtray an' maked me lie to Ma."

Curious, Graham said, "What were you playing?"

"Who could hold their breaths the longest under water. You know that game?"

Graham nodded, wiping a drop of sweat from his eye. "Me and my brother used to do that in the bathtub when we were little."

Aaron grinned. "You're *still* pretty little."

Graham hated it when people said he was small, but with Aaron he didn't mind. He said, "I wasn't very good at it."

"Clay neither. He said it's 'cause he's too little to reach the rain barrel by hisself an' stick his face in so I had to lif' him up, but I was squeezin' 'im too hard'n he couldn't hold his breath long enough. Was his idea to get in."

"He got in the water?"

"Yup. Clay got a Mickey Mouse watch with a second hand for Christmas an' we was usin' that for counting who'd win. A few times I pretended I couldn' hold my breath very long but Clay knew I was cheatin'. Said he wanted to win fair 'n' square. I held his watch an' under he went, but I still was winnin'. So Clay said to *hol'* him under till he won so I did. That time I made *sure* he won, two whole minutes extra." A terrible expression came over Aaron's face then, a kind of scrunched red crying face that made snot shoot out his nose. He wiped it away and said, "But I *drownded* him. I drownded my baby brother..."

Grimly fascinated, Graham said, "Jeez." He didn't know what else to say.

"I pulled him out the barrel, run in'n' showed Pa an' he said, 'Here's what we're gonna tell her. You and Clay was playin' outside an' a big man come out the bush an' cracked you on your empty melon an' when you waked up Clay was gone'." Aaron said, "Then he picked up that ashtray an' brained me *hard.*" He leaned forward, digging in his hair to show Graham the long scar on his scalp. "After that he wrapped Clay up in'n ol' blanket an' put 'im in the hole over to the Misner place what burned down. Put 'im down the rut cellar." He pointed into the distance along the road. There was a policeman over there kneeling in the tall grass. Aaron said, "Pa tore out the ladder an' tol' me never—*never*—to go over there again. But I did.

"When Ma come home I tol' her what Pa tol' me to say an' I seen he was right, it was better keepin' it secret." His face scrunched up again, turning beet red. "I never meant to hurt you, Clay," he said, and started shaking his head again. "I never meant to hurt you…"

Graham put his hand on Aaron's arm and sat with him in silence.

* * *

Rob Laking said, "Hey, Vick, get a load of this."

He'd used a heavy screw driver the chopper pilot loaned him to pry the hasp off the steel door in the summer kitchen. Once inside he and Vickie had split up, Laking checking a series of storage closets ranked against one wall, Vickie heading down a cement-floored corridor to an open area at the end housing a sophisticated home gym with a heavy bag, a multi-station weight machine, a bench and assorted free weights. There was a barbell on the bench with some very serious poundage attached, more than Vickie could roll across the floor, and the heavy bag looked like someone had worked it over with a twenty pound sledge.

She heard Laking say her name and came back along the corridor to a small room near the front. Laking was inside, hunched over a desk supporting a keyboard and a flat screen monitor. The raw particle board walls were literally papered with maps, photos and printed documents, the surface directly behind the monitor plastered with images of boys resembling Clayton Dolan, most of them culled from newspaper articles from places as far away as Alaska and New Mexico. Some were circled repeatedly with red ink, others X-ed out with the same pen.

Lying on the desk next to the screen was a printout of the article Vickie had seen on the Cade's fridge, Graham balancing his huge, gem show door prize under a proud smile. She found one of Jason Mullen too, push-pinned to the wall and faded with age, the boy staring uncertainly into the camera with a flying squirrel perched on his head, the caption reading: LOCAL BOY MAKES FLIGHTY FRIEND AT SUDBURY'S SCIENCE NORTH. The brief article even named the boy's school.

Laking said, "Goddam Internet. That's how she found them." He opened her Favourites list, highlighting a few of the links, saying, "Look at this shit. How to break into a car, how to hotwire a car, lock picking, alarm systems, weapons sites, martial arts sites, those fucking mail-order drug sites. *Bomb Making for Dummies?*" Straightening, Laking pointed at the large, well stocked bookcase next to the computer table. "And check some of these titles. *Crime Scene Investigation, Modern Forensics, Evidence Collection.* The woman turned herself into a world class criminal without ever leaving home."

Vickie said, "Incredible," and heard a raised voice outside, calling her name in alarm. She looked at Laking looking at her, a sick feeling in her stomach, then ran for the screen door, Laking hot on her heels. One of the cops Laking had assigned to the outbuildings was standing at the foot of the porch steps, pointing in the direction of the road.

Vickie saw the officer first, the one Laking had sent in search of Roger Mullen, the man running full out toward the farmhouse now, the gear on his utility belt jangling, one hand holding his cap on his head. He was shouting something Vickie couldn't make out, waving his free hand in the air.

Then she saw Mullen about fifty yards behind the cop. He was running too, a haunted look on his face, a gaunt, emaciated child, naked save a filthy pair of underwear, flopping rag-like in his arms. To Vickie the boy looked dead. It was at once the saddest and most triumphant thing she'd ever witnessed.

Now she could hear what the officer was saying, "Start the chopper, start the *chopper*," but Laking was already running toward the aircraft, shouting the pilot's name.

Vickie headed for the Corolla, hearing the prehistoric whine of the 'copter's ignition, the first low revolutions of its rotors, and now the officer coming up behind her saying, "They were trapped down a hole over there and I heard Mullen shouting." She saw Graham staring at Mullen stumbling through the dirt with his boy, then up at her with tears in his eyes, and opened the car door. "Come on, sweetheart," she said, "let's go see your folks." She took his hand hot in hers and Graham hesitated, looking at Aaron now, Aaron still shaking his head in those vigorous, spastic rhythms, shooting guilty, sidelong glances at Mullen and his boy. She said, "Graham, it's okay, we'll look after Aaron," and Graham stepped out of the car and Vickie picked him up, turning his head away when she saw him staring at Maggie Dolan in the squad car, the woman pounding on the window in there, screaming silently at the frightened boy. Passing one of the officers coming back from the barn she said, "Get her out of here," and ducked under the throbbing rotors, lifting the boy into the chopper.

Laking said, "Heads up," and Vickie turned to see Mullen red-faced and drenched with sweat, scuffing toward them through swirls of dust, his son unconscious in his arms. She made way for him and the pilot went down on one knee in the doorway, arms extended for the child; but Mullen refused, hefting the boy on board under his own flagging steam, then dropping spent into the nearest seat. The pilot got some blankets out of a storage bin and helped Roger swaddle his son.

Over the heightening roar of the chopper Laking told Vickie to go ahead, he'd finish up here. Vickie said she'd contact him as soon as they landed and climbed aboard. She bent to buckle Graham in and the boy said, "Clayton's dead. He's in the hole."

Vickie said, "Did Aaron tell you that?" and Graham nodded. Vickie waved Laking closer and told him. Laking nodded grimly and backed away.

Vickie belted herself in next to Graham and the boy took her hand as the bird lifted off. In the seat behind them Roger Mullen rocked his child, telling the boy he loved him, begging his forgiveness. In the cockpit the pilot spoke into his headset, telling the dispatcher to notify the Children's Hospital in Ottawa, ETA twenty minutes, he was transporting a male patient in critical condition. He turned to tell Vickie she and Graham would be staying on board during the drop off, he had to get the bird back to base ASAP. Vickie asked him to radio ahead for a squad car to meet them at the airport in Toronto and take them to the Credit Valley Hospital in Mississauga, where Graham's parents were patients.

While Vickie was talking to the pilot she saw Graham undo his seat belt and get up, almost losing his balance going to sit

310 · Sean Costello

next to Roger. Belting himself in, he took one of Jason's limp
hands and stroked it, saying, "It's over now, you'll be okay."

Mullen looked at Graham and broke down, making the
most wretched sounds Vickie had ever heard.

* * *

It was full dark before Vickie Taylor got around to calling
her boss. She used a pay phone in the waiting area, her cell
phone dead, gazing with lidded eyes through a narrow window
on the fourth floor of the Credit Valley Hospital, a thin rind of
moon riding the clear sky out there, traffic moving along
smoothly below her on Eglinton Avenue. She was waiting for
the operator to reverse the charges.

Laking came on now, his tone weary, telling her he was still
at the cop shop in Arnprior trying to arrange the Dolan woman's transfer to a lockup in Toronto. He said, "You must be
pooped," and Vickie laughed, sounding a little crazed.

She said, "No worse than you."

Laughing now too, Laking said, "What a day, huh?"

"No shit."

"Where are you now?"

"Credit Valley. Graham's back with his family. It was quite
a scene."

"Did you cry?"

"What do you think."

"Pussy."

"Asshole. Sir."

Laking laughed. They were both on the verge of collapse.

He said, "What about the dad?"

"On a ventilator. They're giving him a fifty-fifty chance he'll ever walk again."

"Jesus."

"Yeah. Four kids."

"And Mullen's boy?"

"I just got off the horn with the doc in Ottawa. She was pretty guarded. Said her best guess was the kid had been down that hole for at least two weeks. Said he'd slipped into a coma from dehydration, malnutrition and exposure. My impression was she couldn't believe the kid was still alive. I asked her what his chances were and she wouldn't say. She told me Mullen's got family there with him now, though, so that's good. And the wife's driving in from Montreal."

"Well, let's pray for a good outcome."

"Already done," Vickie said. "Any word on Peter Croft?"

"Nothing yet. Last I heard he was still in surgery."

"And Clayton Dolan?"

"In the root cellar, like the brother said."

Graham had told Vickie the whole story in the chopper and Vickie gave Laking the highlights now, telling him about the accidental drowning and the father's decision to cover it up.

"Unbelievable," Laking said. "If the son of a bitch had fessed up, none of this would have happened."

"I know. It's a shame."

"Okay, Vick. I've got one last thing I need you to do."

"What's that?"

"Go home."

Vickie smiled. "Ten-four, Rob. See you tomorrow."

"Yeah, Vick, see you tomorrow."

She hit the cut-off button and glanced at her watch, then dialed her home number. Her husband Michael picked up and said hello, asking her when she was coming home. Vickie said she was on her way and asked him to put their daughter on the phone. Michael said he'd just put her down and Vickie said, "Please, Michael, I really need to hear her voice."

Michael said sure and a few moments later a sweet, sleepy voice said, "Hi, Mom."

Vickie said, "Hi, baby," and felt tears film her tired eyes.

epilogue

October 20, 2008

Roger Mullen said, "This is the man who saved your life," but Jason showed no reaction. He'd filled out some in the weeks since they found him, but he was still pale, his gaze somehow vague and unfocused. The new clothes Roger had bought him hung on his brittle frame.

"He hasn't spoken yet," Roger said, a fretting sadness in his eyes, "but I believe he knows who we are, Ellen and me. We've been showing him pictures, telling him about his life...before, but it's difficult to say if we're getting through.

"Ellen's been staying at the house. We've talked about trying again, but I don't know. Even with Jason back, I'm not sure she can ever forgive me. It's hard."

Shivering a little in the autumn breeze, Roger said, "I never got a chance to thank you for finding my son, so I'm doing it now. It breaks my heart that doing it cost you so much, but to have him back...there just aren't any words."

Roger took something out of his pocket now, the toy boxcar Peter had stolen. Shaking his head, he said, "I wanted you to have this. Erika told me how you got it. Sneaky bastard. I told her what you said, about being sorry, and she was glad. She said she'd come visit you soon."

Roger rested the tiny boxcar on the base of Peter's head-stone, gleaming black marble to match his son's. Straightening, he stepped off the damp sod quickly, not liking the spongy feel of it under his feet. A gust sent autumn leaves cartwheeling across the triple gravesite and Roger shivered again, his broad shoulders hunching under his jacket. He felt something cool touch his hand and realized it was Jason's slender fingers lacing through his own. This was the first time since finding him that Jason had touched Roger on his own.

Looking down at Peter Croft's headstone, Jason said, "Dad?"

Roger felt the word vibrate in his son's hand. Biting back tears, he said, "Yeah, Jase?"

"This man saved me?"

"Yes," Roger said, "he did."

He tightened his grip on Jason's hand and turned away from the Crofts laid out all in a row in the earth. He'd already decided he'd never come back.

On their way out through the iron gate, cold spits of Octo-ber rain struck the cobblestones around them. Quickening their pace, Roger and his son made their way back to the Suburban, the only vehicle in the small dirt lot. Roger opened the door for his son and lifted him inside. When he reached for the boy's seatbelt Jason said, "I can do it," and Roger ran his hand through his son's curly hair.

He walked around the hood and got in behind the wheel, resting his hand on Jason's knee as they drove out of the lot, thunder grumbling in the low autumn sky.

As with my every effort,
this book is also dedicated to my family:

Carole, Candace and Steve

Love…to those who possess it,
there exists nothing more priceless or powerful

About the Author

Sean Costello is a practicing physician who lives and works in Sudbury, Ontario, his home since 1981. *Here After* is his sixth novel.

For information on previous and upcoming titles, visit the author's website at **www.seancostello.net**